Forget Me Not

Lisa Anne Davis

PublishAmerica
Baltimore

First printing

ISBN: 1-4137-0393-3
PUBLISHED BY PUBLISHAMERICA, LLLP
www.publishamerica.com
Baltimore

Printed in the United States of America

Dedication

To my father, who always said:
"If you're gonna do it, do it right."
I love you, Dad!

And to my mother who said:
"It's really good! It made me cry!"
I love you, Mom!

Thank you to all the friends and family
who helped make this dream a reality.

Special thanks to my husband for his support and all the long,
lonely nights he endured while I was brainstorming.

Thanks to my sister for finding the path and pushing me forward.

CHAPTER 1

"Don't look back, he's a memory!" The song blazed on the radio. Lauren wiped the streaming tears from her reddened cheeks, *a memory was all it ever was*, she conceded, solemnly. Brian was the love of her life, she thought, at least for the first three weeks of their relationship. He was handsome, sensitive, caring, and everything she had dreamed of, until she found out he was all of those things, and married, to a woman in Philadelphia. He had said he was legally separated and divorce pending, but the relationship trailed on, and the lying continued, until Lauren had to make the break, and hurt herself in the process, but it had been for the best, this she knew. Rain spat upon the windshield of her 1978 Firebird as the wipers brushed it aside in synchrony. Turning a sharp corner her tires caught a pooling of water, causing the vehicle to hydroplane and slide sideways. Jolting the wheel frantically to compensate for the misdirection of the tires, the car slid uncontrollably into the opposing lane, just as a red 1965 Ford Mustang came around toward her. Before she could even blink, Lauren jerked the car back into the right lane, narrowly missing the unsuspecting Mustang, which in turn, swerved into the roadside ditch, and back onto the blacktop, blowing its horn as it flashed by.

"That was close!" she said, staring into the rearview. *Brian's revenge*, the thought crept eerily into her mind, how coincidental, right by one of the many sawmills he'd owned. The fight they had had earlier still lingered on her mind, as she glanced in the mirror, one more time, catching the license of the classic car. POPS it read clearly.

"I hope I didn't send that poor old man to his maker, with a heart attack," Lauren said, biting her lip. She drove on more cautiously now, sniffling her drying tears away. "He's not worth that!"

The rain began to slow, as glints of sunlight filtered between the dark pines that lined the road. How familiar it all looked, but so distant, now. The last time she had seen those magnificent forests, she was only 16, and she had had the worst crush on Billy Malhoun. Funny, she pondered, how back then she had never really noticed the beauty of it all, her thoughts drifted back to the awkward night before she had left. She giggled at the thought, those days were so simple, so innocent, then, it was a sappy letter, or a whispered, I love you, after awhile you moved on with a tear and a goodbye, nowadays, you think you're ready to commit, and if you're wrong? Well, divide this and that, who gets the dog, the house, the car? Your whole life changes. She was never so glad to finally be back to simplicity. No more arguments, no more worries, no more Brian. Now capable of viewing the situation from an outside point of view, she was at last able to realize how relieved she really was.

Sighing with contentment, Lauren turned onto the familiar old driveway of rocks and dust, she was going to spend some quality time now, she determined, without any complications. The cabin was smaller than she remembered, but everything seemed to be intact. The shutters were still closed, a monumental signature to her parent's last visit. Four years of dust, and darkness would be begging to be let out. She stepped out of her car, digging the key out of the pocket of her tight blue jeans; she drew a ragged breath as she peered at the reminiscent structure, *had it really been ten years?* She hoped that everything was still okay inside her new abode.

The door creaked loudly, as it swung open and years of dust and stale air wafted out. Waving it away, Lauren stepped inside. The old overstuffed furniture sat just as she'd remembered it, covered now with sheets.

The large brown and blue Indian rug still lay unmarred in front of the fireplace. She recalled the many times she had lain sleepily there, watching the dancing flames, as her parents talked amongst themselves. The bookshelves and knick-knacks were still in place, as well as the mahogany table and chairs, in the kitchen. A solitary vase, still containing a barren dogwood twig, sat in all conceptuality upon the covered table's center. Everything was in order, it seemed, and Lauren smiled at the warm memories that filled the room. She closed the door behind her, heading toward the pantry, still containing the canned goods and jarred vegetables, her grandmother had made, it would definitely need to be restocked. As she made her way up the open staircase, her eyes followed the banister to the top. She mounted the landing, and peered in each room quietly, her single bed still remained where it had always been and her white-mirrored vanity still harbored the same wall. *How long ago*, she thought in amusement, it still seemed like yesterday. The mattress and box spring, of her parents' king sized bed, had been newly replaced, but sat in the same place it had always. Even the solitary, hunter green, armchair still remained by the bedroom's large window, she could almost see the silhouette of her father, as he sat smoking his pipe, and watching the sunset, after supper. This would be her room, she decided, the warmth of love still radiated in here. She walked across the braided, beige and white, throw rugs that covered the hardwood floors, over to the window.

"What a view!" she conceded, peering out across the lake. She knew of a few neighboring cabins, but she was sure no one would still be in them this late in the year.

She headed back out to get her bags from the car, and quickly decided to make a trip into town, before unpacking. Four years of dust and cobwebs weren't exactly an appealing environment for relaxation.

Aside from the much-needed cleaning supplies, nourishment for a growling stomach, sounded good too. It was a fifteen-minute drive to the nearest convenience store, and by now the rain dampened roads were sure to be drying. Lauren pondered the thought of dinner, it was already after 3 p.m., and she would probably be cleaning for the remainder of the night, she decided, without hesitation, to just eat in town this evening besides, she deserved a treat.

As she pulled into the parking lot, of the town's grocer, a familiar object caught her eye. "POPS," she read, "where have I seen that?" Oh, no! The enlightenment of the recognition, struck her, it was the very same mustang she had almost collided with earlier! "I hope he doesn't recognize my car…" She looked around and realized with sickening obviousness, that she stuck out like a sore thumb. The urge to go elsewhere overwhelmed her, but it was late and this store was a monopoly, out here, miles from any other town. She swallowed her heart, and trod nervously to the store, slipping in unnoticed. Searching the aisles for her supplies, Lauren decided to collect a few groceries, not wanting to have to make any more unnecessary trips than she had to. The sooner she could get back to her solitary comfort, the better. After a half an hour of picking, and choosing, she could no longer bear her growing hunger. As the cashier rung up her items, Lauren glanced out at the parking lot. A strange dark haired man was eyeing her car, he walked around it slowly, and then, precariously, he sat against the rear fender. Perturbed, Lauren stared in awe at his obvious uncouthness, *how rude!*

"$46.50 ma'am!" the clerk repeated loudly.

"Oh, I'm sorry," she jolted back to her present merger with embarrassment. She quickly handed him a fifty-dollar bill, and walked out with her purchases in hand, leaving her change behind.

"Ma'am!" the clerk called after her, his voice trailing away.

As she approached, she noticed the man to be close in age to herself, he ran his long fingers through thick, dark hair, and glanced her direction, a look of agitation on his face.

"Can I help you?" she asked, irritated by his obvious malignancy.

He eyed her thoroughly, his expression softening, as she came toward him. He seemed to be judging her character, with cruel intimacy; the notion brought a flush over her, reddening her cheeks.

"CAN I HELP YOU?" she said again, as she reached the Pontiac.

His blue gaze met hers with quiet assertiveness, "Is this your car?" The softness of his voice, held a deep masculinity, prickling the hairs on the back of her neck.

"Yes ... Why?" she asked, uncertain of herself, beneath his steady scrutiny.

"Well then, I just wanted to thank you, for nearly killing me earlier." Her heart jumped into her throat, this was the "old man" she had nearly run off the road? Her eyes swept quickly over him, a new view of the situation dawning on her now.

"POPS," she recalled, it was no doubt his wealthy father's car, her earlier guilt, transforming into contempt, at the audacity of his actions.

She mustered her best apologetic explanation, hoping to discern the disgruntled man, who was obviously entertained by her discomfort at the confrontation. "Well I'm sorry for that," she began. "It was raining, and..." She was unexpectedly interrupted.

"Where did you learn to drive, anyway? Sorry wouldn't have replaced that car any sooner than it would have me!"

"EXCUSE ME?" Lauren was momentarily shaken. "You have some nerve talking to me like that! Who do you think you ... ?" She was interrupted once more.

"I have some nerve? Where do you get off, incidentally, showing up at the same store as me? Are you so determined to do damage? It wasn't close enough before?"

Mouth agape, in disbelief, Lauren turned and began to load her belongings, vindictively, "I can't believe you!" she fumed. "It wasn't my fault, and I..." She glanced back at him in wonder. "You don't actually think that I meant to..." His look of scrutiny answered her clearly, "For your information, I live here! So don't let your imaginative ego run away with you!" She jammed the last of her belongings angrily into the back seat of her car. "If I had known you were going to be so rude, I wouldn't have apologized!"

With that final word, a loose jar of strawberry jam tumbled out of the car, and crashed, idly, on the ground. Nicholas watched the perturbed young woman picking the glass fragments out of the sticky, red blob on the pavement. He felt a tinge of guilt, as he viewed her small form, maybe he had been too hard on her, and after all, she had apologized. Her dark shining hair was cast away from her eyes, again and again, as she struggled to clear her line of view, crouching over the mess.

"Look," he began, feeling a bit awkward now, "I'm sorry if I … well, seem to be so rough." The look of resentment in her eyes did not go unnoticed, as she glanced at him. The sea-green gaze that met him, caught him off guard, *mesmerizing*, he admitted.

He hadn't truly taken in her features earlier. Her dark, lustrous hair shone like flowing silk, shadowing porcelain skin, and those eyes! Those magnificent sea-green eyes appeared almost transparent turquoise. He watched her fumbling fingers, desperately trying to clean the mess, he was certain, was his.

"Look, I'm really sorry." He bent down to assist her. "This is my fault, let me help you."

"I don't need your help," she hissed, "you've done enough!" Her bitterness was validated, Nicholas conceded, he had been quite rude, now that he reflected on his actions. It had simply been too long since he had even felt remorse for his behavior, any compassion for another. He had become accustomed to his cynical view of life, his pessimism.

As she rose, he met her eyes squarely, sending another prickle up her neck. His stare lingered uncomfortably long, her anger diminishing into discomfort. She looked away, clearing her throat, "If you'll excuse me…" Her facade of prudishness felt transparent. "I have more important things to attend to." She could feel his gaze wash over her, but refrained from looking back at him.

"I really didn't mean to cause such a problem." Nicholas felt a tinge of embarrassment at the whole confrontation; he must have looked like such a fool! A blubbering idiot, arguing with a woman he would have sooner had swoon to him, than to cringe from him. "Maybe I can make it up to you somehow?" His proposal irked her further.

"Don't tell me you're actually going to ask me out? Is that your game? Save it for some other lucky girl! With charm like yours, they should be knocking down the door!"

Nick was surprised by her quick wit. "I meant to pay for the jam." Lauren carefully avoided his amused look of measure; she pulled the heavy door of the firebird toward her, only to find it stilled by the stranger's steady grip.

"But, I like your idea, better." She cast him a look of awe, he'd frightened her, he surmised, maybe he had let his stare linger for too long. He truly hadn't meant to, but those eyes, and the witty personality behind them, were too much of a temptation. She began to back up, intent on leaving the awkward scene. "Wait," he pleaded. He couldn't just let her leave. "Please?" She stopped, even with him, casting him a look of indifferent inquiry. "Would you consider letting me buy you dinner? I mean to make up for this? I do realize it wasn't..."

This time she interrupted, "I'm eating at home." She backed out fully, and stopped again. "Where it's safe!" With that she drove past him, leaving him to ponder on the mysterious newcomer. She was like a breath of fresh air, compared to the locals he had met, and he had blown it. A thought crossed his mind, gingerly, he headed for the store, he was sure he'd see her again; perhaps he could make a better impression next time. Nicholas never was a man to give up easily, and something about her seemed to pull at him. As of late, he would have left well enough alone, but something gnawed at him, the challenge perhaps, or maybe the minute sense of chivalry, he had buried within himself for so long. Either way, he would be sure to seek the answer to the mystery that this newcomer held.

On the way to her cabin, Lauren couldn't help but smile frustratingly, *who was that guy?* What did he think; he would woo her with his debonair rudeness? How odd that encounter had been, and how much of a spectacle he made of them both, nonetheless, she hadn't the time to reminisce about the frivolous event, she had groceries to put away. She glanced at the clock, *was it really 5:30 p.m. already?* Well, it looked like she would have to eat out tonight; she only hoped she wouldn't run into any, well, problems.

CHAPTER 2

Lauren straightened her silken shawl, it was modest, but delicate, and it matched her low cut, silk blouse beautifully. She shut the door of the firebird and brushed her hair back from her shoulders, the lights of the small restaurant, made her feel underdressed, but in this quaint little town, she knew her attire would fit right in. Cautiously, she glanced over the parking lot, hurrying up the broad cedar steps, to the large, wood framed, glass doors. Grasping the brass door handles, she swung them open, and stepped inside, knowing she had subconsciously been searching for a certain, red Mustang, she didn't see it.

Inside the restaurant, Lauren inconspicuously, marveled at the rustic majesty of the small, southern eatery. Rich maroon carpet overlaid the floor; round tinted glass tables lined the walls, which harbored large, heavily draped windows. Glowing chandeliers hung throughout the dining establishment, casting a soft glow over the floor plan. It was larger than she remembered, but then again, it had been ten years. For a moment, she wondered if her black denim pants fit here or not. A waiter in semi casual dress escorted her to her seat, smiling broadly at the eye-catching belle. She was definitely not from these parts, he decided, eyeing her soft curves under the tight denim. Most often there were strangers that vacationed in the area, but it was late August now, and nearly all of the vacationers had filtered back to their suburban homes. The summer cabins that were owned by many of the visitors, were equipped for winter, but here in the mountains, you had to be more than a just a soft handed city dweller to handle it. The cabins were usually left empty until May.

"Shall I bring your menus now?" the waiter probed, "Or wait for your companion to arrive?"

Lauren glanced up at the beaming servant. "Oh, no, no, I'm quite alone this evening, thank you." Alone … , Even the word sounded empty, strange. Lauren cleared her throat, ignoring the emotion. She looked over the menu there were so many choices and decisions weren't her strong point. She grimaced at the thought; even her choice of career had left her wanting. What had ever possessed her to enter into architecture? Maybe it had been that cute teacher her freshman year of college, he had always kept her class interesting. For now, though, until she could work out her personal life, she would enjoy her extended leave from the stressful profession, if she ever went back. Finally she settled on the lemon pepper pheasant, with broccoli tips, basted in garlic butter sauce, and white wine, to unwind.

Motioning her waiter, she handed the menu over, and began nibbling on the complimentary bread. It was every bit of 7:30 p.m. and she thought about what chores were left for her, back at the cabin. She had changed the bed linen, and disposed of the overly ripe canned goods, replacing them with the new. She thought back to the jar of jam, what a great start to her relaxing get away. She wondered who he was, she didn't know of any wealthy locals, but things had changed since her last visit, maybe he was the exception. In any case, she was sure it wouldn't be a good idea to run into that one again, something in his eyes made her apprehensive; there was danger in those deep blue pools.

Nicholas stepped out of the shower, water streaming through his thick hair, for which he had the Greek in his bloodline to thank. He wrapped a towel about his hips, and went into the bedroom, his mother had such a quaint way of reminding him about her, N.C., was inscribed clearly on the tag of his boxers. Nicholas Carmen, he mused, "I guess I couldn't lose these even if I wanted to." He slid the black silk boxers on, tossing the towel into the hamper, he didn't consider his quite massive home to be extravagant, but he kept it well organized. He was relatively new to the area himself, and had bought the summer home at a steal, 8 months earlier. Seclusion was the biggest attraction. He needed time, space and a place to forget the past, to let his wounds heal, out here on the lake it was perfect.

Combing his hair back into his usual coiffeur, he slipped on his blue jeans, and a hunter green cardigan of his choosing, he had begun to feel a hint of claustrophobia in his secluded hiding place. Tonight, he was going out for the first time in the eight months that he had been there. Loneliness was a key factor too, but it went with the territory, and he swallowed it with a grain of salt. Grabbing the keys to his car, he bounded downstairs and out the door, with a jubilance that expressed his hunger, a hunger that he hadn't felt for sometime now. He had had a certain dark headed woman on his mind, and when his blood had flown anew, where it had lain dormant and cold for so long now, he couldn't resist the urge to take on the challenge. He hadn't felt such a heat within him, since he was eighteen years old, ten years had been a long time for curiosity to lay unchallenged.

Lauren glanced at her watch, 8:02 p.m.; people had begun to filter into the restaurant now, mostly the few vacationers that hadn't yet left. Maybe it was a going away meal, or the occasional young couple, imagining the mid-standard restaurant to be of regal proportions. She could understand their reasoning. *Where is that waiter?* She quarried, *and where is my food?* Her impatience was growing, she caught herself, impatience, had been one of Brian's big faults, as she recalled.

"Come on baby, I missed you, just let me have a little sugar..." Brian pulled her against him, hard. He had just come back from another "business" trip, as he called them.

"I don't feel very comfortable with that right now, Brian, let go of me, please?" She struggled away from him, he smelled of light beer, and a cheap perfume. She glared at him, "You've been with her again, haven't you?" His silence betrayed his infidelity, Lauren's heart raced in to her throat, "Brian, how could you?" He smiled awkwardly at her. Her pride was sorely damaged at his betrayal of her, a feeling of ineptitude washing over her, "You said it was over!"

"Laurie, when are you gonna learn to trust me?" He reached for her again, "Look, forget about it okay, I'm here now, with you, would you just relax? I'd like to have some time for us now." His careful response was typical; he always seemed to brush off her concerns, no matter how obvious he was. He pulled her roughly to him, as she tried desperately to pull away. If she cried in front of him, she knew he'd take advantage of her weakness, and although her feelings for him had diminished, her need for companionship was still livid. She turned away, tears brimming her eyes. "Come on Laurie, she's out of my life, I swear!" Her lack of response pushed him farther, "Sheila is gone, all right? Just let me kiss you, okay?" He continued to paw her, despite her protests, "I'll make it all better, baby, you'll stop all this suspicion, just relax..." He tightened his grip and began kissing her neck.

" STOP!" She was at the end of her restraint, tears spilled down her cheeks, "Just leave me alone!"

He pushed her away, "I don't have the time or patience for this!" He gathered his jacket, turning back toward her briefly, "What the hell is wrong with you, Lauren?" With that, he headed to the door, "I'm going out!" Patience, she mused sadly, was truly a virtue.

The memory was still an open wound, she had given him so much of herself, devoted so much of her life helping to rebuild his, to get over his money grubbing wife, Sheila. She'd stood beside him even when his gambling problem had almost caused him a bankruptcy. She had helped him to get his life back on track, when what she really needed was her own life, which had been conveniently pushed to the side. *What a waste, she queried, a terrible waste of time.* She wondered if any man was actually sincere, or if they were all the same, a group of lying, selfish, introverts.

"Your food ma'am." The waiter's voice pulled her from the thought.

"Oh, thank you!" She laid her napkin on her lap, as he placed the dish before her, and poured her wine.

"Enjoy!" He smiled broadly at her once again, "If you need anything else, my name is Mike, and I'd be more than happy to accommodate you." She glanced up for a moment, to thank him, catching more in his eyes than servitude. She looked away with a shudder; she wasn't looking for that anytime soon, and certainly not with him. A disturbing picture formed in her mind, of his thick, plump hands, grasping at her breasts, she shook it away, nearly losing her appetite. Mike turned, walking away in tight uniformity, leaving Lauren's appetite to return with a vengeance.

The pheasant was immeasurable in taste; she savored each morsel of the meal with divine delicacy, she had all she could do to refrain from just picking the bones clean with her teeth, she tasted each morsel of the dinner with divine delicacy, she was hungrier than she'd expected. She had just begun to enjoy herself, watching couples filter in and out; when she heard a voice she was sure she had heard before, "Reservations for Nicholas Carman?" She glanced in the direction of the phrase.

"This way sir." The host walked past her, seating the patron two tables down from hers. To her astonishment, it was the same dark-headed man from the parking lot that followed. Grasping her napkin she threw it in front of her face and nearly choked on a half chewed broccoli tip. She hoped he didn't see her, how odd was it that they had both come to the same establishment again? In all reality, it wasn't that peculiar, in such a small town, but by her standards, it was too strange. So his name was Nicholas, now she knew something he didn't, a name, she wondered if he was looking at her, and if he'd think she had followed him again. This time though, she had been there first and if a confrontation were to come about she would be sure to stress that point. She was nervous, like a kid again, and she didn't know why. Nicholas searched the menu for a suitable meal, he was hungry, but the atmosphere of the restaurant kept his attentions, he looked around, it was a cozy little place, not quite the Ritz, but quite the diamond in the rough, out here. His eyes traveled from table to table, watching each group of people talking and laughing. As he scanned the room, he realized everyone else had at least one companion and he was alone. How foolish he must have looked, dining alone in a room filled with couples and groups, he began to rise, he shouldn't have come, he wasn't ready. Just as he began to rise, he looked directly in front of him, was it her? Only she had that dark, flowing hair that he hadn't been able to get out of his mind, it had to be her! But why was she here? Maybe she had come with someone and he would be along shortly, he sat back down, he would have to see what sort of a man would measure up to her standards.

Lauren wanted to turn so badly, she couldn't stand it, she tried desperately for an excuse, but found none, and moving to the other side of the table would be too obvious. At long last she conspired a plan, she would innocently excuse herself to the ladies room, and if his blue eyes followed her again, her curiosity would be satisfied. Slowly he watched her rise, she was graceful and delicate, her eyes averted his as she walked toward the ladies room, but as she passed him, he caught the mesmerizing, turquoise stealing a glimpse, his blood began to race, she had seen him, but was she so disinterested? She never again looked at him the rest of the way to the powder room, but he had seen that hint of sea green, oh why hadn't he kept his cool earlier, she could've quite possibly been the new start he'd needed.

The door shut long after Lauren had passed through, she hurried to the far end of the room and stared in the mirror, her reflection staring back drenched in obvious nervousness. She blew a breath of relief through her lips, he had watched her the entire way, and what was it in those blue eyes under thick black lashes that frightened her so? Was he so malicious in his revenge that he was following her to torment her? Or was he just another guy trying to pick up the newest thing in town, she guessed the latter. Deciding on her next move she straightened her blouse and shawl, fluffed her hair and headed out to face the fire, or so she thought. She stopped, stunned. *"Where had he gone?"* She stepped a few short steps and looked around, nowhere. Hurriedly she headed over to his table checking for any sign that he'd return, the menu was open, napkin still folded, and his seat was still pushed out, surely he'd be back. What did she care anyway; she was acting like a foolish sixteen year old with a crush. The thought had slipped out carelessly, not actually a crush, what she had meant was, well, all right a crush, so he sparked her interest, so what, what was wrong with that? Everything was, she was setting herself up to be hurt, and she felt helpless against it, Brian had hurt her deeper than she wanted to believe, she was scarred from the experience but the memories were so painful for her that she refused to learn from them, well, she would have to learn, or the pattern was sure to attach itself permanently, and she didn't want to travel that path at all. She had survived the first time, but she was sure a second time would be unbearable, already her faith in love and the all-American romance had dwindled, the next time she most likely would just give it up. With a laugh of satisfied victory, Nicholas came around the potted tree by the men's bathroom and in three long strides he was upon the curious woman, "Looking for me?" His sudden question startled her, she turned, her eyes wide with surprise, her lips parted, soft, tender lips, he began once more " I guess you were following me again?"

A broad white smile gleamed back at her in pure conceit; Lauren's surprise was quickly converted to anger, "How dare you frighten me like that! I wasn't looking for you; I was going back to my seat, when you decided to harass me!"

"Harass you?" Nicholas' smile faded into confusion, he hadn't meant any harm, just a simple jest was all, and he felt like the whole room was watching them.

"Yes, harass me! And besides, I was here first." She sat back down. "You followed me!" Her insinuation was to be final but Nicholas stared at her. "What is it you want?" she asked a bit unsettled now.

"My chair?" His expression was blank as hers turned a shade of deep crimson, she stared at the meal she had ordered just two tables up from where she sat. She rose with mottled dignity and prudishly moved toward her table, playing it cool was out of the question. "Wait." Mocking eyes met hers. "I could always just settle for relocation." His smile wasn't taken lightly as he motioned to the seat opposite his own.

"He's making fun of me," Lauren ascertained, humiliated by the whole charade, her pride wouldn't let her see the offer behind his jest, and truly he meant no insult, why had she glared at him so? With a muffled sneer she turned and walked toward the matre de. "Check please!" she called. Nicholas' disappointment was echoed by his sallow face, maybe she was right, maybe she was too good for him, but he wasn't about to let her get away that easily, turning him into the big bad wolf. No, she had another thing coming. He pushed the chair in with a thud and headed for the door, brushing past her and knocking the shawl from one shoulder, *"How rude,"* she thought as she paid her bill, he probably didn't come to eat anyway, why wouldn't he leave her alone? As she headed out the door she saw him walking from her car, she hurried down the steps wondering what he'd done, if anything was harmed ... Nicholas was filled with anger, more so at himself than anything, he slammed the car door and started the engine. Jamming the mustang in gear, he backed out and sped away from the parking lot, leaving a screeching trail of blackened rubber behind. He should have stayed home, now he felt worse than before, what was the sense in trying when no one would give you a second glance anyway? He'd just go home and start preparing for the fall; it would be easier when all these vacationers left anyway, quiet, calm, and less females to distract him. He shifted gears and thundered down the darkened road wishing he'd never decided to go out tonight, and cursing her for all the emotions that had begun to rise again. Lauren watched the red taillights disappear into darkness as she hurried to her firebird, she just knew he had done something or he wouldn't have left so soon, she wondered why he didn't try to confront her again, maybe he decided to finally give up, but secretly, she hoped not.

As she approached the car she saw an object on the pavement next to her driver's door, what was that? She slowed her pace and squinted in the shadows of the parking lot, trying to focus, it was a small brown paper bag sitting upright in the cool darkness. She lifted it into the light, it was heavier than expected, reaching inside she pulled the contents out and studied them with irked curiosity. A jar of strawberry jam protruded, tied with a yellow ribbon and a small card which, upon opening, she found to read: *Sorry. Could we start over? It was signed Nick.*

CHAPTER 3

Lauren pondered on the small note, was it all a scheme to get to her? Or was he actually a nice guy under it all? Deep inside she kicked herself for being such a shrew, she had lost all her faith in people altogether and she knew it would be a long process to get that back, if she ever did, besides, she wasn't sure she wanted to struggle through that process. It had been three days since the incident at the restaurant, three long, exhausting days at that, between the scrubbing and cleaning and all the unpacking, she was completely worn out, not to mention the lingering thoughts on her mind. She had gone into town twice since that night and hadn't seen so much as a trace of Nick, she wondered if he'd left for good or if she'd see him again sometime around town. She supposed she could be civil to him, that is, if he was to her. She pulled her favorite woolen sweater out of the dryer and folded it, laying it softly on the pile of clean clothes. The washer and dryer set was barely five years old, her parents had had the small washroom added to the cabin when they had come up for their twentieth anniversary while she was away to college. She smiled at the thought and imagined them picking it out together, they weren't always happily married, there was a time when her father had turned to the bottle for support after his car accident, and he still had a limp from that. Then they had come close to separation, but her mother held on and after months of rehabilitation, 18 to be exact, their painstakingly difficult recovery had paid off. She wondered if she would ever find a love like that, she didn't feel so young anymore and life was so short, but she didn't want to settle for the first man to come along, she'd rather be single and lonely than tied to an unhappy marriage.

She loaded her whites and started the machine, looking around she realized in all her errand running she had absent mindedly forgotten to get bleach, *at this rate*, she thought, *I'll have to get more gas too*. Shutting the machine off she headed out to her car once more; the day was clear with a crisp whisper of winter in each breeze, she breathed in the refreshing mountain air and felt newfound buoyancy in her step. Pushing the sleeves back on her oversized sweatshirt she climbed in the driver's seat and started the car, maybe she would see what was playing at the movies tonight, it was a small theatre but it always had the newest movies playing and with no T.V. at the cabin the songs on her stereo were becoming monotonous.

She pulled away from the drive and headed into town, brushing her whispery bangs out of her eyes. The sun was high and bright in the cornflower sky and the trees lining the streets of the small town were starting to turn autumn colors now, Lauren loaded her purchases into the back seat of her firebird, she was a sucker for last-minute buys. Glancing up she saw a small gas station nearby. It was a newer station and hadn't been there when she last visited but it seemed well enough established, she'd go look into it, she needed gas anyway. She pulled up to the pump and began pumping the gas, with intentions of putting five dollars in, when suddenly a voice startled her "Lauren?" The man came out of the station, his mid length brown hair was feathered back from a handsome rugged face, and upon seeing his gleaming crooked smile, Lauren recognized the man instantly. "Billy!" She let go of the pump and came around the car. "Billy Malhoun? Is that you?"

"Well yeah it's me!" He came toward her, arms open. "What are you doin' here girl? You look great, you're all grown up!" She smiled deeply at the familiar old voice as she hugged his neck, a strange feeling of awkwardness came over her, he was bigger than she'd expected and his broad chest and bulging arms intimidated her.

"Billy, what are YOU doing here?" He wasn't a local, his family always vacationed here in the summer but they lived in California.

"Well, I sort of live here," he began to explain. "I own a house in town here, investment property, if you will, and I was renting it out for the summers, until recently. I moved down about two years ago, after my divorce that is."

"You were married?" Her question was of true surprise; she'd never imagined him to settle down, ever.

"Well, sort of, we were doomed from the beginning; I just wasn't ready for that kind of commitment." He looked away briefly as if the subject bothered him, she could understand. "So, anyway, what about you? What are you doing here?"

She hesitated, "Oh … I'm just on a little relaxation trip, I just had to get away for awhile that's all. You know the old cabin of my parents'?"

"How could I forget?" He smiled slyly. Her facial hue deepened at the response, she remembered it well too.

"Well, I'm staying there for a while."

His large hands lingered too long upon her hips where they had settled after their embrace, she cleared her throat and backed up a bit, as his insightful gaze swept over her entirety.

"My God, you've changed." He shook his head smiling broadly again, his eyes lingered yet. "I mean, you always looked great, but wow, you really look good!"

She smiled shyly casting her eyes downward, "Oh Billy, you were always a flirt!" Her outward honesty was a cover for her nervousness; her heart was beating heavily. "Well I never expected to see you again ... so you own a house here?"

Billy finally broke off his stare and directed his gaze to her eyes. "Oh, it's not much, a little place down on Avery Street. Maybe you can stop by sometime?"

"Oh yeah, sure, that'd be great!"

He looked across the lot of the station. "So that's your bird huh? I saw it the other day at the marker, wondered whose it was, I've got that jeep over there." He pointed to a newer CJ-5 Wrangler, red and black with a black leather interior.

"Wow, that's nice!" She headed toward it with curiosity, and a need to escape his intimate eyes; with long powerful strides he was behind her in a flash and commenced to show her all of the jeep's features. After about ten minutes of show and tell Billy's attentions were cast to Lauren once more.

"What are you doing later?" The question caught her off guard.

"Well I ... I'm not sure. I thought about catching a movie."

"Great!" Billy beamed, sitting down in his driver's seat; he started it up. "I'll pick you up at eight!" Before she could say anything, he drove off waving.

"What just happened?" she thought dizzily. Billy was a nice guy, but his persistent authoritative ways made her feel intimidated and nervous, he was older than her by five years and even when she was sixteen and he was twenty one, he was overpowering, but his looks and his charms were enough to woo her innocence away that night, and although she never regretted it, she wouldn't have had it happen quite so soon if she could've helped it.

Her parents were out to dinner on their last night in town, and being a foolish child she invited Billy over anticipating some great romance which turned out to be very awkward and unexpectedly painful, for a virgin ignorant of men. They never did eat the meal she'd prepared that night; as a matter of fact they never even made it into the kitchen. When Billy arrived he brought her into the living room by the fireplace asking her if she was sure she was ready.

"For what?" her innocence was embarrassing to remember.

"For me," he said in his low sultry voice. He began to lead her upstairs. She declined the idea meekly, but his words were clear. "We can do it right here if you want?" He kissed her deeper than before and began caressing her in secret places that no one had ever touched before.

"Billy!" she objected.

"Oh Lauren!" he moaned into her hair. "Touch me! Let me have this one night to remember you by, it would mean so much to me!" His words were like honey to her young heart, he pulled her soft hand to his hardened manhood. "Don't be scared, I won't hurt you." He unfastened his pants and gently brushed her hand to his flesh, knees weak she allowed him to lay her down on the floor and slowly remove each other's clothing, she remembered his hot, moist mouth tugging at her nipples and how it had aroused her so, his stroking fingers probing her and his sudden entrance into her innocence, that was as clear as yesterday, the white hot tearing pain that ripped through her was too, she remembered their sprawled limbs and his violent shuddering as she held back tears of pain due to his swollen throbbing. It wasn't the most enjoyable time she'd ever had, but it was the first and most memorable, it hadn't lasted more than all of fifteen minutes, but it seemed an eternity.

Drifting back from the memory Lauren remembered her gas, she hurried to her car to pump the remaining gas in when she realized it was still slowly pumping and had begun to spill to the ground "Oh no!" she cried as she frantically pulled the pump out. "Twenty-six dollars!" She'd only had fifteen left in her pocket, she leaned in the open window for her purse, maybe they'd accept her credit card, searching she realized she had left it at the cabin, she had been in such a hurry. "How thoughtless," she scorned herself. *"Now what?"* Maybe she could convince the clerk that she'd return with the money, she hurried in the store, maybe if she explained her situation. The clerk frowned at her story, his withered skin was pinched between his brows

"I'm sorry ma'am, but if I dealt everyone who had a run over with gasoline credit I'd be paying more than receiving." His voice was harsh at first but softened upon seeing her frustration, she seemed like an honest girl he thought with a hint of pity.

"But sir really, you can trust me for it!"

"I'm sure you're good for the money ma'am, but ... I don't even know you..."

"Lauren," she said putting out her hand, "Lauren Conklin." She shook his hand desperately. "Here's my license if you want proof."

"Ma'am you don't understand." He motioned her to put it away. "Even with your name, there's no guarantee that..." He was cut short.

"That's all right, Harry." Lauren turned around only to see Nick standing behind her. She wondered how long he'd been there.

"I'll take care of it." He handed the man twenty-six dollars and headed out the door. Lauren blinked in confusion, what was that all about?

"Wait! Nick!" At the sound of his name on her lips he stopped turning to face her, his expression held question. "Wait, please, you didn't have to do that."

"Don't worry about it, I guess I owed you, now we're even." He started to leave again.

"Wait! I wanted to thank you, for the jam that is, and for the gas, really I owe you now." Lauren felt indebted to him for his kindness. As she caught up to him she saw a restlessness in his blue eyes, midnight blue with hints of cerulean ... he looked away from her, casting his gaze downward as if he were uncomfortable, she was puzzled for a moment, what was wrong? Nick's heart was pounding, why was she suddenly so interested in speaking to him, it was the least he could have done to make up for being such an ass, besides, he couldn't leave her thinking she was going to get the upper hand on him, he wouldn't be left with the burden of guilt on his shoulders from their last encounter. He had been home for three days without so much as going into town for a soft drink, and he couldn't seem to get rest for anything, it wasn't obviously her fault, but it was her that had been on his mind.

She stood before him with an amiable expression, her tight buckskin colored leggings revealed her thin shapely legs, she looked so young with her hair tied back, he wondered her true age.

"Are you all right?" Her question was a bit too personal for the moment and Nicholas' perturbed expression, revealed his discomfort, if she only knew ... She changed the subject. "I found the jam." She smiled and looked away, "You are Nick, right?"

He looked up sharply "Yeah, that's ... me." His smile was a flash of embarrassment.

"Look I..." they both started.

"Go ahead." Lauren smiled again.

"No, you first." Nick's smile was genuine this time, his attention was hers again.

"Well, I just wanted to apologize, for being rude in the restaurant, I didn't know." She fidgeted with her sweatshirt like a nervous child, catching herself, she put her hands behind her back. "What you wrote, about starting over. I think it's a good idea."

He studied her for a moment, he wished she hadn't said that, he wasn't sure he could handle her personality matching her looks, she had already begun to get to him, creeping into his dreams, her unknowing presence violating his intimate secrets, could he handle the reality of her, when the imaginary was already too much? Swallowing his pride and praying his growing attraction wasn't obvious he extended his handshake to her. "Nicholas Carmen."

She smiled. "Lauren Conklin."

"I know." His eyes held a sudden Mystery, "I couldn't help but overhear…" He motioned toward the station. Lauren glanced back remembering the clerk and her license, she nodded her head. The situation was tense; neither knew what to say next, when Nicholas' courage spoke up, "You're new in town, aren't you?"

"Well sort of, my family used to vacation here."

"So what brings you back." He felt a little obvious in his intentions. "If I may ask?"

She knew Nick meant well but she wasn't open to sharing her true personal reasons with anyone, her own mother hadn't even known about it. There was too much turmoil right now to get that personal, and besides she wasn't about to just throw her trust to him and set herself up for a fall, that she was certain of. By the expression on her face Nicholas knew he had turned over the wrong stone, he recounted gracefully, "It must've been the great scenery and solitaire splendor." He jested playfully, "At least that's what they said in the brochure!" She met his reassuring gaze squarely, the smile in his eyes was open and caring, he was rusty at this, he grimaced, and it simply had been too long since he had been remotely friendly to anyone.

That same feeling came over her, but she couldn't help to smile. "Something like that."

"Me too," he said, grinning.

Lauren started again, "So are you a vacationer then?" Her tension began easing.

"Not quite, I won't be leaving this winter." Secretly she was glad of it, this trip was beginning to get a little more interesting.

"Me neither." She sounded a little too hopeful for her own good, she thought. "I mean, that is why I'm here, you know, the solitary splendor."

So she was alone, Nicholas' heart skipped a beat, he sensed her nervousness, maybe now wasn't the best time to talk, he didn't want to push it. "Well, I guess I'll let you get on with your business, I didn't mean to interrupt your schedule." He turned and began to walk toward his mustang. "Maybe I'll see you later?"

"Sure." Lauren chirped out a little too anxiously, she scorned her obvious interest. She sounded so foolish, "Maybe we'll bump into each other again." As she walked toward her car Nick got the feeling he may not see her again for some time, he really hadn't wanted to let her go so soon, could he bear another night wondering about her, about himself, he knew it was now or never.

"Lauren!" Her name from his lips melted inside her fluttering heart, she turned. "How about lunch?" The question hung in the crisp air, she knew she wanted to see him, she'd been day dreaming about him since Thursday night, but was she sure she was ready, could she trust herself, trust him? "There's a great little diner around the corner?" His offer was openly genuine, and Lauren just couldn't let him get the wrong impression by refusing.

"Well, I guess I could use a bite to eat, meet me over there." She got in her car and headed toward the diner. Wondering if he had made the right choice, and scorning himself for doing this to himself again, he jumped in his mustang and followed her lead. He knew that part of him had just overrun his mind, but was it his heart or his loins? And like a typical male, at the thought of being close to her both were pounding. Nicholas sat with his chin resting on his palm, staring across the plaid covered table at the dark headed belle before him; he studied her features and movements, trying not to give himself away. She delicately blotted her napkin to her soft, puckered lips and her dark, lashed eyes darted to his and fluttered like shy butterflies, she smiled meekly.

"What are you thinking?" She put her elbow on the table and rested her cheek softly on her palm; he stared at her velvet skin and had an urge to reach out to her and softly stroke her face. "Nick?"

He snapped back to reality. "Oh, just thinking." He smiled and quickly shook his fantasy away. "Thanks for lunch."

She was searching for conversation, "Do you come here often?"

Nick grinned guiltily, sipping the last of his coffee. "Actually, this is the first time I've been here." Lauren's surprise turned to amusement, at his blatant honesty, "I really just wanted to see you."

Her mind clouded over with thought, she wondered if she had made the right decision by accepting his offer so soon, her earlier curiosity may have just gotten her into further trouble, and she was beginning to get cold feet about the venture. She'd never led him to believe she would actually be interested in a deeper attachment, right? There were no strings attached, but now came the awkward part, the meal was over, and the decision to see him again or not was close at hand. She knew he'd want an answer, that's how men worked, and she'd been well rehearsed with being hit on and turning her pursuers down.

Nick pondered his next move, so they had had lunch, lots of people did, it didn't mean anything, or did it? All the qualms of dating were a nuisance to him, he had always been the kind of man to just go straight for his goals, and games weren't a strong point for him.

"I'm glad we had the chance to meet each other under better circumstances." Lauren seemed a little uneasy her words were followed by an averted gaze, he could tell by her expressions that if he pushed things, she would most likely flee, perhaps he knew that he would push things a little too far for his own good. No matter how perfect she seemed, this attraction to her was dangerous, and he could feel himself teetering on the edge, he wanted to keep it a physical one before it was too late. Besides, weren't they all perfect in the beginning? It was later when their true colors would show.

"I'm sorry," he started, "I just didn't want to give you the wrong impression, I'm not usually so gruff, thank you for the second chance." His eyes seemed to measure her, glancing at his watch he began to stand. "I'd better let you go, it's getting late, I'm sure you have plans that I'm keeping you from." His blank statement surprised Lauren; her prepared dismissal was disintegrated before it came. That was it? He was done with her? Her vanity was suddenly diminished to embarrassment as her face reddened.

She remembered Billy, "Sort of." She realized that she had obviously assumed too quickly. She liked Nick, she liked him a lot, and that was the bad part, the realization that it was she who had read more into the lunch than what it had actually been filled her with embarrassment. How foolish of her to expect the attraction to be mutual, she felt nude, he obviously only wanted to clear up the misunderstanding between them, he was simply being nice, he probably only viewed her as an arrogant fool, after the way she had behaved at the restaurant. Her decision to avoid further embarrassment left her leading a foolish charade of casualness, all the while suppressing a growing curiosity of the one man she'd met that really had lost interest in her, what was it that had turned him away? The question bothered her; did he not find her attractive? Wasn't she good enough for a man like him? Although she was a bit relieved that she hadn't made a complete fool of herself by interrupting him and letting him down gently. Her disappointment was a sore kick from behind, she hadn't ever had the chance to decide if she was interested or not, indeed he had thrown her a curve.

Nick studied her reaction; she didn't seem to be surprised, in fact her cool demeanor held a hint of relief that tinged his pride. Perhaps she had accepted his invitation only to let him know once more of her disinterest in him, so that he would know to stop now, before he embarrassed himself. The thought ate at him, how cruel to tease with such a wanton prize, he didn't need her pity, or her games, after all, all she really was, was a pretty face, an accessory to a cashmere suit, an accessory he didn't need. What conceit she'd had to assume he would fall for her devious plot. It was obvious that she had planned to assault his pride all along, well, he would show her, someone needed to teach her a lesson in humility, and he would enjoy turning the tables on her. Nick could feel his ire rising with every quaint movement she made, as if she were flaunting what he could not touch, taunting him further. Did she really think herself to be too good for him? Maybe he was being a bit too paranoid, or maybe he was right. The sway of her delicate body as she rose seemed almost too graceful to not have been deliberate, and the swift gentle movements of her slender arms, as she began to clear their mess, seemed to be a prelude of how her soft fingertips might caress her lover's body. She had to be teasing with her movements; it was all too erotic to be simple. Lauren flashed an awkward smile at him as he watched her gathering their mess, it was all he could take, he felt the cold callousness seeping back into his chest at the notion of the deceit, but it was laced with an aching need he ruthlessly denied. He wouldn't let her get to him, he concluded, the charade needed to end.

"That's quite enough." Nicholas sounded so cold and business like that Lauren stopped short and put everything down, her nervousness and perturbed confidence in her self image left her trying to keep busy, avoiding the situation, as usual.

"You're right," she explained, "I'm sorry, it's a habit." She motioned to the table. Nick glared at her, she was either ignorant of the charisma she displayed, or very good at playing innocent, he guessed the latter. So that's how she wanted to play, well two could play at this game, he could pretend not to notice how she flaunted herself so obviously in front of him, she was simply a tease, and she was mocking him for his confrontation when they'd met.

"Well, let me not keep you from whatever it is that you must get to." Lauren sensed a glimpse of sarcasm behind his stony features. She reflected for a moment in slight confusion, for someone who was trying to be nice, that certainly was a strange thing to say.

"Well, I'm really not..." she paused, he was no longer looking at her, as if trying to avoid her totally, he was now looking around the room. His actions agitated her, it was one thing to find her boring or be disinterested, but quite another to be so blatantly rude, after all he was the one who had invited her to lunch. She no longer felt the need to explain anything to him. "Yes, well," she began, her prudish facade returning now. "I must be going, thank you again."

As their server laid their bill on the table, they simultaneously reached for the slip. "I'll get it..." the momentary union of touch startled them both, as their hands met unexpectedly. Sparks flew through Nick's body as never before, crumbling the hardened mask he wore to hide his interest. Their eyes met revealing to them both the inexplicable truth of the attraction. What Lauren saw in this virtual strangers eyes frightened her more than anything, Nick's eyes held something, not anything like her ex or any other man had ever held when they'd looked at her, this was a deep intensity, too deep for her to handle at the moment. She felt her knees weaken and her stomach knot up when his touch lingered, "Lauren..." Nick began, his voice low and sultry, mimicking the seriousness in his eyes. She pulled away from him. She had to seek refuge. "Lauren, wait! Please!" The urgency in his voice revealed itself unintentionally.

Lauren hurried faster now, her mind reeling, her heart pounding. "I've got to go!" she called back, her voice trembling. "It's not you, really!" Reaching the safety of her firebird, she tried desperately to start the car.

Nick tossed a few bills on to the table, oblivious to the exceptional tip he'd left, as he hurried out to Laurens car he was upon her in a few strides, "Lauren, please don't go..."

Her fumbling fingers betrayed her as she dropped her keys to the floor. "You don't understand..." She pleaded, searching for the fallen keys; escape was all she wanted at the moment. Something in his eyes had enlivened her, parts of her that had never been awakened before now bombarded her senses cruelly. Nick ascertained the situation as clearly as possible, the beautiful creature was human after all, and he had seen it undoubtedly within her eyes. A hunger, much like his own, clouded with a desperate, untrusting pain and hidden, blocking her from life much like it had done to him for so long. He couldn't let her go like this, he had to act now, and he had to know. The engine was turning over now, beginning to run ...

Opening her door, Nick knelt beside her, "Lauren, I'm sorry, things are so complicated, I can't explain right now, but if you'll just give me a chance." His soft words were too much, Lauren needed something, someone, being alone with him was just too dangerous. She felt trapped, trapped within herself, something was happening, it was all too much, too fast, she couldn't look at him again, She had grown so accustomed to Brian's constant mind games, that she didn't know how to react to Nick or how he made her feel. Nick's hand touched her shoulder, his warmth penetrated her and she began to unravel. "Lauren?" His voice was hypnotizing, her world was quaking beneath her, and she had to escape. Lauren's eyes met his, locking now, and disabling her from looking away. Softly, her lips parted, Nicks gaze flashed to them briefly, and her eyes seemed to hold a mutual longing. A feeling of nervous excitement came over her, she wanted to be taken, to feel helpless, so that she wouldn't blame herself for the consequences, wouldn't have to think anymore. Nick didn't know his next move; he didn't want to let the moment go. "Give me a chance," he breathed against her skin. Remembering Brian's words the feeling of excitement diminished for a moment, if only Nick were truly genuine. How she longed for just one man to actually want more from her than something physical, someone she could confide in, tell them anything and everything, things she'd never told anyone, never wanted to even admit to herself, but that kind of trust would never find her, she resolved. She closed her eyes from the bombardment of her senses, her pain was still too real to allow her heart the exposure he presented, and she felt weakened, vulnerable and, to some degree, scared.

Leaning toward her, Nick's lips brushed hers, gently, softly, bringing a startled gasp from her at his actions. His soft lips caressed hers once again as he wondered what she must have been thinking of him at that moment, their eyes met, revealing the blazing fire that had ignited from the glowing embers within. Nick's blood raced wildly, he longed to kiss her again, deeper, stronger, but would she allow it, had he gone too far already?

Lauren's breasts peaked at the flush that washed over her body, Nick's face was aglow with desire that even she could read, his blue eyes held a deep tension that changed his expression audibly as he cradled her face in his hands. Lauren's heart was pounding fiercely at the notion of what was to come next, the intimate closeness of his body was draining the last of her reserve, she was like a wanton girl once again, unable to protest the matter at hand, and unsure if she would have, even if she could. Softly his lips claimed hers and her body began to melt. Spinning dizzily into his arms, they both knew he could have her in any way he wanted, but the need to hold her, revel in her very scent overwhelmed him. So much pain had been suppressed, so much need for human touch … The kiss lingered too long, and he could feel his aching manhood begin to rise, he broke free of the embrace, only to have his hunger return two fold. Lauren opened her eyes slowly still askew from the sultry kiss.

"You drive me crazy, woman," Nick breathed raggedly. His desire obvious with every breath. "One minute I think you're setting me up for a heartache, and the next you're like some sappy kid at prom. I have to know, Lauren…" His hungry mouth sought hers once more, but Lauren's hesitance toward him now, stopped him; he cursed himself for his weakness. He'd set himself up again! He had to leave … he couldn't face her. Standing slowly he stiffly headed for his mustang, there was too much to handle, too much to sort out for himself; he needed time, space, and refuge.

Lauren didn't try to stop him, she thought about the kiss and where it left her now. She couldn't believe what had just happened, what she had allowed! Now he could see how vulnerable and weak she really was, why had she let that happen?

The guilt was already seeping into her mind, she could have kicked herself, this was Brian all over again, and why couldn't she learn? But what she couldn't deny was that the kiss they had shared had been like no other, even the memory of it still engulfed her desires, and strangely enough she hadn't even thought of Brian the entire time, as lovers often do on rebound excursions. He had kissed her, and worse, she had kissed him back, and though she inwardly warned herself against the emotions that circulated now, undeniably, the heat of their union still burned within her.

CHAPTER 4

Speeding down the gravel road, Billy's shining jeep gleamed, reflecting the faded sunset all around. He was early, he knew that, but that was his style. As he grew closer to the old cabin he turned his blaring music down and peered into the rearview mirror, brushing his sandy hair back in place, *"yeah,"* he thought confidently, *"you still got it."* He pulled up to the drive beside her firebird and turned the key off. Stepping out he looked up and noticed the master bedroom light on, he smiled and trod up to the door, slipping in.

Lauren was upstairs putting her laundry away when she heard a small creak behind her, she turned quickly and gasped, Billy stood cocked in the doorway, "Billy!" she cried. "What are you doing..." suddenly she remembered their "date."

Smiling he unfolded his thick arms and leaned an elbow in the doorway. "Gee, I was hoping I'd catch you dressing."

The sly laughter in his eyes eased her tension. "Oh Billy," she explained apologetically, "I'm so sorry, I forgot!" Her face told the truth and Billy read it clearly, his ego was bruised.

"Well, I guess it's a good thing I came early then." He backed out the door. "Go ahead and get dressed I'll wait downstairs."

"No, really, I've got a lot to do still and..." Lauren really didn't want to go out again, especially after this afternoon, but Billy wouldn't accept rejection.

"I won't take no for an answer," he cut in. "If you're not downstairs and ready in 25 minutes, I'll drag you out..." His eyes held a hint of seriousness amongst his obvious playfulness, and Lauren wasn't up to arguing, he shut the door and she turned slowly to find an appropriate outfit. She decided on her black party dress, it fit her curves perfectly and the thin spaghetti straps accented her slender neck and shoulders, besides she needed something to boost her spirits, she had been depressed and tired most of the day maybe it would be nice to catch up with an old friend, and surely the icon of her nervousness wouldn't be out and about tonight. She doubted she would see him anytime too soon after the way he'd left her earlier, and she secretly hoped her resistance wouldn't be tested again for a while. She slipped off her sweater and leggings and laid her brazier on the bed, she dabbed her softly scented perfume on various pulse marks and began searching for her sandal toed stockings, she'd need them with her black suede pumps.

Billy's eyes were filled with lust as he peered through the small crack in the bedroom door, he watched as Lauren removed her garments and dropped them to the floor one by one, her milky white skin shone with radiance in the dim bedroom light, he hungrily licked his lips as he watched her remove her brazier revealing her full breasts and rosy nipples that peaked at the sudden coolness, the hairs of his neck prickled up as his arousal heightened. His eyes ran down her soft curves and down her thighs imaging what he would do between them., *My you have grown up haven't you?* he thought to himself. *Everywhere.* Lauren turned suddenly feeling as if someone were watching her, she shook the feeling away as quickly as it had come and finished dressing.

As she walked to the door she shut the light off in the room and called out to Billy that she was ready and he wouldn't have to drag her out after all, but as she passed through the doorway a strange sense came over her, someone was watching her!

She could feel eyes upon her and she wrapped her arms protectively against herself, "Billy!" she called out stepping to the banister, the room seemed to be empty, her heart began to thud as she searched frantically with her eyes for some sort of movement in the cabin besides herself. Did he leave? She thought, confused, surely not.

"Billy!" she called again. *Where was he?* A movement caught her eye behind her and she spun around as Billy came toward her.

Clasping her hand to her pounding chest she sighed in relief, "Where were you?" she asked in nervous wonder.

Billy grinned and straightened his black and white western patterned shirt, "I hope you don't mind, I borrowed your restroom?"

Lauren gathered her nerves and smoothed out her dress. "I called for you," she explained as she watched him tugging at the legs of his black denim jeans. He straightened the cuffs of his pants and brushed the dust off his newly polished cowboy boots. Laurens face showed disapproval, "You could have answered."

He glanced at her shaken features. "Oh, I'm sorry, how thoughtless of me, forgive me?" She cast him a look of sarcasm and started for the stairs. "I'm ready."

Billy caught her arm, and not realizing his own strength, spun her around, Lauren gasped at his sudden roughness. "I said I was sorry Lauren, I didn't mean to frighten you?" His brow was furrowed apologetically, "I mean it, I'm sorry. Can we try to have a good time now?"

"Sure." Lauren felt strangely nervous, but it wasn't the nervousness of a crush like she had felt with Nick, he intimidated her.

On the way to the movies Billy spoke casually and nonstop, which was fine by Lauren, she didn't have much to say anyway, something wasn't right but she didn't know what it was. The movie theater was surprisingly crowded for a Sunday, and Lauren watched the young locals filter in and out in couples while Billy bought their tickets. As she watched him in line, she noticed a young girl that looked to be 16 or17 years old eyeing him, she walked past him brushing against his arm and casting him a flirtatious look. He smiled and motioned her over, the girl timidly crept over to him grinning as Billy chatted with her for a moment, then she swayed closer to his masculine form as if she were swooning to him, Lauren wondered if he knew her, and what their conversation consisted of, *wasn't he a little old to be flirting with teenagers?* Truthfully she would just as soon have given them her blessing and bid them a good life, than to be stuck in the discomfort of a "date" she hadn't wanted. Billy noticed Lauren watching him, he flashed a smile her direction and pointed to her, the girls adoring expression quickly soured as she glared at her apparent competition, her eyes seemed to measure Laurens stature for a moment then flitted back to Billy's, frowning, she whispered something to him and laughed! Tossing her auburn curls about her shoulders. Billy's features darkened and the girl hurried off. Lauren didn't watch the charade any longer, something about it sickened her, a few moments later her sandy haired companion found her.

"Ready?" His question was toned amiably, she walked stiffly with him toward the theater entrance.

"So who was that?" she asked him quietly.

"Oh, just a girl, she tried to pick me up can you believe it?" Billy beamed at her question, jealousy he mused. "I told her I was with you and she left me alone. She tried to say she was eighteen but you saw her, jail-bait." Something was amidst, he had had a longer talk with the "jail-bait" than that, but it didn't matter, she was beginning to wish she hadn't asked. A large thick arm wrapped around her shoulders and slid possessively to her hip "jealous?" Billy's lips barely brushed her ear as he whispered the insinuation.

Lauren turned to face him squarely. "No." By the look on his face she could see his visible bruise, pride was an ugly thing. They walked into the dark room and sought out their seats, this would be a long night, she thought, she hoped the movie was good.

Orange tentacles of flame danced seductively casting dark shadows throughout the room that crept and crawled as nocturnal creatures do, a pop of scorching bark created a minute explosion of bright yellow sparks, that fizzled out as fast as they had erupted, breaking the silence of the solemn dark room. Nick poked at the flickering fire, and then laid the cast iron rod back in its place; there would be no sleep tonight. His mind was filled with too much turmoil; too many conflicting interests were haunting his thoughts. He had kissed her and by doing so, had driven her away. Maybe he was better off, he had fallen too fast and he knew that couldn't be good, why wouldn't she leave him alone, her face kept running through his mind, his name on her lips lingered still … he couldn't go on like this. He stood up stretching his legs, and the urge to flex all of his aching muscles overcame him. He extended his lean muscular arms over his head raising on his toes and tightening each muscle up his back and abdomen; it was a refreshing sensation and helped to boost his energies. He stepped into the kitchen and poured himself another cup of coffee; cappuccino sounded better, he thought, a good smooth relaxing beer even better! But drinking was something he had sworn off, never again, not after what had happened, not after that …

… The nights chill was all around him as he bounded through the emergency room doors. "Where is he!" he called out as he rushed to the desk, from the nurses expression he could tell her next question. "Jack," he cried out, "Jack Carmon!"

"Fifth floor," she breathed as Nick rushed past, "but you can't go up there! That's the I.C.U.!" he frantically pushed the elevator button, but its progress wasn't fast enough for him, he dashed for the stairs and in minutes he was stepping onto the 5th floor, he rushed for the front desk.

"Tell me which room Jack Carmon is in!" he demanded.

"Relation?" The melancholy nurse barely looked up at him.

"Which room!" He grew louder with impatience.

"Sir, I cannot give that information without proof of relation…"

Nick pounded the desk with his fists. "NOW!" he roared ...

"Nick!" His name came from behind him, he spun around.

"Mom!" He rushed to her, his arms open. "Oh God! Mom, what happened?"

"I'm not sure," she started, " I got a call this evening around 6:30 saying there'd been an accident, your father was on his way home when a drunk

driver, well he came out of nowhere and..."

"Is he all right? How bad is it?"

"Now, Nick, you have to listen carefully, he didn't have his seat belt on, he's sustained a lot of head trauma." Tears weld up in her eyes. "They're not sure if he..." Her voice broke off. "Even if he pulls through there's going to be some damage." Tears spilled down her face.

Nick turned away clasping his hands to his temples. "Oh God, Mom, oh God!!" He could feel his emotions rising, he didn't want to accept this sudden tragedy, he couldn't imagine his father, a vegetable or a paraplegic, not the man who had been so strong in life, who had lifted him high as a boy, taught him right from wrong. Memories flashed through his mind, learning to ride a bike, to drive a car, all the arguing.

"Nick." His mother's gentle hand smoothed over his shoulder. "He knows you love him." Her voice quivered but held its assurance. "He's always known."

Turning he fell apart in his mothers embrace. "I have to see him Mom, I have to, I need to tell him myself!" His burning tears melted away the stubborn pride that had plagued their relationship. It didn't matter any longer who had been right or wrong, if only he could have seen that before.

Entering his father room he noticed the cold harshness of his surroundings, as if the patients that harbored the room were already gone, with no hint of warmth or of home, Pulling the slate-blue curtain back he saw a man lying amongst various machines and hoses that attached to his body everywhere, the faint sound of the monitors and rhythmic wheezing of the respiratory equipment filled the room. It scarcely resembled the man he had known as his father, his features were slurred and swollen, bandages covered his head and most all of his appendages, his eyes were closed and blackened and Nick felt a growing pain deep in his chest as he looked on he stepped beside the bed looking down at the fallen man, so many years of anger and pain, he had seen his father as a stubborn dominating monster of man, but looking back and looking upon him now, he only saw the truth, he was only a man who was scared of growing old, scared of losing his son, his family.

"Father?" Nicks words were scarcely a whisper. "If you can hear me, I have to tell you something." He tried to hold back his tears but he felt his throat swelling at the rise of a forming lump, his tears spilt down his cheeks and fell to his fathers hand, reaching out to him, Nick took hold of the broad hand, holding it tightly as if he would hold him back from death, at least long enough to say goodbye, one last time ... "I love you Dad!" he cried. "I love

you and I'm sorry! I'm so sorry!" His fathers heart rate suddenly increased and his hand tightened to his sons, Nicks shock held his tongue, he couldn't move, let alone call out for a nurse, as he watched with wonder a single tear ran down his fathers face and suddenly a flat-line. Doctors and nurses swarmed in pushing Nick farther and farther away but he just stood in awe blinking through his tears, he had been holding on just to hear those words from his son, suffering through indescribable pain just to hear those words, and he had set him free, he had been released from his hellish darkness, but it was Nick now, who felt the pain, more than imaginable, a pain never to be forgotten. The days after were a blur, the funeral, the wake and then the reading of the will, his father had left them a substantial life insurance policy and to Nick he left his pride and joy, his 1965 Cherry red hard top Ford Mustang. Nick and his family pursued the drunken driver but to no avail, his lawyer got him off on the charge of reckless endangerment and manslaughter, they claimed that Mr. Carmen was partly responsible because he did not have his seat belt on, and if the seat belt had been worn, he would have sustained less serious injuries, therefore his death was not due to the mans drunken state but his own negligence, he got off with a slap on the wrist. He never forgot the lawyer, his name was Vincent Malhoun and he was a slick snake, someday he vowed revenge, and someday he would have it. They also managed to get a restraining order against Nick from the driver so as not to put him in danger of any later confrontations. Since Nick had lost his temper at the police station the night his father died. He remembered how his fiancé Gretchen had changed after his father had died too, she was distant always gone, always spending his inheritance. Then came the night when he had broken down in her arms, she had no warm comforting words, no reassuring touch, she pushed him away from her, screaming that a real man wouldn't act so childish a real man would have sued for more money. She refused to take care of him any longer; she cursed him and his father for ruining their life. "I thought you two didn't get along anyway!" she'd screamed when he'd confided his deepest pains to her. After she left, he never saw her again, along with $10,000.00 of his inheritance, He never did pursue her, and it didn't matter, although he knew his father would roll over in his grave if he knew it! He had never trusted her from the beginning, although he would never elaborate his reasons. She was one of the arguments they had never been able to reconcile.

A sudden flash crossed his eyes, bringing him back to reality, a vehicle was pulling in across the way, someone had moved into the cabin around the bend from his. There usually wasn't much movement over there this late at night, but Nick wasn't one to pry into anyone's personal business unless there was a good reason to. He stepped back into the den and sat in his easy chair by the fireplace, sipping at his coffee, and pondering on what he could do to keep himself occupied, Lauren stepped hurriedly toward the door of her cabin, she needed away from her clinging companion, who however, was right on her heels.

"What's your hurry?" Billy asked, raising his eyebrows, he was hopeful that she would invite him in.

Turning toward him, Lauren grinned awkwardly. "I've got a lot to do still," she stammered out. "It's really gotten late, and I've got to get some sleep."

His tall muscular form towered close to her. "Well, do I even get a goodnight hug?" His large hands felt for her waist, as they had all evening. She was wary to allow him very close to her purposely; she had a feeling if she gave an inch he'd take a mile.

"I've really got to get to bed." She needed an excuse.

"I could always join you?" His crooked smile gleamed in the pale moon light, Lauren stared at him for a moment, aghast, she knew he was a flirt, but this was ridiculous, At seeing her reaction, Billy played his statement off as a joke. "Come on, Lauren, loosen up, it was a joke. Don't I even get a thank you. I've had a good night?"

Lauren thought for a moment. "You're right Billy, I'm sorry, where are my manners?" He smiled again arms open. "Thank you for taking me out tonight, I'm sorry if I wasn't the perfect date, I just have a lot on my mind." She feigned a small hug on his neck, hoping she could pull away from him before his thick arms caught her. Billy felt Laurens warmth against him as she hurriedly encircled his neck, her soft breasts pressed against him and he could feel heat spreading up his body, he crushed her to him as she released a small grunt of discomfort.

Pressing his temple to hers his lips began to trail her revealed shoulder, she squirmed from him for a moment. "What are you doing!" she demanded.

"Oh Lauren, can't I have just one kiss, for old times sake?" His arms still held her close and his breath was on her lips, she stared at him for a moment, wondering what her next move should be, he was an old friend, and she had had fond memories of him, but her fondness of him was beginning to unravel, and quickly, maybe if she gave him a small kiss, maybe then he would leave, after all that was usually how dates ended.

"All right Billy, but just a small one, I don't want you to think…" she was cut short by his hot searing mouth; fiercely he claimed her lips, thrusting his large coursing tongue in deeply. Lauren nearly gagged on him before she could even think, she hadn't anticipated this at all, she tried desperately to pull away, but to no avail, he pressed harder upon her mouth, she felt her plump lower lip tear under his excessive pressure, hot salty liquid began to flow from the newly obtained injury. Pushing his large body back she tried to concentrate on a weak point of his anatomy so as to fend him off, he was like an animal, pawing and crushing her feminine features. Billy's blood coursed rapidly as his hands found her breasts and hungrily tried to release them from there binds.

"Oh, Lauren!" he moaned against her ear. Laurens heel came down hard on his right foot sending a sudden shooting pain through him, relinquishing his lustful thoughts, he released her with a quick thrust. "Sonofabitch!" he spat venomously, grabbing for his throbbing appendage. Wiping the blood and saliva from her mouth, Lauren stared at him in disgust.

"Get the hell out of here!" she threatened. "Or next it'll be something a little more delicate!"

"What in Sam Hill is wrong with you?" Billy seemed genuinely confused for a moment, then noticing her torn lip, he came toward her. "Lauren, I … I didn't mean to hurt…"

"Save it!" she retorted. "Just leave."

He attempted again, "I would never…" turning away she closed the door behind her and locked it. Listening for proof of his leaving, she heard his Jeep start and pull away releasing a soft breath of relief, she went slowly into the kitchen, she'd never be able to go to sleep now, she'd be petrified of every little bump in the night. She prayed he wouldn't be back. Lauren laid out her deli sliced turkey and rye bread, she was starving and hadn't had a bite to eat since lunch, she began to put her sandwich together when she heard a knock at the door, her heart seemed to stop, was it Billy? She crept toward the door and peered out the window in the den, it was a man but not Billy, she wondered for a moment who it could be out here this late?

Nick had heard a commotion coming from the cabin near his and the vehicle that had pulled in prior to the scuffle had sped away a little too quickly for his liking, he wanted to make sure that everything was all right. Lauren leaned against the thick wooden door, her heart still pounding wildly. "Who is it?" she called wondering if he could hear the tremor in her voice.

"Ma'am." Nick heard the woman's faint voice trembling. "Is everything all right?" No answer. "I heard some noises over here a few minutes ago, I was just checking to see if everything was all right"

"Oh." Her response was of surprise. "Yeah, everything's fine, thank you."

"Just checking ma'am." As the door opened, Lauren peered upon the man, who was now leaving, his tight blue jeans revealed his muscular legs and tight buttocks, she stared unintentionally for a moment.

"Excuse me?" she started. She intended to thank him for his concern, when suddenly her breath stopped, as the mysterious man turned, their eyes met, and instantly she recognized his deep blue gaze. "Nick?" Her shock was openly stated, as was his.

"Lauren?" The embarrassment of the situation earlier was almost lost in the familiarity of their meeting. Laurens relief was followed by a flush of security in the fact that she knew her would be rescuer, but their earlier confrontation left an unanswered question between them, and a void that was dangerously closing in, already his presence had drained the exhaustion from her and replaced it with a new found buoyancy reflected by the small ember within her eyes.

"How did you know I was here?" She seemed almost as agitated with him, as she was shocked at his presence. They stared for a moment neither understanding their strange situation, nor questioning it. Nick traced over her features as he had so many times in his mind, why hadn't he realized sooner, he knew someone had moved in beside him but he never imagined how close she'd been to him all along.

"I heard a commotion over here," he explained motioning toward his cabin. "I live just over there." Lauren followed his extended arm to the dark structure behind the thick pines over the way, as she focused, she saw the faint glowing lights coming from apparent windows and slowly she could make out the slight lines that framed off a cabin, how could she have not known he was there? A dead silence fell between them, the tension as thick as the pine tar that scented the cool night air, neither dared to recant on their earlier affair, Lauren glanced back at her newfound neighbor, only to find his gaze upon her once more, she felt herself reddening as a result of his bold actions, Nick looked away. "Sorry if I startled you, I'd better go now."

Lauren nodded. "Yes, I do have to get to bed." She knew she couldn't afford another incident with him, and after her ordeal with Billy, she didn't need any more insomnia causing situations. It would be hard enough to sleep as it was.

Nick hadn't expected to see her again, ever, let alone so soon, when she had opened the door and he turned only to see the last face he had expected to see in the world, he felt his heart stop, now he needed to get away before the entanglement began again. Heading toward his cabin, they bid each other goodnight and both wrestled with emotions that neither knew of.

After finishing her late night snack, Lauren picked up one of the dime store novels she had bought earlier, she thumbed through it for a few moments and then decided on writing some thoughts down to help release some of the built up tension that was pounding in her back, this often helped to soothe her. An hour passed by unnoticed and glancing at the clock on the mantle of the fireplace, she hurriedly folded the paper and placed it in the book laying it back beside the large chair she was sitting in, stretching; she headed for bed knowing it would be a restless night.

CHAPTER 5

Billy took the last drag off of his cigarette and flicked it carelessly on to the pavement; he glanced at his watch and fumed with impatience. "What the hell is taking her so long!" he hissed. He began pacing, his stature became like that of a caged lion, but his increasingly violent train of thought, twice as vicious. He bitterly thought back to the events that took place with Lauren. She had rejected him, the little wench, and he never took no for an answer, not from her, not from anyone. She was just like his ex, a tease, well he would show her, Billy Malhoun always got the last word! This rekindled obsession with her wouldn't allow him to forget his pride so easily.

Footsteps hurriedly scurried down the pavement toward Billy, he turned sharply toward the sound. "Sorry I'm late Billy!" the young girl whispered hoarsely. "My folks stayed up later than usual." As she neared him she noticed the sneer in his eyes, before she could wince she felt him clasp her arms with a vice-like grip.

"Do you have any idea how long I've been waiting here!" he shook her viciously.

"I ... I'm sorry Billy!"

He shook her again, "I don't wait on ANYBODY!" His words bit through the night air with an eerie psychotic ring, the girl trembled beneath his gaze, he stared at her briefly, she knew who was in control and that satisfied him for the moment, his grip eased and she breathed a little easier now.

"Did you get the room?" Her eyes never met his as she asked the question.

"Of course I did!" he growled. "I can't afford to be seen with you around that neighborhood!" He tugged roughly on her arm, pulling her after him. "Let's go!" he ordered gruffly as she stumbled behind him. They hurried over to Billy's Jeep, concealed by the dark shadows behind the theater and headed out toward the motel on the edge of town.

Checking in at the desk earlier, Billy had paid for a single room, as usual, and led his partner in secretively, he couldn't afford to get caught, publicly, with her, she was merely a child, but he had seen to it months earlier that the curious 14-year-old learned the ways of womanhood. Although his actions weren't public knowledge, they were blatantly obvious to the desk clerk at the Motel Rendezvous, he shook his head in disgust as he watched the red jeep Cherokee pull into the parking lot of the motel, now carrying two passengers, one of which he knew to be Sabrina Ellington, the daughter of the towns Chief of Police, but Billy was also a well respected member of their community, and his "charitable" donations, every year, to various organizations that kept the small town on the map, were enough to keep heads turned and mouths shut.

Entering the small room of the motel, Billy closed the door quickly before turning on the light; its walls were gloomily decorated and covered with a thick, yellowish blanket of generations of cigarette smoke. Sabrina stepped forward and laid her purse on the nightstand beside the shoddy made bed.

"Get undressed," he roughly demanded of her as he pulled at his shirt tails. The command was strangely exciting to her, the games they would sometimes play included cast roles of dominance and submission.

Casting him a look of seduction she now commanded him. "Make me!" she dared. Billy looked at her for a moment and then was upon her, pulling her clothes carelessly off of her still ripening body.

"Oh, Billy!" she cried. "If my daddy knew…" she reveled in her rebellion against him. Billy was bad and all her girlfriends knew it. She was the envy of all of them, which also put her at the top of the list of all the boys in her school. But, boys weren't the reigning interest in her life. When Billy had moved into the house down the street from hers, she had, had no interest in boyfriends or sex, at least not openly, his flirting had started their affair, and boys seemed immature after that. She needed men, powerful men, like Billy someone who would take her away from this one horse town and treat her like a woman, not a child. She didn't plan to stay in the woods all her life, and she was learning all too well how to use all her assets to best suit herself, and no one, not even her father would stand in her way. Billy hungrily claimed the girl, Lauren weighed so heavily still on his mind that he needed an outlet for his tensions, and if he were to take her in darkness he would be able to visualize Lauren instead. Sabrina's soft young body would never do tonight, his needs were twisted, with obsession and she was no Lauren. As the last pieces of clothing were removed, Sabrina reached for her purse to extract the protection Billy would wear, but he had other plans, forcefully clasping her wrists above her head he held them fast with one of his large hands.

Sabrina's confusion was evident. "Billy? What are you doing? You know we need to…"

His broad forearm muffled her words. "Shut-up." His voice was dangerously bitter, the girl struggled to remove herself from his grasp but to no avail, she began to panic. It wasn't supposed to be like this!! He had made love to her before, and she felt she was safe with him. He'd never made her do anything she didn't want to after the first time, but she couldn't do anything without assurance that there would be no mistakes.

"Billy," she tried, "p-please I don't like this game..." Her soft mouth was snuffed out once more. Billy forced the wanton young woman's thighs apart. His urgent needs would hear of no bonds, not this time. He cast her face out of his mind and absorbed himself into the memories of Lauren, creating his own sexual fantasy world. Wrapping his mind into this work of nymphonic pleasures, Sabrina was gone and her body served as a blank canvas on which he would create his fantastic effigy.

"You'll not deny me this time Lauren! Not this time!"

Morning came with a flash of bright sunlight and the sound of chirping birds. Lauren sighed with relief, she had made it through the night, and her aching neck and shoulders painfully revealed her tense evening, as she winced at the pain. Rising to get dressed she noticed that she had left her bedroom window open all night, how thoughtless of her, she scorned herself, a raccoon or some other curious snooper could have gotten in last night, she closed it sleepily, a falling object, from the window sill caught her eye. "What on earth ... ?" She bent down, retrieving the small item. Turning it over in her hand she studied it briefly. "Now how did this get here?" she mused. A crushed cigarette butt was indeed a foreign object to any home of her parents; her father kept a pipe, but never cigarettes. She hoped he hadn't picked up the habit since they'd last been there! Tossing it in the wastebasket, she shrugged it off, the small brown burn mark on the sill, going unnoticed. Yawning, she began searching her closet for what attire she would be displaying today, she knew she would have to head into town this morning, she needed to find the hardware store so she could price the roofing supplies, she had noticed some missing shingles on the backside of the house and she wanted to make sure she could stay on top of things before winter hit. The mountain winters could sometimes be fierce, and she had never actually stayed long enough to know what to expect. After a quick breakfast, Lauren headed to her car, the thought of Nick being so close made her anxious to leave, she wondered for a moment what his night had been like, if he had tossed and turned all night as well. Heading toward town Lauren began changing through the stations on her car radio, she needed something up beat to keep her awake, the rumble of the car and gentle loping of the hills worked like a sleeping pill on her exhausted person, she found herself drifting, her eyes heavy and aching, she wondered if she should pull over for a moment, but the town was only a few more miles away … suddenly Lauren jumped awake, a diesel truck was blowing its horn wildly, realizing what was happening Lauren over compensated her turn, swerving out of the oncoming traffics lane and barely missing the 20 ton 18 wheeler. She frantically jerked the wheel again trying desperately to control the speeding car but to no avail, she slammed her foot to the break pedal only to find that her breaks were non-existent, to her horror Lauren watched the approaching curb, for a moment she wondered what was on the other side of the guard rail, and then terrifyingly recalled, the river!

As the Firebird hit the railing Lauren cast her arms over her face, a shriek of terror rang through the tall darkly nettled pines, but ended abruptly as the vehicle dove onto the icy water below. Inside the steel death trap, Lauren sat barely conscious, unable to interpret her situation, water poured in rapidly as the car sank deeper and deeper into the flowing river. As it reached a depth of nearly 12 feet it collided sharply with a fallen tree that had been wedged into the river bottom, some 4 yards further down, scraping along the log the rear axle of the car caught a large boulder and the car stopped inches from the black chasm below. The icy water raised Lauren from her unconscious state, her eyes fixed on the scene before her, the water nearly engulfed the entirety of the Pontiac and it swallowed Lauren's stricken features quickly, she struggled with her seatbelt, releasing it seconds before she ran out of breath. Frantically she shot toward the rear of the car, emerging, she found herself trapped in an air pocket the size of a breadbox. Gasping for air she began to panic. Feeling the claustrophobia begin to sink in she pounded on the rear glass in a painstakingly futile effort to reach freedom from the icy cell. Under the incredible pressure the car lurched forward and Lauren screamed. Remembering the complete blackness that she faced if she went any farther, closing her eyes she breathed deeply for a moment, she had to calm down, she had to think. If she could open one of the doors, without too much movement, she might be able to make it to the surface, but she had no idea how deep she had sunk thus far. She decided it was her only choice, if she stayed much longer she would run out of air anyway, taking in two deep breaths she pushed herself to the front of the car, blindly she reached for the drivers door handle pulling on it roughly and pushing outward in sequence, she found it was wedged into the fallen timber that she had struck, she quickly tried the passenger door no progress, she seemed to be wedged in between the log and the large rocks that harbored the edge of the underwater drop off, she was trapped, emerging again she found that her air pocket was gradually shrinking, what now? Would this be how she would die? Immersed in a cold watery grave forever? She couldn't die! She didn't want to give up, not yet, not while she still breathed. Pondering her next move she wondered if she could squeeze out of the windows, but the passenger window was broken and pinned to the rocks outside, maybe the driver's window? She was sure if she caused too much movement the vehicle would surely drop to the bottom. As she began to realize her grim situation a sound brought her to attention, a rhythmic ping from outside, someone was rapping on her car! She desperately tried to see out of the darkened rear glass, but only caught a glimpse of a silhouette swimming toward the distant sunlight.

"Help me!" she cried. "I'm here!" *It must be the truck driver,* she thought. *He saw me crash!* "Down here!" she yelled. The silhouette appeared again. Laurens desperation increased, the air was becoming stale and her head was beginning to pound, peering out the window the man's plan became evident, he held a large rock in his hands and he was coming toward the glass at an incredible speed. Diving under the water, Lauren felt the sudden jolt of the car and the tight vacuum that was suddenly released she dashed for the opening quickly, her breath was running low, the firebird lurched forward and broke free from the restraints that held it. Reaching for the broken glass Lauren grasped hold of the opening and threw herself out of the sinking prison. She felt the jagged glass slice into her flesh and tear her fragile hand, releasing deep red fluid into the dark water, her legs and arms were numb from cold, and she hadn't noticed before that she could scarcely move them. Hypothermia was quickly setting in, her lungs aching with a need for oxygen, she found herself at a loss for energy, a deep cold set in to her joints, *No!* she thought desperately. *I'm this close!* Extending her throbbing appendage toward the light at the surface, she felt her legs stop kicking. Her eyes grew clouded, *It's over,* she realized solemnly. *It's all over*. Out of nowhere Lauren felt herself being grabbed. A strong arm wrapped around her waist, pulling her rapidly upwards, until finally she broke surface. Gasping she found it almost impossible to breathe, the raging waters quickly pulled her under again along with her newfound hero. She was pulled upward again, this time she began to struggle to stay afloat.

"Hold on, Lauren!" the man's voice cried over the roaring water. "Don't fight me! I'm trying to help!" The words rang clear as Lauren stilled herself, glancing up she noticed her surroundings were foreign, she was far from the curb she had flown off of, all around were trees and densely thickened forests, the water became rougher as the two struggling beings drifted, several times Lauren nearly lost hold of her mysterious savior, but his steel grip held tight. Only now did she feel his strength beginning to weaken, the water was swift and icy cold, she knew they had to get to shore soon or they would surely perish. The roar of the water increased in it's intensity the farther they went, large jagged rocks emerged gradually growing in numbers, Lauren felt her rescuers heart beat quicken suddenly. "Hold on to me!" he commanded. Through barely conscious eyes Lauren stared in awe at what lay before them, the river stopped abruptly, breaking off at the edge of a cliff, a seemingly large drop off at the sound of the hollowness below, she couldn't escape this time, the river was determined to swallow her and it seemed that it would, when suddenly out of nowhere she was jerked up from the deadly rapids and swung viciously onto the rocky shore where she finally collapsed, unconscious and exhausted.

CHAPTER 6

Laurens eyes fluttered as she began to move about, she rolled onto her side and began gasping and choking on the water that remained in her throat, she felt cold and sore and the coolness all around her nipped at her bare skin. She tried to rise but found that she was dizzy and disoriented, moaning she clasped her hand to her head, a sharp sting of pain shot at her from the appendage. Lurching her arm back she focused on her palm, it was jaggedly slashed in a deep vertical tear. She thought for a moment, confusion still reigning in her mind, what had happened? A cold gust of wind caught her, sending an icy chill through her entirety, she glanced down at herself, she was clothed only in her undergarments and was damp from head to toe, she brushed the locks of saturated hair out of her eyes and began to examine her surroundings, the sun was fading in the west and dusk was settling in, trees and rocks surrounded her and to her right she noticed a smoldering brush pile, concentrating on it she found she could not recall where it had come from. Something wasn't right, why was she here? Why was she sleeping half nude on the riverbank? The riverbank! Something was familiar about it, but what was it? She tried to recall the events that had led up to her current situation, but shockingly found that she couldn't, not a trace of them remained, she thought for a moment and began to panic, where was she? And more importantly, who was she? Suddenly she was lost, alone and frightened in a world that she couldn't recall, trapped in an identity that she knew nothing of, she struggled to think, desperate for a single memory, anything, anything at all? Everything was slurred and incomprehensible, nothing fit or matched. A rustling in the nearby growth startled the disoriented woman, she jumped at the disturbance and gasped when a man appeared out of the foliage, he stared for a brief moment his blue eyes mesmerized by the sight of her.

"Thank God!" he breathed as he dropped the bundle of sticks he had been carrying. "Are you all right?" The dazed young woman squinted in confusion, no answer came to her lips, she wasn't sure how exactly to answer, physically she felt as though she had been put through hell, but she was in one piece. Mentally, well, that was another story, she had no idea who he was or if she should trust him or not. Lauren seemed to be shaken up pretty badly, her long dark locks surrounded her oval face and blanketed her bare shoulders, her eyes held a hint of fear and confusion, as if she didn't know him, the innocents they reflected brought to mind that of a child.

Nick considered her reaction to him for a moment, she seemed genuinely confused. “Lauren? Are you all right?” He stepped toward her.

Struggling to stand, Lauren drug herself back from him. “You stay back!” she ordered, casting her finger toward him.

“Lauren, it’s me, Nick!” He tried toward her again, followed by the same reaction. “What’s happened?” His concern seemed honest enough, yet something was wrong, a flash of a memory came to her, she tried to start her car, he was next to her, kneeling … it was done, so maybe she knew him somehow, but whether he was dangerous or not she didn’t know, only frenzied feelings were felt in that quick flash, a nervousness from something, she didn’t understand.

“Where are my clothes?” The question felt odd. She wasn’t even sure that she had had any on to begin with; she hoped she hadn’t given away her secret ailment of the lost memories; he might use that against her.

Nick knew something was wrong; she wasn’t behaving normally. “They’re not exactly dry yet.” She felt his eyes roving down her body and embarrassingly she tried to cover herself. She peered at him for a moment, he, himself was only wearing a pair of red boxer shorts. She caught herself staring a little too long at his bared flesh, he was attractive, she thought to herself, but what connection did he have to her? Nick watched her try unsuccessfully to cover her barely clothed body, he felt a flush of red go over him recalling how he had removed her soaked clothing while she was in an unconscious state. He hadn’t thought a thing of it then because he really had no choice in the matter, hypothermia had begun to set in after he pulled them both from the icy river. The tree branch that hung low over the water had been their beacon in the storm then, he reflected on how he had lain beside her frail body, flesh upon flesh, while their shared heat coursed between them until her tremors subsided and her heart beat steadied, he hadn’t even considered his explanation when she awoke.

Their now obvious state, of little if any concealment left both of them feeling a bit uncomfortable in the presence of the other, embarrassment became an unsurpassable factor. Nick cast his eyes upward and rubbed the back of his head awkwardly, clearing his throat he suggested that she don his shirt until her clothing finished drying, the thick sweatshirt she had been wearing held the saturation deeply. It would possibly be dry by morning or mid-afternoon, as for the denim pants she had worn, they too still held moisture, but nearing them to the fires warmth they would soon have, they would dry by late that night. Nicks shirt was soft cotton blended flannel and had quickly dried in that afternoon's sunlight, he picked it off of the tree branch where it hung solemnly and shook off any loose bark or creeping insects. Trying not to look in her direction, so as not to cause any further embarrassment he handed the garment to the shivering woman and she quickly put it on.

"Sorry about the clothes," Nick began. "It was the only chance we had, and it couldn't be helped, really." Lauren shook her head for a moment, he seemed earnest enough, but she couldn't piece together what had happened, or where he fit in. Seeing her obvious confusion Nicholas began to feel the tension between them, she didn't seem to trust him, to know him … "Lauren," he started, "I don't want to seem opportunistic, but what choice do you have but to trust me? I'm the only link you have to getting out of here and if you'll give me a chance, I'd like to help you with, whatever, is wrong."

"Lauren," she repeated back to him, buttoning the shirt. "That's my name." The statement seemed more of a question, but held its assurance.

Nick stared at her for a moment disbelieving her dilemma. "You mean, you don't know?" Lauren looked away, his blatant remark somehow hit home, tears welled up her eyes, she started to speak, but the lump in her throat interfered with the passage of her words.

"I just…" she cleared her throat. "…I just can't remember…" her tears spilt down her dirt strewn cheeks and she looked to Nick for some kind of reassurance, some morsel of relief. Nick's heart went out to her. "It's Nick," he began. "Nicholas Carmen, and you can trust me." He walked to her and touched her shoulder tenderly, the warmth of his touch emanated throughout her, something, briefly familiar, rang clear for a moment, something good, something safe.

"Yes! I think … I think I remember…" It was gone, she looked up at him, his bright blue eyes burned into hers, was he her lover? She didn't know, but the way she felt under that blue gaze she knew that there was something between them, whatever it was. Nick started the fire with flint stones he had found, soon it was blazing warmly and aside from the flickering flames darkness blanketed the land. Nick and Lauren sat close, to absorb the welcomed heat.

"So you're telling me that I was involved in a wreck, and my car along with my identification is still in the river somewhere?"

"Yes," returned Nick. "I was a few minutes behind you when it happened, I'm glad I decided to go into town when I did because the driver of the truck never even stopped."

Lauren wondered for a moment, what had happened before all of this, before her apparent amnesia, a memory began to emerge, icy steel surrounded her as the water engulfed her, her heart pounded as the memory began to subside, she remembered the accident! *What a wretched prize to hold so dear,* she thought to herself. She shook the feeling away, wrapping her trembling limbs about herself, she was still here, and she knew she was grateful for that, no matter what her life had been before. Nick watched Laurens features change, she stared dreamily into the fire, her expression riddled with dazed fear, she began to tremble as she blinked away from the fire, the urge to wrap his arms around her for reassurance became unfathomable, he resisted remorsefully. Lauren turned toward him, she didn't know how well they had known each other or if they had ever been anymore than friends, but the disturbing reenactment had shaken her so.

"It's getting colder, I think," she began as she inched closer to his warmth.

He leaned toward her. "Here." Opening his arms he wrapped them warmly around her, she leaned into him comfortably. His heat emanating into her.

"Lauren Conklin, it just sounds so foreign." She unknowingly fanned her fingers over his chest, he was so warm, so soft … quickly sleep overcame her and she drifted into his strong embrace, Nicks heart beat rapidly as Laurens soft body melded into his, her tender fingers still burned his taught and supple flesh, the moment had gripped him deeply, he was quickly becoming too protective and he knew that, but in these conditions he had no alternative, she was lost in her own world, not to mention the mountains too. He had to help her, he was all she had, and in her state anyone could take advantage of her, he didn't know enough about her to help piece her life back together, but he knew enough to help her start. Pressing his lips to her velvety soft temple he whispered goodnight and leaned against the log behind him, settling in for the night. If he was setting himself up for heartache, so be it, all he wanted was here and now, however short lived it might be.

The night was long and cold, with no shelter of any kind or even dry clothing, yet it held a certain bliss that hung dreamily in the atmosphere, it was as if the two huddling refugees were the only two left in this untamed wilderness, and that they were, aside from the quiet town that was quite possibly several miles away. Nick schemed half the night away trying to contemplate an escape from the harsh environment, he knew that the river ran slightly parallel to the town but he wasn't sure if they needed to go upstream or down to reach civilization, during their icy escapade down river he couldn't be sure if they had surpassed the town or not, most of the trip had been blindingly confusing and only when they approached the falls did he regain stature enough to evaluate their situation. The swollen river could have taken them miles away in the time they were submerged. His main concern at the time was to get Lauren and himself out of the water, and now that he knew she was safe and healthy, save the memory loss, he knew he would have to get her home and soon before anything else happened.

When dawn finally broke, Lauren sleepily stretched while yawning; she brushed the sleep away from her eyes and sat up slowly, examining anew her surroundings. The fire had died down and had begun to smolder under the thick morning dew that covered the shore, she turned toward her companion, he smiled tiredly as she batted her sea green eyes, she was so beautiful, he thought.

"Good morning." He folded his powerfully built arms abroad of his chest. "And how did you sleep?"

Smiling openly at his sweet personal question Lauren responded, "Actually, I can't compare it to any previous nights, but I'd be lying if I said that my bedding wasn't comfortable." Nicholas laughed at her remark; she seemed to be opening up to him a little more. He watched her stand and extend her arms above her head, releasing the tension that ached her stiff joints, his large flannel actually was very seductive on her shapely figure, it pulled high on her thighs as she stretched, revealing more of her bare flesh than he needed to see. He felt himself involuntarily becoming aroused, and his boxers did little to conceal this, his eyes darted away from her flesh, traveling toward her face, but as she bent downward brushing of the dirt from her calves, the open flannel sagged low on her chest revealing the womanly curves of her ripened breasts. Her brassiere was removed, something she must have done without his knowledge, and her nipples were hardened and obvious from the morning chill, his rising appendage coursed. He stood, quickly turning from her, and hurriedly sought out his now dry blue jeans and t-shirt. He could feel the sweat beading on his brow as a powerful flash of heat swept over him, the things she did to him were unbearable, and yet she seemed to have not the slightest idea. Lauren gathered her clothing, her denim pants were dry, but her sweatshirt still held heavy dampness.

"Nick?" she called. "My shirt is still wet!" Nick thought for a moment, if she wore his flannel, he wasn't sure he would be able to handle his constant arousal, but he guessed it was a matter he would have to deal with.

"Just wear mine! It's okay!" They were shouting across the clearing they had spent the night in, both dressing in concealing foliage opposite one another. Nick struggled with his pants, his uncomfortable state made dressing difficult, he reached for his scarcely white T-shirt, when suddenly a jolting shriek bombarded his senses, and rushing over to Lauren he crashed through to her no longer private dressing area.

"What is it?" he breathed harshly. Lauren clasped her hand to her chest

"It was just a spider, a big spider, it was in my…" She held the garment in the air and Nicholas peered upon it, quickly she removed the article from display, her embarrassment shown abundantly, as well as his. She stashed the brassiere out of sight, and suddenly realized her topless state. She grabbed up Nick's oversized shirt, covering her bare breasts. "It's all right, it's gone now." Her reddened cheeks made Nicholas feel as if he shouldn't have barged in.

He turned from her. "I'm sorry, I just came rushing in on you like that, it's my fault, don't be embarrassed, really. You've got nothing to be ashamed of, trust me." His words were true, but yet a little too out right for the moment, Lauren felt humiliated. Nick realized his verbal mistake seconds too late, he felt like kicking himself. "Well, I'll be over here if, if anything else should happen." He headed quickly back to his shirt. It was going to be a long day and the outcome, he hoped, would be a productive one.

CHAPTER 7

The mid afternoon sun was particularly hot this day but both travelers knew it wouldn't last, the chill in the breeze told of winters return that was soon to be close at hand, the mountain nights were growing longer, and temperatures dropped below fifty, they were followed by frosty mornings filled with heavy dew, it seemed that here the mountains held substantial moisture and that made nights dangerous without shelter. Hunger became an increasingly nagging issue as they ventured along the winding riverbank; they were headed downstream after deciding that it was wiser to travel down the mountain than higher into it. They hadn't stopped to rest for nearly six hours and Laurens fatigue was becoming increasingly evident, Nick noticed her heavy breathing and more obvious clumsiness now as she stumbled along behind him. She was strong, and he admired that in the small-determined woman, not once had she complained, not even after falling once or twice and scraping her knee on a jagged stone. Nicholas decided they should rest for a moment, perhaps he could find them something to eat, maybe some late season berries or walnuts. Lauren agreed, after their exasperatingly long walk her feet burned from the stumbling they were being forced to withstand. Sitting down on a large flat stone she began removing her shoes, the outlet of the river they had stopped by looked like a good spot to soak them in. She discovered a large raw blister on her left heel, drawing in a sharp breath as she removed her sweat dampened sock; she glanced up to see Nick watching her.

"What is it?" he asked with concern.

"It's just a blister," she returned nonchalantly, "It's nothing really." She placed her quaintly arched foot in the cool mountain spring water and closed her eyes reveling in the icy soak, a gentle but sudden contact upon her sore appendage spooked her, she jumped, her eyes snapping open, only to reveal her handsome companion kneeling before her, his strong, meek hands tenderly caressed her throbbing feet, first the right foot then the left, softly massaging the pain away, she objected at first, not sure to allow him too much leeway, she didn't want to let her guard down yet, but he was firm about his actions, she needed some relief from the tension that he was sure surrounded her, his large thumbs bore into the soles of her feet, slowly releasing her built up troubles. Long sturdy fingers wrapped around her heels, kneading the various pleasure zones along the dainty protrusions his broad hands fanned over the tops of them as he stroked each phalange from base to tip, the movement was quite sexual for a mere massage and Lauren felt herself becoming wanton and soft, she yearned for other pleasures but held her composure.

"I don't think I could carry us both down the mountain," he said grinning, as he watched her tightened features relax while his gentle hands stroked her swollen ankles. She began to soften under his constant attentions and strangely the movements excited him, he cradled her attractively shaped feet and pleasured them as if he were making love to them with his fingertips, his coy strokes seducing her into quiet ecstasy. Lauren felt Nicks warm hands traveling upward to her calves, sliding her tattered pant legs up to her knees, his bold actions stirred in her trembling abdomen; he caressed her stiff muscles with deep penetrating strokes kneading her composure away. She felt gooseflesh rising as he traveled up her calf in his seductive circular motions

"How does that feel?" His deep voice sent a tremor through her, she choked on her reply, swallowing she answered hoarsely, her mouth dry from nervousness.

"G-good, thank you." Nick smiled devilishly, she was enjoying this as much as he, his kind gesture was beginning to transform itself into another situation and Lauren was quickly losing her composure under his seductive stroking, a moan threatened to escape her thin facade of casualness, as she bit her lower lip, closing her eyes she lost herself in the moment.

A soft release of breath escaped her, "God that feels good!" she panted, eyes flashing open, she chided herself for caving and struggled for composure once more. The situation was revealing a deep intimacy, a feeling that neither of them could deny nor accept. Nick's hands longed for more they wanted to wander upon forbidden flesh, kept only where mutual acceptance and assured permission dared to pass, he longed to brush her soft skin with his urgently burning lips to show her how much more pleasure he could bring her, so much greater than a mere foot massage. He reveled in her slight reactions that held so much more than gratitude for the release of pressure, but loathed himself for such an inappropriate seduction, if she only knew the thoughts on his mind she wouldn't dare allow him to touch her tender flesh, or would she … he needed an escape from his growing fever, before he did something he'd regret. He released her gently, drawing himself back from her softened form. She studied him, wondering what his next move would be when suddenly, to her surprise, he swiftly stooped over her, his body merely inches from hers, her breath quickened as she stared at his mouth nearly brushing the revealed flesh of her shoulder, his extended arm sought an object below the rock she now lain upon, pressed unexpectedly to it by Nicks actions. As his eyes traveled to hers, Lauren held her breath, her heart pounding impossibly hard in her ears, he shifted himself evenly above her, placing his free arm upon his elbow and leaning beside her shoulder, she felt his searching hand touch her tangled hair, brushing it back from her ear, he placed a brightly colored autumn bloom behind the tender lobe. Drawing in the deep floral scent of the flower he paused.

"It's a royal red Hydrangea, they're rare around here." His fingertips traced her ear resting gently upon her rose petal cheek. "Rare and beautiful, much like the woman that dons it." He noticed her flushed features. Perhaps he was being a bit dangerous. He backed away, "You'd better get your feet dressed, I'll see what I can find for us to eat."

Lauren released her kept breath as she watched him head into the forest, what had just happened? She sat up, removing the floral cluster from her hair, she studied it delicately its dainty petals were softly pointed on the ends much like rounded arrow heads. Signs of wilting were evident at the tips of the petals, probably due to the changing climate. She would remember the plant long after this, she was certain, the moment had been a dizzying excitement and she knew it was far from over. As the day progressed the wanderers got little farther, the terrain had become increasingly rough, and their speed inevitably declined. Darkness was quickly falling when Lauren and Nick began to build up another fire, Nick had discovered a lone hot spring beside the steep bluff they had come down, and decided they would be best to camp near it for extra warmth. They had found little to eat, aside from a few late season berries and wild onions, but it was some nourishment for their growling stomachs. While Lauren warmed herself by the crackling fire, Nick sharpened a long stick on one end, creating a primitive ensemble of a spear, the streams were filled with trout and tomorrow he didn't plan on being hungry, he peered over at the hot spring beside them, the rising steam was quite inviting to his tired muscles and he knew another night on the cold hard ground would do little to relax them, he set his weapon down beside the fire and began to remove his soiled clothing. Lauren stared into the dancing flames before her, she was tired, but a growing restlessness plagued her, glancing toward Nick she shockingly focused on the scene before her, the naked form of a man waded into the clouded waters of the steaming spring. His stature was eye catching and Lauren tried not to stare, but his physique was truly perfect. She followed the hard lines that formed his broad shoulders and back, down to the firm suppleness of his submerging buttocks, as the water swallowed him slowly, her eyes traveled back to his rugged handsome face, which she discovered was now facing her. Her eyes met his for a brief moment and then darted away with embarassment. Smiling, Nick playfully splashed at the stunned woman.

"What's wrong, Lauren? Don't you remember what a naked man looks like?"

Lauren blushed incredibly and fought the nervous laughter that pressed her. "What are you doing?" she asked seriously. "You could have warned me."

"Oh come now," he lowered his bare torso deeper into the soothing water. "We are the only two out here, and besides after these past two days, we're hardly strangers." His tactful statement deepened her crimson hue.

"Nick," she started, "I don't know how well we knew each before, but please forgive my shyness, I feel as if I just met you yesterday." Yet, since that day it was as if she had known him a lifetime, he was right, it was foolish of her to try and cling to the civilized modesty she felt she should have, it had no place nor meaning out here. The water was tantalizingly warm and Nicks aching muscles were soon relaxed and supple, he peered at Laurens seemingly uncomfortable position, if she could only relax, enjoy their situation a little, he knew it wouldn't be long before they would make their way home, back to civilization, where precious time was scarce, and modesty was watching every move made. Right now all they had was each other and he was beginning to feel satisfied with that, but it wasn't fair to her, and that was something he had to accept.

Lauren stood, stretching, she was tired and she knew she would be lucky to get any sleep this night, she walked toward a patch of thick green moss it seemed to be the best choice of bedding in the area.

"Goodnight Nick," Lauren yawned, her muscles were stiff and sore and she wished she had a hot bath to crawl into.

As if he had read her mind Nick spoke up, "You're not going to sleep yet are you?" His question struck her. "This spring really helps." He was leaning casually against the rocky ledge that harbored the water hole.

For a moment her astonishment was echoed in her features. "But if I get my clothes wet they'll never dry by morning, what would I wear tommor…"she stopped at the thought and watched Nicks amused smile rising.

"Lauren, we're both adults here and like I've said, it's not like we're strangers." He motioned her to come over, the invitation left her momentarily aghast but the longing to ease her tense muscles quickly smoldered her lighted fuse. "You need to relax your muscles tonight or you'll never make it tomorrow." Her uncomfortable response was made clear. "If it makes you feel any better I'll turn away while you undress, you can't see through all this steam anyway, don't be embarrassed, look I'll keep *my* hands behind my back if it helps?" His playful grin helped ease the issue. He turned his back to the suspicious woman and Lauren waited a moment to be sure of her temporary privacy, quickly she stripped her tender limbs of the soiled sweaty clothing and gingerly entered the water, the hot soothing liquid sent a wave of pleasure through her that was unexpectedly numbing to her senses. The deep warm fluid surrounded her now eased body and she forgot about her nude state briefly.

Nick turned, the scene that appeared before him beginning an ache that no amount of bubbling water could avert, an ache that held no ties with exhaustion. He stared, mesmerized by her naked beauty, she stood hip high in the heated pool, her eyes closed in ecstasy as she slowly waded deeper, she opened them sleepily as she sunk into the intoxicating sensations. Quickly the baffled man turned away once more, he wondered if her coming in had been such a good idea, an unexpected wave of nervousness struck him, could he trust himself? Lauren waded toward him, her body emerged up to her shoulders. "Nick?" Her question broke the silence that lingered between them. "You're right, I do feel better, thank you." He turned slightly, she was hidden beneath the steaming camouflage. He faced her, a bit unsure at first, he couldn't escape the burning picture in his mind, her supple curves of dewy flesh, taking in a deep breath he leaned, once more, casually against the surrounding stones. Lauren kept her distance, the hot spring was intoxicating and after the foot rub earlier she knew she would be putty in his hands if he tried anything else. She leaned herself against the farthest part of the ledge, consuming her thoughts into the natural hot tub, how exhilarating it was to feel the cool breeze on her exposed skin while she remained comfortably in the 120 degree water. Her relaxed state loosed her tongue, "So how did you know those flowers earlier?" she inquired. "Are you some kind of botanist?"

Nick chuckled, relieved at her casual conversation. "Hardly," he replied. "We studied some botany in the art academy."

Lauren's eyebrows rose in interest. "So you're an artist?"

"Not exactly," he answered.

Rustling behind her interrupted the comfort of the conversation that embraced her, she turned toward the sound only to come face to face with a pair of curious round black eyes, screaming, she dove toward Nick, desperate for the safety he had come to represent, the scurrying raccoon that had crept down to the strange creatures in the spring, quickly retreated back into the forest.

Nick laughed at the situation. “It’s only a raccoon.” He held the shaken woman tenderly, he could feel her heart pounding against his bare chest. “It’s all right now, it’s gone.” She seemed genuinely scared and reluctant to leave his security, Lauren lingered too long upon Nick’s bare flesh and the heat that began between them far surpassed their steamy hideaway. Lauren backed away quickly, trying not to look at the seriousness in Nick’s eyes, she could feel her exposed breasts peaking at the sudden coolness that seized them, she felt she should hide herself from him, she should cover her now visible arousal, but truly she didn’t want to, it felt right to be here, to be with Nick and the mountain, and no one else.

Nick’s breath quickened as he watched Lauren’s eyes softly meet his, she showed no intentions of hiding herself any longer and her naked breasts rested gently on the stirring water, she started to speak but instead looked away, her arms wrapping protectively around her chest.

“I’m sorry,” she spoke, “I just can’t…” Nick watched her for a moment, she turned from him, obviously she had gotten the wrong impression of his invitation.

“Lauren, I don’t expect anything to happen here, if that’s what you thought.” He studied her response. She was motionless as he spoke. “You don’t have to do anything that you don’t want to, I care about you, Lauren, I have since we first met, I only want to help you, that’s all I’ve ever wanted.” He waded over to her and gently placed his large hands reassuringly upon her shoulders, his burning touch melted her. Turning a bit too quickly, Lauren found herself pressed closely upon his masculine chest, beads of moisture trickled down his bronzed body tracing a pathway over his flesh that led to the core of his male pride. She fanned her long slender fingers over his hardening nipples. Catching her wrists; Nick searched her eyes for the answer to a question he didn’t know how to ask. Lauren peered deeply into the blue depths that sought desperately for her truth to free them, both of them.

She stepped forward, her body gliding against his. “I never said I didn’t want to…” her words burrowed into him like a twisting whirlwind of emotion, he felt his manhood reach a painful height as her soft flesh smoldered against him, the storm behind his cerulean gaze brewed unstoppably strong, as Lauren slowly brought his palms to her breasts as they rose and fell quickly with her heightened anxiety. She slid her fingers to his tense bulging biceps and closed her eyes as she felt his grip tighten to her. Her situation had her spinning with mixed emotions, she was certain she could never have been this bold before and the liberating freedom of it all sent chills over her, reeling her hormones further. Nick began softly to stroke her womanly curves as she succumbed to his dominance; he released her breasts and pressed her body hard to his, drawing in deeply the sweet scent of her.

"Please Lauren," he breathed, "forgive my weakness, do you know what you're doing to me?" Lauren's gentle hand sought deeper, searching beyond his hardened abdomen and brushing fully against his aching member, the shooting sensation brought a deep moan to his parched lips. "Lauren..." he breathed, "Are you sure?" Her daring fingers answered. Claiming her soft mouth, his tongue sought hers as their kiss deepened. Nick's hands pressed her tighter to him sliding over her buttocks and lifting her against his hips, the movement set her ablaze with desire as her legs wrapped around him. Turning to the ledge Nick lifted her higher upon his hips and thrust her upon a moss covered stone, kissing the soft skin of her slender neck. His knee stopped abruptly upon a rocky ledge halfway down into the pool, pulling her over atop him. Nick sat upon the protruding seat and drew her down over his hardened manhood, entering her tightly. Lauren gasped at the sudden entry, she found that it had apparently been a while since her last encounter with a man and his exceptional gift had proven it to be all the more evident. Nick thrust himself deeply into her, his excitement rising with every moan that erupted from her soft lips his hunger for Lauren exploding in a fiery rush of passion. Fiercely he claimed her, his mouth urgently claiming each breast with flames of desire that licked and teased, her world was spinning, tumbling, crashing in all around her.

In one swift movement Lauren was pressed to the stony wall. Nick's smoldering body upon hers, rising and falling rhythmically as his desire carried her away. Soon his uncontrollable thirst for her rendered him helpless against his own actions, the sweet salty taste of her velvety flesh lingered upon his tongue, as the scent of her entangled his mind, twisting and turning within him as he struggled to maintain some small amount of control. It had been well over a year since he had last been with a woman and never had his passion run this deep, every movement she made, every small breath that brushed his tender ear, sent incredible waves of thunder through his entirety, his world ended here with this woman, never would he find another to surpass this moment, ecstasy in this paradox of paradise and hell. He needed nothing more to complete him, with her he was whole, the empty void that had plagued him for so long had been filled, she was his now, and would, forever be a part of him, no matter how destiny should twist their lives. Lauren clung desperately to Nick's powerful arms, she no longer cared about her past, she didn't need to, all she ever would need was in her arms, she closed her eyes tightly to the thoughts and emotions that seized her, pushing them away and refusing to believe that anything that happened in paradise should prove to be a mistake in the future, a prelude to a painful regret. The pleasure that coursed through her left her breathless and longing for more, dreams of lost loves and deep rooted pain were filtering through her straining mind. Nicks escalating thrusts quickly dissolved the uncomfortable memories as he neared his climax. Their eyes fixed upon one another, locking in an entrancing embrace that held their souls as one, the sea-green embers seemed to plead to Nick for reassurance, desperate for a love to hold her safely from the tearing rains, deep within the raging storm that consumed them. Throwing her head back in complete euphoria, Lauren felt herself thrusting upon his throbbing member, as she peaked within her climax, tumbling and falling she felt as though Nick were charting the course of her pleasure, he stiffened upon her, enveloping her body to him as if he would draw himself within her completely, their very beings melting into one another, crashing together in a hurricane of desperate passion until at last they lay, spent of any and all energies left to them.

Exhausted by the rush of satisfaction that now harbored their Gaelic atmosphere, the moment was a magical one for the weary travelers, but filled with a deep fear of now losing any bit of the purity they had found and desperately trying to keep faith that even in the world outside, their newfound happiness would never be tainted by loves sometimes poison arrow.

CHAPTER 8

Lauren lay awake staring at the fading diamonds that hung in the early morning sky, the two lovers had slept peacefully in each others arms throughout the night, but the nervous trembling in her stomach had awoken her early that morning. Uncertainty played on her emotions as she lay cradled in her saviors arms, in her heart she felt she had done nothing wrong, what they had shared that night had been pure bliss, but somewhere deep inside, already a small seed of doubt had begun to grow. Her past was a vast darkness, an uncharted chasm of secrets and mysteries she could not comprehend.

A name came to her briefly, but was gone again before it could mean anything to her, before she could fit it into the broken jigsaw puzzle of her life. *Brian* ... she pondered on it for a moment, whoever he was she was sure he'd had an important role in her life; she only prayed there had been no commitments there. She glanced up at Nicks quietly sleeping features, her heart racing at the thought of the newly shared passion they had had. She wondered again if she had made a mistake.

The slumbering man began to stir, and Lauren gazed at the spreading smile that touched his lips.

"Good morning," he sighed tiredly, as he tightened his arm around her. He brushed his lips gently to her forehead, the sweet feel of her filling him again. "After last night I wasn't sure if you would really be here when I woke..." Her timid grin told of the magenta hue that would soon follow, and Nicks' amusement shone through his eyes. Lauren rose upon her elbows and perched herself above Nicks' broad chest, so as to face him directly.

"How much farther do you think we'll have to go?"

Nick was quiet for a moment. "Are you in such a hurry?" He looked at her questioningly. Struck by confusion, she glanced around at the raw wilderness that surrounded them, her meaning evident. "I'm sorry," he followed, "It shouldn't be much farther." A hidden sadness seemed to dwell behind the hard lines forming in his chiseled features. He stood and began to dress, leaving Lauren to ponder, once more, on her actions.

The mornings' coolness brought on a hunger more ferocious than the previous mornings' had been, and the shimmering, silvery trout, which darted below the transparent surface of the nearby outlet, seemed more enticing than ever. Lauren knelt down by the clear brook, drawing the cool, mountain spring water into her hand and tasting its freshness. The soothing liquid ran carelessly down her plump lips, and spilled along her slender neck, it so reminded her of the trailing kisses that still seared in her mind.

Nick stood, statue like, knee deep in the icy water, his bare skin glistening in the sunlight as he aimed his sharpened spear at the unsuspecting prey. The curios fish dared ever closer as it studied the strange object before it, alien to its underwater domain. A sudden rush of fizzling foam, and clouding blood, filled the scene, as the jagged weapon pierced the animals' flesh. With precision marksmanship, the proud hunter snatched his trophy from the clearing waters and gingerly removed it from the spear, tossing it upon the shore. Lauren jumped at the quick thud beside her and stumbled back at the sight of the bloodied fish.

"Are you hungry?" her companion called as he waded toward her, his teasing smile mocking her dazed reactions.

Lauren grinned at him, gritting her teeth, "I'll teach you!" she declared. Delving her open hands into the water, she quickly threw them aptly in his direction, splattering his sun-baked torso with the icy liquid. Drawing in a broken gasp from the shock of the sensation, Nick rapidly retorted, soaking her face and shoulders. The shirt she donned caught the full blast of the chilling retort, and the icy water clung to her noon-warmed skin with vengeance. Quickly the article fell to the ground, as Lauren sought refuge from the cold blast. Glaring back at him, with an astonished look of retribution, she threw her denim pants to the side, and charged after the laughing man.

Nicks escape was slowed by the overwhelming laughter that consumed him, as the perturbed woman came at him. Another icy blow was sustained, which in turn he retaliated, until the stream was amuck with gusts of spraying water, and squeals of screaming laughter that echoed through the hills. Unable to accommodate Nicks' large handfuls, Lauren dove into his sturdy form, knocking them both into the chilly waters of the gentle stream. Surfacing, the laughter erupted between them, at the reality of their folly.

The recapping of the events slowly dwindled, along with their laughter, an amiable calmness falling as the last morsels of the charade tumbled gently by. An equally felt tremor traveled through them as they stared helplessly into one another's eyes. Drawing ever closer, Nick traced a finger over Laurens soft lips, igniting the fire that blazed within her racing heart. Capturing her face within his hands, he claimed her mouth once again, softly probing his searching tongue within her, and triumphantly seeking out what was sought. Lauren grasped his muscular forearms, as he tenderly kissed her, and found herself drawing him in deeply and returning his actions. He brought her to him, hard against his tense body, as their limbs entwined. A mere thin layer of under-clothing lay between them, as the heat stirred once more. Pulling her upon the sandy shore, near the forest, he desperately tore at the coverings between them, removing the last obstacle to her sweet flesh. Lauren moaned as Nicks gentle hand found her core, he began to stroke her wantonly, bringing waves of pleasure through her, as he made certain of her acceptance of him. Reaching for him, Lauren held no resistance to his guiding hands, as he pressed her arms above her head, exposing her fully to him. Hungrily he kissed her full breasts, tasting the sweetness of her tender flesh, and reveling in the trembling desire she held for him. His arousal ached with need, but he refrained from entering her, he wanted to pleasure her this time, to revel in her ecstasy, to feel her quake before him and crash down into the whirlwind of divine bliss that she deserved. Traveling slowly down her naked flesh, Nick licked and teased her twitching body. She felt his hot mouth trail over her, lower and lower, until his coursing tongue found her center.

A dizzying flush washed over her as he softly stroked her pleasure.

"Oh Nick," she sighed breathlessly, "please make love to me..." Upon her words, Nick glided easily atop her, slipping into her, pulsing, as she wrapped herself around him. His strides were slow and steady, fully pleasuring the gasping woman as she tried desperately to hold on. As his climax neared he rose above her, and his thrusts grew intense. A sharp moan erupted from his parted lips as he filled her with seed once more. Lauren could feel herself falling, her quiet reserve washed away with the sudden increase in thrusts, "OH NICK!" she cried, as her peaking climax spilt over. She clung to his tightened body, desperately, as her dizzying moans slowly subsided.

Her multiple pleasures were evident to the satisfied man, and he lay for a moment, tenderly kissing her sweat-strewn brow. Her hold on him lingered, revealing her reluctance to release him yet, but at last her exhaustion prevailed.

A few hours later, the slain fish crackled and fizzled atop the open flame that danced in the afternoon breeze. The weather-grayed, beechnut skewer, which it harbored, was slowly blackening, due to the extensive heat, and the rich heady scent of the meal filled the air, increasing the steadily growing impatience of the hungry pair.

Lauren rose from her woodland perch, the weathered stump was becoming slightly irritating to her tender rump, and she paced by the tempting meat.

"It smells delicious; don't you think it's done?" She stopped pacing, and stared exasperatingly at Nick, who in turn came toward the roasting trout as well.

"I think it's been on there long enough." He poked at the bubbled flesh with a pointed twig, inserting it easily. "Yes it's done, would you mind handing me that slab of bark?" He motioned to a sliver of birch tree bark he had cleaned and burned slightly, it would serve as their serving plate for now. Stealthily he drew the fish from the flames, and converted it to the slab, hot steam rising from the scalding meat, as he palmed the birch tree server, motioning it toward Lauren as if he were a diligent waiter.

"Your meal my dear," he accented jestfully; Lauren giggled at his senseless behavior.

"Lets eat now, all right?" She smiled, her stomach growling with anticipation.

The lunch was exceptional, and disappeared rapidly, each bite leaving a cruel wanting for more, Lauren had never tasted a meal so good.

"Where did you learn to cook so well, especially in the wilderness?" Her question was earnest, she had had a feeling that if she were the one to have cooked it, a bundle of wild onions and pungent wild gooseberries would have been more appetizing.

"When I was younger my father took me camping…" He paused, staring up into the densely forested mountains. "…he brought me to a place much like this, high in the mountains. I remember him saying, 'Boy, if you're gonna survive in the real world, there's nothing more real than nature,' he said, 'she can be beautiful, and she can be cruel, but you've got to learn to exist here, because if you can make it out here, the *real* world is no more than a walk in the park.' Back then I was fourteen, and all I cared about was what I wanted, but he taught me a thing or two up there, even though I never let him know that, I'll never forget it. His methods were sometimes rough, but I guess that was the only way I would listen." He gazed solemnly away, as if he were entranced in a deep memory, it lingered for a moment and then he shook it away with masked dignity.

"We'd better get moving," he stood and began smothering the fire with handfuls of the soft dirt that lie around the sight. Lauren assisted his cause and soon they were on the move once more. This time Nick carried his sharpened spear ahead of them, he wasn't sure if he'd need it but the deeper into the wilderness they got, the more dangerous the predators became. As they moved on, the terrain grew rockier than ever, and they found themselves climbing downward more than walking, soon they had to veer to the right, traveling away from the river, which had already forked several times during their journey. The new trail they followed seemed to be more traveled than the others, perhaps a deer trail, or wild hogs, whichever the case their traveling certainly eased.

Up ahead Lauren strained to see their destination, the wooded path opened broadly, revealing a large field before them, it fronted a large stretch of mountains that seemed endless, and there journey suddenly seemed quite minuscule. Lauren was beginning to wonder what she had gotten herself into.

As they started for the field, a sudden commotion caught Nicks eye, a cloud of falling rocks scattered behind them as a shrieking scream rang through the tall pines. The proprietor to the ruckus came to a halt on a rocky ledge above them, with an ominous thud.

"Lauren!" Nick cried as he clutched her forearm. "Run!" It was their only chance to escape from the ravenous creature above, and without thought she obeyed.

"What is it?" she screamed, her lungs aching as she darted beside the fleeing man. Before he could answer, the beast charged after them, plunging itself a sure eighteen feet to the ground, and not once pausing in the chase.

It's sleek, khaki-brown, body was tense with pure adrenalin as its blackened lips tore back to reveal dagger like teeth. Another shrieking cry tore through the air, as it bounded quickly after its prey, razor sharp claws extended as it closed in.

Awestricken, Lauren screamed in terror as the huge cat struck at her, catching the sagging sleeve of the sweater, she had donned after the water fight, and tearing it, nearly dragging her down.

"NO!" she cried. Nick thrust her to the side, as the monstrous cougar attacked. It sunk its three-inch fangs into Nicks extended arm, grasping him with ferocious accuracy and knocking him to the ground. As it tore at him with its jagged nails, he tried desperately to free himself of the ravenous beast. Lauren watched the occurrence in horror, as she searched frantically for some means of defense. The sharpened spear was tossed beside the struggling man and Lauren seized the chance, clutching the weapon fiercely, her shaking hands drove it straight and true for the panther's spine.

As contact was made, the rod sank deeply into the mountain cats flesh. It shrieked with pain, hurtling itself upward, and knocking the spear out of the newly founded wound.

"Nick!" Lauren screamed. He lay very still, bloodied from the unprovoked attack. She cast herself beside him. "Nick!" A moment later the injured lion turned to the terrified woman, without hesitation it sprung, its hot breath bearing down her bare neck. She closed her eyes, throwing herself over the wounded man, and waiting for her untimely demise to come. A rocketing shot rang through the air, silencing the frenzied commotion, as the cougar dropped suddenly, motionless. Trembling with fear, Lauren remained, huddled against Nicks injured form.

Slowly she looked up; a lone rider was galloping toward them, shotgun in hand. As the stranger neared, Lauren squinted against the sunlight that was falling behind him; it appeared to be a woman. She wore a dipping leather hat, which resembled a tattered Stetson, and a long darkened poncho of the same material. As she approached the couple, she saw the large wound on the downed man, and quickly dismounted her exceptional steed.

"Oh m'God!" she exclaimed, her accent seemingly of southern origin. "Is he all right?" She stooped over Nick's torn body, examining the wounds thoroughly.

"It looks like mostly surface scratches, but that bite on his arm is pretty deep, that'll need a few sutures." She glanced at Lauren, furrowing her brow for a moment; she looked to be in her late fifties, maybe even early sixties, by the defining lines that accented her features. Her appearance was harsh, even rough at first, but as her expressions changed, a hint of genteel femininity shown clearly.

"What on earth are you two kids doin' way the hell out here?" She waited for a response, but could see that the young woman was still shaken from the attack. She began to notice the girls' appearance more so than before, she was ragged and dreadfully soiled, her dark hair a tangled mess that covered part of her sun-browned face. The torn jeans that she wore, told of an inexperienced travel, apparently down the mountain. She puzzled on this for a moment, the nearest town was forty-three miles from her place, and up the mountain it was still a sure thirty-five, or so, although the mountain route was impassable. She looked again at the woman's face, which she found oddly familiar. "What's your name, child?" The question was eerily strange, the only one else who knew the answer, was Nick, and he lay unconscious between them. He had said her name was Lauren, and up until now, she had assumed him to be right, but all the confusion, and commotion had her wondering again.

"Lauren," she managed out. She hoped the woman wouldn't ask her last name, she had forgotten what Nick had said.

The old woman's eyes lit up., "Lauren Conklin!" she hollered, slapping her knee, with a broad toothy smile. "I knew I saw you somewhere before! Land sakes child! What in earth are you doin' out here?"

Laurens hope rocketed. "You mean you know who I am?" Her excitement was bewildering.

"Well, I used to know your mama."

Lauren was ecstatic. "Do you know how I can reach her?"

A look of pure confusion settled on the older woman's face. "Don't you?" she asked suspiciously. Lauren glanced at Nick, a need for safety creeping over her; she wasn't ready to divulge too much information to this woman yet.

"We should get him some help. Do you know of anyone who would take us into town?" Lauren looked back to the woman, who rose to her feet.

"Lets get 'em up on my horse, she's strong enough to carry us all." The two struggled the injured man onto the horse's back. "That's the beauty of Clydesdales. They're one helluva' good pack horse."

She mounted the intimidating beast, and reached her gloved hand out to Lauren, swinging her roughly upon the animals' rump. Nickering, she drew up the horses' reigns, and they began across the field.

"Names Mildred," the rider started, "Mildred Evans, round' here folks call me doc' Evans, I'm the local vet. My place is about twenty minutes away from here; don't mind the mess when we get there. Damn mountain lions are bad this year. Yer' lucky I was out ti'day, I was lookin' fer that bugger, it killed a couple sheep yesterday, o'er the Johnsons' place. They come n' got me when they found 'em." Mildred was lively and full of spunk, from what Lauren could surmise, and her chipper attitude helped to compensate for Laurens silence, she only wished that Nick would be all right, if only she had found them before the attack, Nick would have known better what to ask, surely he would have been more adequate than she.

About five minutes into their journey, large, dark, clouds began to accumulate above, splintering branches of lightening spider webbing through them as the threatening storm brewed thickly ahead.

"I hope we get there before that hits!" Mildred mused, her concern showing through her light-heartedness, as she kicked the horse into a quick paced trot.

Already the wind was picking up, and the broad fields, which stretched on along their journey, danced eerily in the tumbling gusts. Lauren tightened her hold on Nick, she could feel the oncoming storm brewing dangerously, and was grateful that Mildred had found them when she did. They wouldn't have survived the attack, let alone a storm on top of that. The atmosphere was growing dark, and the increased pressure, of the falling clouds, pressed on the inner ears of the travelers.

"We're almost there!" Mildred shouted communication was growing more difficult as the blasting wind carried their words away with the storm. Nick began to stir, his reflexes seized him, and he jumped suddenly, confused and dazed.

"Nick, it's all right, we've been found!" He pressed his hands to the horses' sides, but a sharp, jolting, pain refused to let him rise. He moaned in agony, his vision blurred, and his head pounded where it had apparently met an unfriendly mass, when he had been knocked to the ground. Lauren saw his struggle to rise, and promptly lent him a hand, twisting him up vertically and against the softness of her body. Nick thrust himself upward with his undamaged arm, and with the added assistance, sat upright, leaning dizzily against his companion. Unable to ascertain the situation, he grasped the supportive arms that wrapped protectively around him, grateful for the familiarity.

As the rain broke through, Lauren spotted a small cottage just ahead. Mildred pointed assuredly in its direction, but her explanatory message was shouted in vain. The raging storm was upon them, and the howling wind and pounding rain, now filled the air, muffling any other sounds that were before distantly clear.

"We're almost there Nick, just hold on!" Laurens words were scarcely noticed, even to her own ears, and the light-headed man fell unconscious once more.

They reached the house as the full force of the torrential rainstorm hit. Hurrying in for cover, the soaking wet women struggled with the dead weight, of their injured peer. "I've got an idea!" Mildred shouted, running to a small wooden shed that stood nearby. Rolling out an old wheelbarrow, she quickly assisted Lauren, as they successfully transferred him to the rusted stretcher.

Once inside, Mildred hurriedly removed her wet poncho and hat, and together they placed Nick on an old sofa, that strained under his weight. A large clap of thunder barreled over them, as lightning made contact somewhere nearby. The lights flashed out suddenly, and Lauren jumped, she hated storms and she found that inclination, quite hastily, to be true. A moment later the room was lit up once more, as Mildred placed a large hurricane lamp upon the honey colored, dining room table, in the open room. "I always come prepared!" she chuckled, and promptly she lit its twin and headed into a back room. Lauren looked about as thunder rolled ominously by outside, the pouring rain beating against the thinly pained windows, which were throughout the house.

A flash of lightning lit the room, briefly revealing countless pictures and figurines that harbored the walls. A stone fireplace sat rigidly into the east wall, its ashy contents swirling in the slight breeze, which escaped into the room by means of the open chute. Atop the mantle were various plaques, and small trophies, along with several oddly sized candles, scattered between them. On the west of the room was an open doorway, leading into a room she was certain was a restroom, the glowing flame that lit the area, seemed to reveal a bluish wall in that space. The tiny den they stood in was comfortable, and snug, with a lazy chair near the fireplace that was adjacent to the sunken couch, pillows lay about the furniture, and an idle rocker stood, alone, by the largest window in the room, an unfinished crochet in a basket at the foot of it.

Lauren wondered if the woman was lonely here, she seemed to be alone and a bit up in her years, but perhaps that was why she was here, perhaps she enjoyed the quiet place. As her eyes followed the structure of the house, they fell upon a large shelf that contained, what looked to be, books. Stepping up to the structure, she traced her fingers over the literature; they ranged from medical journals, to romance novels, with several classics in amongst them.

A wide range of stories, were displayed in the case, and Lauren was caught up in the titles, momentarily.

"Tom Sawyer was always one of my favorites."

The voice startled her, she turned to see Mildred, carrying several medical supplies in her arms, along with a white blouse, and a flowing teal-green skirt. "I think these will fit you, they were my daughters, of course that was years ago, but they've been well kept." She handed them to her, revealing a hand basket full of toiletries. "When the power comes back on, you're more than welcome to get a shower, and clean yerself up, but right now would you mind givin' me a hand?"

Lauren hurried over. "OH, of course!" She took half of the supplies, from Mildred's arms, and carried them into the den, setting them on the coffee table. "It's the least I can do, to repay you."

"Nonsense!" she scolded. "Seeing you two get back home safe will be plenty enough payment for me, now will you please remove that boys shirt, and throw it in the trash, before it walks off by itself?"

Lauren knelt beside Nick's damp body, and carefully began to take the soiled cloth off of him, the extent of his lacerations was more evident beneath the clothing, and each movement of the shirt tore at the drying wounds.

"Here, hon." She handed a pair of surgical scissors to her. "You might as well just cut the rest off." Lauren snipped the material easily, and it fell away into her hands, the bloodstained fabric sent a chill through her, Nick's blood. She hurriedly took the articles to the wastebasket in the kitchen, where Mildred had directed her, and tossed it in.

Upon returning, she noticed that the thrifty, old woman, had already cleaned the surface scratches, and was preparing the sutures, arranging to dress the large gash.

"I'll need to numb it a lil', or he might come to a' swingin'." She produced a sharp needle, that contained a small amount of anesthetic. "This'll numb the surface skin, just enough…" She pricked the edges of the tear in several spots, and placed the spent syringe, to the side. Quickly she maneuvered the curved stitching needle and, with several steady strokes, closed the wound securely. "There might be a small scar, when it heals, but I'm sure there'll be no infection. Now he just needs to rest, I've got a spare bed in the back if we can get him there." Lauren agreed, and somehow they managed him into the back room. "I'll leave you two alone, so you can take those horrid clothes off of him, that'd sure breed germs by those open wounds…" she closed the door behind her, leaving a lantern on the nearby chest of drawers, that lit the room dimly. Lauren looked to Nick; he was so close, but yet so distant. She wished he would wake, but knew he needed his sleep. She resolved to taking off his soiled garments, and cleansing his dirt-strewn skin. With the terrycloth rag Mildred had laid beside the bed, in a bowl of clean water, Lauren followed the sturdy structure of Nick's physique. Gently she dabbed his burning skin, removing the built soil, and streaks of perspiration, that covered him. Nick stirred briefly, but stilled as quickly as he had moved.

He had mumbled something unintelligible, as if he were in a complicated dream, one that pulled at his consciousness. Lauren could only imagine what it might be, after all of the past events, leading up until now, she was certain his dreams weren't unlike her own, mixed patterns of confusing events, that crossed over each other in delirious arrays of senselessness. She drew the blankets over him and pressed her lips to his brow,

"Sleep well," she whispered upon his ear.

As he turned to his left side, in a slumbering attempt to find comfort, a soft growl rumbled from his unconscious form, a barely audible word. Lauren leaned closer, briefly, trying to decipher his moaning, again he spoke, softly, dazed, but clearly this time. Her quick intake of breath revealed her comprehension, his statement was clear, echoing in her mind, as her heart beat raced, filling her ears with the pounding.

A name had been uttered, but not her own, and his involvement in her life seemed to take on a new aspect. His reluctance to return to reality, from their adventurous journey, seemed to suddenly become all to clear. Stepping back from him, she stifled the tears that threatened to spill, and swallowed hard, trying not to let her imagination run rampant. A sudden flash of emotion hit her like a tidal wave …

"Don't look back! He's a memory…" Tears blurred her vision … he was married … smelled of cheap beer … her heart ached at the thought of losing him … crying … crying and driving in the rain to get to … to get away … away from … The memory was gone. A choking sob pressed on Laurens chest, was the memory of Nick? It couldn't be, but it was so clear, the pain the heartache, but hadn't they just met? Perhaps he had told her that in hopes that she would accept him, she had been leaving someone … but whom? Nick? Was that the reason he had conveniently been there to save her? The turmoil within her was devastating, why hadn't she remembered the entire memory? Frustration was following suit, whatever had happened out there would simply have to be left behind them, her life was still ahead and she couldn't be certain what she would find.

As Lauren entered the den, Mildred popped her head around from the kitchen, "Would you like a hot cup a' tea? My gas lines are still a workin'."

Lauren smiled at her cheerful invite. "I would love one," she replied kindly as the cheerful gray-headed woman disappeared once more.

The warmth of the now crackling fire smoothed the chill out of the darkened room, and illuminated it ever so much clearer. Pictures of children were hung variously, some photographs, some drawings.

"Are these your children?" the curious onlooker presented.

"Heavens no!" cried the elderly woman as she entered the room, stepping down into it, and handing the hot tea over. "My Sarah's over there." She motioned to a painting near the book shelve. "I only ever had one, then the Doc said no more."

Lauren appeared surprised for a moment. "Were there complications?"

"Only with me." Her attitude remained amiable. "They said the pregnancy put too much strain on my inerts that they dropped, my ovaries were under too much pressure, and when I was seven and a half months along, I started bleedin', they stopped it, but it was a miracle. See honey back then that was pretty complicated. So, anyway, they cleaned me all out after she was born, took out all o' those female parts, you know, and that was that. Well … I got one ovary left, but without that ol' uterus, it's pretty useless!"

The story should have been a serious one, in Laurens mind, but Mildred seemed to take it in stride, a smile still touching her lips. "Those are my nephews and nieces, that dark-headed boy is my grandson, Charlie, he's eight now."

Looking at the boy, she could see the family resemblance; he harbored the same determined eyes that laughed with his smile. "He's very handsome," Lauren complimented.

"He's a good kid," the woman replied, taking a sip of the chamomile tea she held.

They sat upon the sofa, by the fireplace, and Lauren drank deeply, the soft sweet taste of her tea, a hint of honey, lingering in her mouth, as she stared into the dancing flames. A flash crossed her thoughts ...

She was young, a teen, she pretended to be asleep as she listened to her parents quietly arguing ... "Bill, I don't care. I don't think you should choose who she sees, he seems like a nice young man, besides, his parents are respectable country club members, not like some of these locals..."

"Sandy! I've told you, I saw him with that, Deborah woman, she's married, and to that police officer, Ell ... Ellington! That's it! I've heard rumors about those two..."

"Don't be silly, she's almost thirty-five and he's barely twenty-one. Don't you want the best for your daughter? He comes from a very successful bloodline..."

"Sandy, that girl of hers, Sabrina, they say it's his! Besides a wealthy pocket only leaves room for lawlessness, people like that think they are above the rules of common folks ... I've worked for all we've acquired, and I'll be damned if that rich, snobbish S.O.B. is going to take any of it away, he's trouble, Sandy, I'm telling you, he better stay away from Lauren!"

The memory vanished suddenly, leaving her to ponder on the thought, the conversation made little sense, and she hadn't the strength to try harder on remembering.

"So child." The woman's voice reflected her concern. "Tell me now, what on earth happened out there?"

Lauren sighed, casting her eyes downward and then looking squarely at her newfound acquaintance, "it's a long story…"

Mildred nestled back against the softly worn arm of the couch, drawing her legs upward, and tucking her white-socked feet beside herself, comfortably.

"I've got time…" her reassuring smile left little need for any further coaxing.

Lauren explained her situation, to the best of her abilities, though she knew little of what took place prior to the accident. Mildred listened patiently, nodding her head in understanding, and shaking it in disbelief of the amazing story. After the distraught young woman was finished, Mildred began filling in some of the spaces in her past. Her confused recipient inexplicably appreciated the little that she knew.

Photos were brought out, of her and her mother on horseback, with the sun on their faces, and the wind catching their hair. Her mother rode sidesaddle, as a proper lady should, but Lauren seemed as if she were determined to break that mold, her face showed love, for her mother, but it seemed she harbored a deep rooted defiance.

"You were sixteen here," Mildred pointed out, "it was the last summer you came down, your mother wanted so badly for you to have fun that summer, it was as if she knew you wouldn't be back the following year."

"But why didn't I come back?" she didn't understand, it appeared she was happy, in the photos … surely she would have wanted to return?

"You were growin' up my dear, an' yer' mother knew that, she didn't want to keep you from yer' aspirations."

"Aspirations?" she enquired.

"Well, you went off to college, that next fall, somewhere out west. Yer' mama said you were studying to be an architect, you know, modern design, n' all that … she said you were good." The idea seemed incredible, what would an aspiring architect be doing out here? She wasn't sure if she felt relief at knowing more now, then before, or if she wanted to sit down and cry? The confusion, over her emotions, shown through her features, summoning Mildred to explain further; her parents owned a summer home, somewhere in the seasonal resort, on the mountain. She had never been to it, but she had been told of it.

The cabin Nick had spoken of, Lauren thought tactfully, it must have been her parents' summer home! The elation was a relief, but there were still so many unanswered questions, what of the name that had come to her? Who was Brian? What was her relationship to Nick, if there had ever been one? Would anyone have even known?

"Do you know if I had any recent beaus, any serious commitments?"

Mildred thought for a moment, a question lingering on her lips, that was quickly reconsidered, "the only one I know of, was young man named Billy, Billy Malhoun. If I recollect, you were pretty hung up on that one, I guess you could say it was serious, he was a bit older than you, you know."

"Billy Malhoun? It doesn't sound familiar…" Lauren waved it away, "What about a, Brian?"

The woman paused in thought, "no…" she considered, "no, your mother never mentioned a Brian."

Lauren recapped, "And you don't have her number either?"

The woman shook her head; "I don't have a phone either, Hon, not since last Friday."

Lauren chewed her lip, in deep thought, the storm was subsiding, and the wind was carrying it away twofold. The lights flickered, and then sprang on, the full force of their brightness, struck the women's dilated pupils, harshly, and both flinched at the sudden shock.

"Well, it's about time!" Mildred stood up, stretching her legs, as she began blowing out the lamps, "Are you hungry?" she gave a questioning look in Laurens' direction, "I've still got to eat supper yet, an' I wouldn't mind the company'."

Lauren smiled. "I'm starving!" she confessed eagerly, her stomach growled contemptuously at her, as they headed into the kitchen.

As Mildred began preparing the meal, Lauren offered her assistance, but the hearty woman refused it, and bid her exhausted guest to go cleanse her parched skin. Lauren insisted on her helping, but Mildred prevailed. Gathering the toiletries, and clean garments, she headed tiredly toward the bathing room, peering in on her sleeping companion, along the way, whom remained still, and settled.

The bathroom was a brightly lit room, painted a robins' egg blue, with white and blue tiles along the floor and halfway up the walls. A cornflower-blue bath rug fronted the claw-footed tub that stood idly against the back wall. Lauren stripped her clothing and ran the steaming bath water, adding a bit of the teal colored bath foam, from the toiletry basket. The floral accent filled the small room, as the steam rose.

Upon the shelf, beside the full-length mirror, lay a broad, wooden handled, hairbrush. She borrowed it eagerly, and commenced combing her tangled hair. Immersing herself into the soothing bath, she lay back against the slanted porcelain, reveling in the hot liquid, and consuming fragrance.

A new sense of confidence came over her, as she unwound her tensed nerves, she would find her way back to herself, and if not, then she would be content with the life she would make, starting today. Either way, she would seek out her happiness, and she was determined she would find it.

CHAPTER 9

Lauren bandaged the small cut on her delicate ankle; it had been acquired accidentally while shaving her legs. They were quite honestly becoming a trifle out of sorts. She peered at her reflection in the mirror, aside from her thinning structure and obvious weight loss, the blouse and skirt fit her as if they had been made for her. The flowing garments slipped easily over her petite frame, clinging to her womanly curves, and softly drifting against her slender limbs, she looked good, she considered, healthy.

The soft cotton material was satin upon her weary flesh, and she gathered it to her, embracing the sensation of cleanliness. Her senses were caressed by the gentle scent of lilac and gardenia, while the heady scent of peony touched her pulse points, mixing with her own warm scent, and creating a relaxing collage of colorful aromas. Tying her damp hair back in a tight, thick braid, she intently headed out to the warm glow of the kitchen.

Mildred was busily setting the last of the meal upon the table, as she entered the room timidly. Yellow cornbread lay to the side of the butcher-block table, cut into small squares, and placed on a rose-colored serving plate. Beside it a butter knife and dish, lay, open to reveal the golden, creamy, spread within. A solitary pot was centered on the table, its contents steamy and bubbling.

Lauren watched as the busy-bodied woman promptly removed the lid of the pot, and commenced to stir the thickened liquid. She drew in the hearty, rich aroma of the stew.

"I hope you like chickin' n' dumplins', cause I made enough of 'em to feed an army!" She motioned to the table, pulling out a chair, and then hurriedly stepped to the china cabinet, drawing out the rose colored dishes to set places for the meal. Refusing Laurens helpful offers once more, Mildred continued to lay the feast about the table, as Lauren gave in, finally taking her seat.

Laurens stomach roared with hunger as she peered over the delectable dressings, she thought back to Nick, helplessly unconscious in the other room, a tinge of guilt panged at her, she hoped the meal would keep until morning. She hadn't noticed a microwave in the kitchen, if only he were able to join her in consuming the fresh, hot meal, cold food was better than nothing, but the disappointment still ebbed at her.

Mildred placed a long, shallow casserole on the table, containing whipped potatoes with herbs blended evenly through them. She then seated herself across from Lauren, and began spooning the courses onto her plate.

Lauren spoke now. "You didn't have to go through all this on my account!" she scolded, feeling even guiltier over not aiding the older woman.

"Oh pish!" Mildred returned "I was going to have to cook supper anyway! This is nuthin'! Now you eat up!"

Lauren glanced at the woman, apologetically. "Now don't tell me you always make this much!"

Smiling broadly, the older woman winked in her direction, and continued to fill her plate, "Don't let it get cold," she advised.

Shaking her head in amusement, Lauren hungrily began to pile her plate high with each scrumptious dish, she was famished and each revealed course looked more delicious than the last. Caught up in the process of fixing her plate, Lauren glanced up at her companion, only to find her staring adoringly past her, her eyes smiling with approval, "well now, those fit ya' just fine, don't they!" following the woman's gaze, Lauren found the subject of her statement, a dark figure loomed, largely, in the doorway, the mans' face in shadows as he stepped forward. The surprise shown in her features, as she sized up the stranger. Glancing down at the start of him, a pair of burnt umber cowboy boots based his sturdy ensemble, overlaying them was a pair of blue jeans that clung to two long, noticeably muscled, legs.

"Nick?" Laurens surprise was baffling, as he stood in the light now, tiredly smiling at her, her eyes washed over him once more, pausing at his partially revealed chest, at the open neck of the white shirt that he wore, the darkly tanned skin that was revealed was accented noticeably, by the bright clothing, stirring thoughts of what lay beneath them … Tucked securely into his tight fitting jeans, the garments complimented his narrow hips and broad shoulders.

"But when did … where did … are you all right?" She stood suddenly, forgetting her hunger completely, and starting toward the injured man.

"Now, don't get up on my account," he laughed, throwing up his arm to reveal a new bandage and tourniquet, Lauren began to examine his injuries once again, needing to know he was all right. "Lauren?" he pleaded, "Lauren, I'm fine, really." Her concern for him brought an unexpected satisfaction that deepened his smile, reflecting through his features. "Really, Lauren, it's all right." He brought her eyes up to his, capturing her gaze briefly. "I couldn't sleep after I smelled this delicious meal." He looked to Mildred's grinning face, and gave her a wink.

"Now you two kids better sit down and eat, while it's hot!" she directed, motioning to the open chairs. The two seated themselves with courteous haste, and began devouring the home cooked meal. Afterwards all three sat comfortably around the table, allowing the food to digest.

"Well, you certainly do heal fast enough," Lauren began. "When I went by, on my way into the shower, you were out cold!"

Mildred glanced at the six-foot-three man, and then back to Lauren. "He jes' came a wanderin' out here, right after I started cookin', wasn't wearin' nothin' but a sheet! Nearly sent my poor ol' heart to failure! Seein' such a sight..." Lauren blushed; she could understand the reaction.

Glancing over at Nick, she noticed that he was staring at her profusely, as if he longed to speak of something to her. She reflected on the incident in the bedroom earlier, the flash of emotions ... dreading the answers she sought.

"He was rantin' an a' ravin' an demandin' t' see you!" Mildred continued, "I had all I could do t' keep im' outta' that bathroom, an' convince im' you were all right!"

She expressed herself easily. "I divvied up some old clothes o' my husband, he looked about the same size, when Earl was young, anyway! I've got enough things stored around this place to start my own thrift shop!" She chuckled amusingly to herself, shaking her head comically, and glancing at the two of them, "Honey, if you were wonderin' about any serious beaus, this one seems pretty serious to me!" Nicks eyes glanced away at the statement, leaving Lauren feeling a little awkward now; she had never really considered him a beau.

What had happened out there, between them, seemed to be of another nature. They each had been under a tremendous amount of stress, and fear, the pressure to survive was incredible! With all of these factors combined, added to a mutual attraction, of course something was bound to happen! Lauren needed to convince herself that it had been nothing more than a fling, if her heart wasn't involved, then it couldn't be broken, but yet, even now, she could feel her pulse quicken at the thought of their encounters. It was more than an affair, more than she wanted to admit, and his obvious reaction to the idea was all too noticeable.

The reddening complexion, of the quiet girl, set a clue of understanding into the old woman's mind; she swallowed her foot with a grain of salt, and decided it was time to clear the table.

Rising, she recanted as gracefully as she had began, "You two would make a charmin' couple..." Nicks expression was of stone, as if he had cut off all emotion, Lauren could not meet his eyes as he faced her now, something about his sullen appearance brewed a deep pain within her.

Secretly, she mirrored his loss of emotion, their prior lives were close at hand, society was close at hand, and with society came rules, rules neither knew if they had broken or not. Gretchen, he had said, one word, one name, but in it the answer to so much lingered, her heart ached at the thought, the emotion she had fought to extinguish, now threatened to consume her. No, she decided, it was better left behind, back in the mountains. She wasn't ashamed of what had happened, but the uncertainty of her awaiting life left a worry of commitments. Rising she headed eagerly to the sink to assist Mildred in her cause. She didn't want to let their relationship go any further until the truth was abroad.

Nick found himself at a binding pivotal moment. He watched as the skirt that Lauren wore, swayed gracefully about her slender limbs, the white cotton blouse, which clung tightly to her full bust, was tied loosely at the low bodice. Its criss-crossing pattern traveling downward between her breasts, revealed that she wore no brazier; the thought enticed him. His eyes followed the small teal flowers that bordered the open peasant front, up to her revealed shoulders. Their browned color reminded him of the nude excursions they had shared, and of the other places that were also browned, in some cases, stiffly burned.

Turning toward the den, a stifling pain gripped his injured limb. He despised the feeling of helplessness that followed an injury, loathed the thought of anything standing in the way of his physical soundness. It made him feel trapped condemned to a bleak impairment, of which he had no control. Gritting his teeth, he strode onward into the den, embracing the stinging pain, and casting it away by boldly defying its existence.

He was no longer concerned with his physical impairments; a matter of the heart now constrained him. But as with the bodily limitations, he loathed the truth of his lack of control, and detested the fact of his utter defenselessness. If she had remembered anything from her past, she hadn't disclosed it to him, but from the evident statement Mildred had made, it was obvious that she had. The reason for her silence was obvious to him now; there must have been someone, someone waiting for her return.

The answer was becoming painfully clear, her reason for rejecting him at the diner, she must have been involved with someone. Perhaps she had kept that secret from him all along, after all, HE had been the one to proposition her in the hot spring, her reluctance to be with him was clearer now than before. It was he who had pressured her into making a rash decision, and by doing so, opened himself up for another astounding blow to the heart. Try as he may to view their encounter as nothing more than a fling, something that might happen between two people forced to lean on one another, while facing impossible odds, he could not.

The night was still as Nick lie awake in the double bed, he stared quietly out of the large, side window in the room, and into the millions of tiny bright stars that filled the broad sky. The moon was fully aglow, and shone brightly on the underlying land, casting an iridescent, silvery glow over the scene. The door opened and he quickly closed his eyes, mocking sleep, he knew it would be Lauren, entering after she finished combing her thick, dark hair.

"Nick?" she whispered as she crossed the room. "Are you awake?" Her delicate hands pressed on to the bed, as she peered at him, trying to focus through the darkness. A cool breeze caught her hair, as it streamed in through the open window, sending a chill over her as it wafted beneath the long vanilla gown she wore. Mildred had insisted she wear it, despite Laurens objections, the garment had belonged to Mildred's daughter, and was a keepsake of sorts. Shivering, she rounded the bed and closed the window, peering for a moment out into the starry sky.

Nick gazed secretly at her delicate silhouette, outlined in the silvery glow, he longed to reach out to her, to touch her velvety flesh, and claim her body once again, but regrettably he refrained, silently cursing his weakness. Closing his eyes, he shut her out once more, allowing his stone cold façade to imprison him once again, as it had before, for so long.

Nicholas hadn't spoken to her since supper and Lauren was growing worried, his features had begun to take on a dark, solemn appearance and one she couldn't decipher, no matter how tactfully she sought the answer. Whatever was plaguing the quiet man, it was coming between them, and Lauren struggled desperately within to convince herself that it shouldn't matter. The truth was growing more clear though, and harder to deny, there was more than a mere encounter that had taken place, and she could not write it off as easily as she had hoped, after all it had been Mildred whom had disclosed the obvious, and if others could see through them so easily, how could she hide it from herself?

But while Lauren was trying to come to terms with that, Nick seemed to be pulling away, far away, and out of her reach. No matter if he did belong to another, they would have to come to terms with what was happening, she couldn't bear to be brushed aside, like some kind of mistake.

"Nick?" Her whisper held a tremor that filled him with guilt. Disappointed, Lauren climbed beside the apparently sleeping man, and drew the thick, down comforter over her forlorn body, she felt like weeping, but knew it would solve nothing. Tiredly she sought the comfort of her dreams, perhaps the morning would bring about the answer, she comforted, but invariably she knew that the answers would only be found when they reached their destination, only when she knew for certain her binds, would she be able to justify her feelings.

Sleep came quickly for the weary woman, but the comfort of her dreams was non-existent, instead her mind was mobbed with flashes of inconclusive memories, and bits of tangled thought, she felt as though she were falling down a bottomless pit, filled with unknown dangers and frightening darkness. Along the uncharted course, sprang forth an intense rush of memories and faces, that were foreign to her, until at last a name found a face … she woke with a start as the memory teetered on the edge of conscious thought, suddenly plummeting forward into reality. A man, someone she knew, someone close by a strange twist of fate, the hard chiseled features of his face held many varying emotions that burst forth at the sight of him, but strongest of them all was an uncertain fear, that kept at her racing mind. The sandy brown hair that feathered at his forelock and his crooked gleaming smile were suspended in her searching mind, but the sudden familiarity that seized her recognized only one name, Billy Malhoun. The name Mildred had mentioned, but what was her startling fear all about?

Lauren lay back down upon her pillow, glancing at the clock, she realized that she was alone in the room, it was already five after seven in the morning, and Nick had apparently risen sometime earlier, leaving a cold and empty bed as evidence. She thought for a moment about the recapment that had stunned her so, from what Mildred had told her, she hadn't been with Billy since she was sixteen?

Although, the memory seemed quite recent, in it he appeared to be nearly thirty, and not at all a 'boy' as Mildred had described. What it all meant was unclear, but she harbored a secret fear that he may have some link to her.

Tossing the covers to the side, she quickly rose and dressed, combing her hair expeditiously, and hurrying into the warm glow of the kitchen. Mildred sat at the small table, sipping on a cup of coffee, and reading through a worn book, of which she had most likely read several times before. She glanced up at Lauren and then continued with her literature.

"Have some breakfast, hon?" She motioned to several covered platters in the center of the straw-colored butcher block. Lauren glanced inconspicuously through the room, not seeing Nicholas anywhere.

Upon lifting the, unexpectedly heavy, covers, she discovered an assortment of breakfast dishes, pancakes, sausage and eggs were among them, but her appetite was non-existent, she glanced around once more, making certain she had gone unnoticed by her hostess, she was beginning to feel a bit anxious, where had he gone?

"He's out at the stables." Mildred's words were unexpectedly spoken, as she continued to read. "They're down back."

Lauren studied her for a moment, grinning with embarrassment, "Was I that obvious?" she queried.

The other woman peered over her book, "You had better hurry, he's takin' one o the Clydes out, fer a clear yer mind mornin' ride." Snatching a piece of sausage from the plate, she hurried for the rear door.

"THANK YOU MILDRED!" The old woman looked up from her book, and smiled, knowingly.

As Lauren made her way down the winding earthen path, that crossed a mossy green pasture, she began to wonder if her presence would only serve as a bother to him right now. She approached the barn slowly, worrying what his reaction to her might be; perhaps she was becoming a nuisance, like that of a useless piece of baggage.

She placed an unsure hand upon the graying barn door, as the plaguing thoughts struck her once again, Nick had spoken of his knowledge of her, but reluctance was evident where his profile was concerned.

Perhaps his silence did not lie with his feelings for her, but with his own dilemma, he knew what lie ahead of them, he was quite witty, and handsome, a pillar of stability in her eyes, but what about to his someone else? Gretchen perhaps, was she lost without him by her side, without his arms to hold her? Waiting, worrying, over her missing husband? Was he riddled with indecision or guilt over what had happened? Could that be the cause of his held tongue? A picture of another woman in his arms flashed through her mind, Gretchen, she pondered, blonde? Thin? Athletic? Swedish … her heart began to race, what had she done? The memory of their first encounter was still vivid on her mind … *"I don't expect anything to happen here, if that is what you thought…"* his words seemed to ring more clearly now, as did hers … *"I never said I didn't want to…"*

She had seduced him! She now felt like a complete harlot, to have given herself so readily, she had placed him in a situation with which he had no control, a situation that he had had no resistance in, it wasn't his fault, it was hers. She knew she would have to tell him that she had discovered his ailing secret, and that she didn't want him to take the blame for her wantonness, but exactly how she would tell him, was another problem.

Opening the large door, she resolved to attempt the matter unorthodox; she would just have to let her honesty come forthright in the process. She entered the large, wooden structure warily.

"Nick?" His name echoed ominously throughout the room. The floor, she noticed, consisted of soft earth and sawdust, bits of straw bedding and dropped hay, were scattered amongst it, along with the large footprints, of the long-stridden man. Lauren followed the prints up to a stall, in the back, that smelled of fresh horse. It was unoccupied, but the saddle stand, which stood just outside, still held the large western saddle that Doc Evans had rode up to them on.

She strode past the long hall of stables; several of them harbored other horses, the bulk of which were Clydesdales, but some Quarter horses, and a few Paints. She followed the slight trail of prints in the loose flooring, which led to the rear door of the towering barn. It had been left slightly ajar, and a group of fluttering, barn swallows were busily chattering their warnings at an entering cat. Hurrying to the door, she cast it open, flooding the room with the incoming, morning sunlight. Briefly she was blinded, but shielding her eyes with an extended arm, she focused on a large corral, and adjoining pasture, fully surrounded by a large, sturdy, fence, which disappeared over the distant hill.

The scattered trees, that covered the land, were basked in autumn colors; their leaves danced on the crisp breeze, and tumbled along the stretching hills. To the west of the scene, a golden wheat field swayed with the wind, as the last of the buzzing September insects wistfully played along its glistening tips. A movement caught her eye, and she glanced quickly toward it. Along the edge of the pasture a bubbling brook trickled, gleefully, its borders thick with yellow, autumn, wildflowers, and daintily fluttering butterflies. Crossing the stream was a magnificent, black, Clydesdale, the long shining strands of his tail, flowing out like black silk. Upon the glistening steed, sat the handsome nobleman she sought, his thick, dark hair shone much like the gleaming coat of his mount. He was astride the looming beast, bareback, and his large hands were entwined in the animal's long, shimmering, mane.

The sight was incredible, reminding her of some fantasy painting, or some dream-like effigy come to life. He was too far from her to call out to him, and the rush of the wind through the trees would have drowned out any sound that should attempt the journey. He was headed toward the warmly colored forest, and she suddenly felt the urge to be with him on his travels. Nimbly she reentered the barn and began searching the stalls, stopping on a chestnut quarter horse, whose eyes seemed gentle. The horse whinnied and stomped its hooves as if it were hungry. Petting its softly coated slender neck, she fed it a few scattered strands of hay that were lying before the entrance.

She thought of heading to the tack room for a saddle, but then noticed another large saddle before one of the other stable doors, perhaps the obvious saddles marked the horses that could be ridden, she schemed, she didn't want to attempt a green broke filly and risk further injury.

Peering into the room, she saw the rump of a seemingly large mare; she was rummaging in the musky straw of her stall, and picking at the bits of oats that had apparently fallen there after her last feeding. Her coat was a deep bay color, with darkening forelocks that were splashed with a bright white sock, at each immense hoof. She slowly raised her exceptionally large head and turned to look at the curious woman, another splash of white took its place as a wide blaze upon the arch of her broad nose, emanating from the shock of white, was a burnt sienna hue that darkened quickly into a dark brown, close to the likeness of black, which covered the remainder of her large head.

Her gentle brown eyes were thickly lashed, and her long mane and tail, were a black-brown shade with streaks of sun-ripened auburn streaming through them. The horse softly stepped toward the gate, snorting the scent of Laurens hand out of its nostrils, the woman was unfamiliar, but the mare seemed to be drawn to her.

"And what's your name?" she presented quietly, as she stroked the animals thick coat. "You're so large, I hope you're friendly." She slowly opened the gate and stepped inside, praying her instincts wouldn't fail her.

Looking around for something to step onto, to mount the horse, she noticed a stepping stool outside of the stable. She grasped it readily, and placed it beside the mare. "Now please have patience with me, it's been awhile you know." She petted the mare softly and tested her weight on the bare back of the horse, continuing to speak gently to her, the animal stood quietly, as if expecting her to climb up. Lauren lay over her back, breathing shallowly out of nervousness, she hadn't realized just how high the horse was, but luckily, the gentle steed never moved a muscle while she mounted.

Swinging her leg gracefully over its back, she sat swiftly upward, and grasped onto her long thick mane. The height was dizzying abroad the huge mare, she was nearly eight feet above the ground, from her perch, and her heart bounded into her throat when the animal stepped forward.

"Whoa!" she called unsteadily, and the horse halted obediently, the unexpectedly positive reaction brought a breath of relief. Slowly she brought the mare into the hall and out the opened door, into the fresh autumn air. Upon entering the open hillside, the large mare raised her head with a new alertness, she took in the scents of the land, snorting several times and pawing in the direction of the stallion.

"My thoughts exactly!" Lauren mused as she patted the neck of her steed. A buoyant sense of adventure came over her as she peered in the direction the two had gone.

"Get up, girl!" she called, nickering and spurring at the mares flanks with her bare feet. The horse let out a shrill whinny and jolted forward into a steady trot, wavering Laurens balance for a moment, which was quickly caught, as she entwined her hands deeper into the horse's thick, dark hair.

"Yah!" she called out, spurring the animal once again, and steadying herself for the jolt, the graceful mare loomed ever faster, the soft canter transforming into a steady gallop.

Lauren devoured the moment, she basked in the rush of freedom it brought forth, the cool morning air rushing through her hair, the gentle steady rhythm of the enormous steed, and the glittering morning dew that embellished the rolling hills in the bright clear morning sun, all combined, surrounding her hyper tuned senses to create an impossible, fantastic, moment of paradise likeness. In no time she was across the wide-open pasture and barreling toward the brook. As she neared the body of water, she realized that she had greatly underestimated its size, peering down upon it from the peak of the hill. She was certain that the charging horse would falter on one of the protruding stones, from the flooded creek, only to stumble, and injure itself, along with its rider. Before she could call out her halt, they were upon the stream, the mare jolted suddenly, and closing her eyes; Lauren clenched her hands tighter to the hold of mane she grasped. Gasping, she felt the animal soar smoothly upward, and connect easily once again with a thud, upon the solid earth. Opening her eyes, she stared in disbelief, behind them, as she realized she had cleared the expanse with ease, a deep excitement bubbled up within her, after the nervousness subsided, she felt as if she had crossed over into her youth once again. Faster, she thought, faster! The speeding mare was quickly exposing itself to be the escape she had needed from the pressing issues that bore into her mind.

She charged recklessly on, past thick groves of trees and knotting twisting binds of roots, moving onward she realized they were traveling a well beaten path, which led deep into the valley beyond the pastures boundaries. The filtered morning sun cast pillars of light through the entangled branches that overshadowed the earthen trail, revealing clouds of dancing pollen that erupted as the horse and rider flew past. Ahead lay another crossing of stream, this one shallower, and broad. Lauren spurred onward, drawing herself against the thick neck of the beast, crossing the outlet swiftly. She could feel the gusts of spraying water, splash against her bare legs, catching the burning flanks of the horse, and quickly dispersing into the rushing draft they left behind them.

The speed was exhilarating, and Lauren barely noticed when they barreled past Nicholas and the black Clydesdale, the baffled man stared in awe at the shocking revelation that unfolded before him in a flash.

"Lauren!?" he mused, as she disappeared into the thick forest, he laughed in astonishment at the amazing girl; she never ceased to surprise him. His laughter stopped abruptly as he suddenly wondered if everything was all right, perhaps she had lost control of the large horse. He spurred his mount with the faded boots, and called out an order of speed as the towering stallion charged forward.

"Lauren!" he called as he plummeted after her, in a moment he was upon the two, as they flew together swiftly, deeper and deeper into the valley.

The beaten path they followed dispersed into an old riverbed, which was shallowly filled from the night's rain.

"Lauren!" he called again, she turned briefly toward him, her face aglow with a child-like happiness. Her eyes caught his momentarily, and filled him with a frightening exuberance, as well. "Where are you going?" he called to her.

"I don't care!" she returned, with a careless laugh. They charged on through the stream bed, their pace slowing a bit with the dragline of water. The bed widened as they traveled, leading to high walls of earth on either embankment.

They were side by side, at a quick trot, when they reached a breaking point that forced them to slow to a stop. Lauren looked around, the mares' nostrils flaring as her heaving sides revealed the strain of the run, the impossible view around them was exceptional. Low-hanging weeping willows lined the riverbed, their drooping foliage brushing the surface of the shallow water. Autumn hued leaves drifted on the air, falling to the ground, and into the flowing stream all around them, along with the remnants of the wilting, late season, wildflowers that thickly bordered the brook.

The new winter birds happily sang of the seasons end, and joyfully fluttered from branch to branch, as the woodland creatures busily harvested their supplies of winter food. Before them, a softly dropping array of small waterfalls, expanded, weaving right, then left, down into a shallow pool, about twelve feet away. It was a gradual slant, down the various large flat stones, and ledges, but Lauren had no intentions of pushing the animal any further. She had escaped her dilemmas successfully for a few moments, and she only wished to hold on to the moment while she still could. Above the large, hollowed, grove, the towering pines and oaks swayed gently in the mountain breeze, the scent of the looming trees, drifted in, mixing with the soft, floral oils, which touched Laurens velvet skin, and the musky scent of the horses. The animals stood close to one another, snorting, and tossing their heads, as the riders followed the borders of their surroundings, with awe-stricken eyes.

Nicholas leaned close to Laurens side. "Why did you come here?" he whispered, startling the engrossed woman. She turned toward him, only to find him looming closely to her, studying her. Turning away, to escape his closeness, she looked again out into the thick groves of dark pines, and fiery splashes of autumn foliage.

"I think I know this place," she revealed, softly. It seemed she had run to this thicket before, needing comfort from something, but again, the memory clung to the precipice of her conscious mind, still blurred and gapped as the bodies of her memories were. Nickering at her mount, she steered her away from the stallion, by means of pulling at a high point, in her long mane. The horse stepped heavily, a few paces to the left, turning broadside to the black Clydesdale. Lauren looked to Nick briefly, her eyes finding his, and then flickering away, she found it difficult to keep a steady gaze, when his deep blue eyes burned into her.

"Why did you follow?" she challenged, daringly, her eyes still averting his.

"I thought you might be in trouble," he began.

She smiled spitefully, "I'm not a child, I can take care of myself." She didn't know why she was being so very smart to him, perhaps it was the growing pain she felt, when he was near her, and even stronger when he wasn't. The thought of him belonging to another was slowly choking the life from her, and she couldn't bear his compassion where she was concerned.

Her bitterness cut him deeply. “So, I guess you didn’t need me when you were twelve feet under the river then?”

She could sense the tension between them, but could not hold her tongue from a sassy retort, “You’re not my keeper!” The emotion stirred within her. “You’re not … you’re not anything to me!” She knew she hadn’t meant it, but her quick words sent a blow he hadn’t expected. He was silent, too silent, and she could feel his eyes burning through her, she couldn’t bear to look at him, not now, she hadn’t meant it, she hadn’t, but if she let him continue this charade, if she let him go on playing with her emotions … She wanted desperately to turn to him, to scream at him for letting her love him, to clear her mind of all the anger she felt at the situation, but she held her tongue, she had to let it end before it went any farther.

Nicholas stared hard at her, why wouldn’t she look at him? Perhaps his silence had botched up any chance he may have had, or was this to be the truth of their relationship, had they merely used one another? Had all the emotion he had felt for her, been a figment of his mind? Something he had wanted to be, needed? Even with no memory of the folly he had caused at their first meeting, she would not succumb to him.

He recalled that cool night, her dark hair falling over her shoulders, as her sea-green gaze found his, he had been truly enchanted by her, and still he ached for her sweetness. Scorning himself for the weakness, he reflected on their situation, obviously there was a chance that someone would be waiting for her return, she herself had been enquiring about it, he longed to hold her but knew that it would only accomplish a deeper pain, why had he been so easy to open himself up, only to be hurt again.

She was far away now, too far for him to reach, like the wind drifting through the pines, she captured his heart and ran with it, she was unattainable, a wild soul, too good for him.

“You’re right,” he sighed, “and you’re nothing to me.” Lauren felt the rising lump in her throat, she fought it desperately but the tears began to well up in her eyes, she couldn’t bear that, not his agreeing with her. She hadn’t meant what she had said, but apparently had stumbled upon the truth between them, it was over then, no more of the searing kisses she had become so accepting of, so hungry for. It was over. He would return to his wife, and she would remain only a glimpse of his life, regret, a symbol of his infidelity, the thought ate at her heart.

Nick could feel the anger welling up within him, how could he agree to such a ludicrous ensemble? No matter what lie ahead of them, no matter how she felt at that moment, it was imperative that she know exactly how he felt about her.

"Lauren, I…"

She waved a hand at his words. "Don't, Nick," she choked out. "Don't do this…"

"Lauren, please let me finish."

Tears spilled down her face, she didn't want to hear what he had to say, she couldn't bear to hear of his other life, before her.

"You don't have to tell me!" she stammered out. "I know! I already know!" Her words made little sense to him, what was it she knew?

The searing pain within her plummeted out of control, she had to run, she had to do something to get away. Gathering, tightly, the horses mane, she spurred the horse, wildly, crying out an order to go. The startled creature reared up, suddenly, spooking the stallion into frenzy, and charging forward, toward the rocky slope of falls. The sudden jolt knocked the woman's point of balance off, and as the mare barreled on, Lauren began to waver, uncontrollably. Nick gained control of the stallion quickly, and turned back towards the stumbling mare, she was blinded by the spray of the splashing water, and was charging toward the gradual drop-off before them, without thought, he hurriedly charged after her. He knew if the horse faltered, Lauren would be cast to the stones below, and her wavering balance grew increasingly more dangerous, by the moment.

At full gallop he tore beside them, the blinding spray stinging his tense flesh, and the dropping falls only several yards ahead, *"Hold on!"* he prayed, *"Hold on!"* he slashed his arm out reaching frantically for the faltering woman. Missing, he was forced to adjust his weight, and grasp the stallions' mane once again. Rapidly, he reached again, a miss! She was tossed uncontrollably, backwards, bounding hard against the horses rump, the foaming water came hurtling at her, as she plummeted down toward the slashing hooves of the mare. An unexpected jolt caught her, and she was thrown on to the stallions back, colliding hard against Nicks' solid body, he swooped her up just seconds before they met the falls. The speeding horses could not stop, as inertia took over, the pair soared over the stony slope, landing squarely below, girth high in the rushing waters that followed. The icy sensation left them gasping, and hurriedly heading for the shore. Nicks' strong arm tightened protectively around Laurens waist, as the stallion bounded nervously toward the nearing land. Dazed and confused, she was aghast with shock, it had all happened so suddenly, she was just beginning to comprehend the situation, he had done it again he'd saved her! Somewhere inside, a tinge of anger flared, how could she show him that she didn't need him, if he kept on rescuing her like some damsel in distress!? How could she convince him it was all right to go back to his life, and leave her to hers, if she kept proving otherwise? The horse reached the dry shore, and trotted away from the chilling pool, stopping when Nicholas strongly pulled on his now dampened mane.

Lauren was fuming, she struggled against his strong embrace, "Let go!" she cried angrily, his hold on her remained.

"You just can't stay out of the water, can you?" he mused mockingly, as he watched her squirming against him.

"Would you stop that!" she demanded seriously as she pried at his large hand.

"Stop what?" he mused again, the perturbed young woman, was quite a comical sight under the circumstances.

"Stop, saving me!" With that final word she broke free of his arm and nearly fell to the ground.

Nick gathered her to him once more. "I'm afraid I can't do that," he said as he pressed her to him once again.

"Why not!" she demanded. Turning abruptly, she faced him, only to find his lips dangerously close to hers ...

"I just can't..." He breathed softly against her, the moment lingered, and then softly, slowly, their lips met. She needed to object, but his tender kiss held her, deepening as she turned toward him fully. Her hand found his clean-shaven face, without intention, she found herself unable to resist him, no matter how hard she tried to convince herself it was wrong.

As the encounter broke away, their eyes met evenly. "What of your commitments?" Lauren asked softly. "What about your life before me?"

Nicholas thought for a moment, his gaze outlining her features.

"Why must you insist on torturing me?" she asked desperately, her eyes beginning to mist, as her lips trembled.

"My life?" Nick began, as he stroked her soft hair. "I've never felt more alive than I have when I'm with you; I'm not even close to the same person I used to be!"

"But how can you just leave it all behind you? Don't you think she misses you?"

Nick was momentarily confused. "Who?"

Lauren shook her head, "Don't pretend with me, Nick! Gretchen! What about her?" The name left a dry feeling in her mouth.

How she knew about Gretchen, he didn't know, but nevertheless, she did, and she deserved to hear the truth from him now,

"My life before you, if you can call it that, was the reason that I left. She didn't care about me, or the relationship, that was clear." His face took on a deep sadness, as he looked away from her. "Before you, I was always so cold, so empty, I guess it reflected on how I looked at life, how I handled it." He quickly captured her eyes once more. "I don't want that again, not with you, Lauren, I couldn't bear it."

Lauren searched his eyes, she began to understand his silence, Mildred had mentioned that she had been wondering about any serious beaus, he was afraid that he would lose her, afraid to be alone again.

"Nick." She shook her head apologetically. "I'm sorry." Reaching up to him, she softly touched his face once more. "I guess I feel the same, all of this excitement has been so confusing, you've been the only constant in my life since the accident, if you leave me too, I don't know..." The heartfelt emotion, was shining through her blue-green, eyes along with the now obvious, fear.

She began to speak, when Nicholas pressed a finger to her soft lips.

"Whatever happens," he began, "I'll always be here for you, right by your side, and we'll get through this together." Their lips met again, the passion flaring between them, raging like the river that had brought them together, and drowning them both with the flowing emotion that they shared.

CHAPTER 10

The road into town was long and winding, it was partially washed away by the bout of rain, which had been driven so viciously by the night's storm. Mildred had bid them farewell and wished them luck, on their journey into town, she knew it would be a long one. The old animal doctor would have taken them herself, but a desperate patient called for her attention. When Bill Shaddock brought to her an injured calf, she agreed to mend the poor beast if Bill would drive the travelers into town. He agreed, and so the two were finally on their way.

Lauren was nervous, but excited, she fidgeted with the soft, black, moccasins that Mildred had given her, the woman had been so kind to them, she took a mental note to visit her after the ordeal was over. She only prayed that the journey would assist in resurfacing her lost life, perhaps when she got into town someone would recognize her, or she them, either way she hoped for some means of familiarity.

Nick remained idly solemn the entire trip, his arm wrapped possessively around her, as he stared incandescently out the window of the old farm truck. Mr. Shaddock glanced at the pair; they were a mighty handsome couple, he confessed, although their attire was a bit out of style for their ages.

"So you two from around these parts?" He continued watching the road as he spoke. "Actually, we're new." Nick spoke cautiously; he didn't want to explain any farther.

"Well I haven't lived here my whole life," Bill explained, "but most of it anyway, say, are you two goin' to the fall festival in town?" He paused glancing again at the pair. "It's an annual thing."

Lauren was grinning; obviously he had assumed them to be a couple, and why not? They had been together through so much, both needing each other for safety, comfort, so much had been shared between them, but now a deep anxiety held them apart. Separate fears plagued them, delving a wedge between their relationship, each fearing what lie ahead, wondering if they would share a future, or if this would be their last moments together as a 'couple'. Lauren glanced at Nick, his features had softened as he held her gaze, question in his eyes, he looked older, Lauren reflected, stressed. Their silence held Bills tongue from prying any further. Nick turned away once again, what lie ahead was unknown, but while they were together, he needed her to know how he felt. Softly he slid his hand over hers, hampering the fidgeting that had started again, and renewing the confidence she had begun to lose. He would be with her, she confided, no matter what, and with this in mind, her fears were somewhat subsided. The truck continued on, with the trip seeming impossibly long, and increasingly uncomfortable, with each agonizing bump, that patterned the road. Soon they entered the town, and Mr. Shaddock pulled into the local grocery.

"Do you folks need anything else?" he gestured neighborly. "I'd be much obliged to help ya' out." They declined, asking only for directions to the police department, which they were readily given.

"Chief Ellington?" The female officer stepped into the office warily, as the chief looked up from his paperwork.

"Yeah, what?" he answered gruffly.

"I think you should hear this…" She motioned the couple into the small room, "This here is Lauren Conklin, and Nicholas Carmen, sir, they seem to have a problem…" She waved them into the room fully, and headed out, closing the door behind her. Lauren stood nervously before the chief's desk; he rose, extending a hand, as Nicholas moved closer to the distressed woman.

"Bruce Ellington," he presented, Lauren studied him briefly, he seemed to be a trustworthy man, with an air of authority, which was most likely the reason he acquired his job. A picture of a young girl was displayed on his desk, and another that displayed him and the same girl, with a woman that appeared to be an older version of her. She looked again to his face, it appeared to be hard and stressed, but not with the drawn and tired lines of old age, but rather the withering of a difficult life. His dark gray hair was still thick and full; it was his eyes that told of the troubled years, as he firmly shook her hand.

"What can I do for you?" Seating himself once more, he motioned for the strangers to do the same.

Nick began, "Well, I'm not quite sure what you can do, but right now you seem to be our only resource."

Raising his brows, in interest, he leaned closer to the pair.

"This is Lauren Conklin, she is staying up at the resort in a cabin that belongs to her parents, we are assuming their names to be Sandy and Bill Conklin, we think they are from Wisconsin, but so far, that's all we know."

Chief Ellington squinted his face in confusion. "And?" he asked, assessing the situation. "And, that's all Lauren knows too, she's lost a great deal of her memories, she was involved in a severe accident several days ago, and now, well, now I'm the only link she has to her prior life."

The chief leaned back in his chair, rubbing his now tense forehead. "I see," he sighed, "well let's hear it from the beginning..."

The taillights of the patrol car disappeared into the darkness, as Nick and Lauren stood on the front porch of his cabin; they had spent hours down at the station explaining time and time again what had occurred. The department had impounded Nicks' vehicle after it had been found on the roadside, abandoned, two days after the incident. He would be able to get it out by morning, after the paperwork and reports were filed. They had found a record of residency on her parents, it had been written up when the community started a neighborhood watch system, all residents were asked to fill out a form, explaining their location and number of family members, they had listed only themselves, it was apparently during the time Lauren had been away at school.

Their Wisconsin phone number had been written in ink on the form, just in case of any problems during their absence, but the numbers were written illegibly, and the paperwork displayed no address. Lauren had been informed that she would be able to receive more information the following day, but that she should get some rest before being subjected to any further stress, she found the statement to be quite ironic, after her prior excursion.

They complied with the decision to post fliers of her all over the town, and to post ads in the local paper, until they could reach a relative or at least a proven acquaintance. To safeguard against fraudulence, they resigned to not print her name, but only a photo of her, and a statement explaining her situation. Chief Ellington decided it best not to let her identity out, so as not to put her in danger.

"There are a lot of sickos out there," he explained. After they filled out their statements, and signed document after document, Lauren was sent to the local doctor to be examined. Other than the slightly infected cut on her hand, and the loss of memory, of course, she was physically sound.

The doctor's name was Junior Cratchet, which in itself was a bit bizarre, his legal name was Timothy Cratchet Junior, and her thoughts were constantly turning to the classic character of tiny Tim, from the timeless novel, Scrooge, by Charles Dickens. The doctor was a jolly old man, with a shining bald head, and crimson hued cheeks that set high on his round face, his bright white beard was neatly trimmed, but protruded past his small chin like a wind-blown snowdrift, and he was anything but tiny she mused. He caught her small chuckle as she read his name.

"That's quite all right Miss." His voice was ominously cheerful, and loud. "I have friends that have called me tiny Tim since I was a boy! It is unique, don't you agree?" Surprisingly he spoke with a distinctly English accent, which left Lauren pondering on the fact for a moment. She herself hadn't a southern accent either, and she mused that the locals most likely thought her strange as well.

In all of their ramblings, of that afternoon, neither had had a bite to eat, it was nearly eight pm now, and their stomachs growled vehemently with famished hunger. Lauren watched the taillights as they disappeared into the night, focusing now on the consuming darkness that the mountain evenings brought forth. She stared hard in the direction of her cabin, but the structure was almost invisible in the dusky atmosphere, it seemed cold, lonely ... Nicks warmth enveloped her as he pulled her to him, she gasped softly with the sudden motion, smiling trustingly at him through lowered lashes.

"Are you as hungry as I am?" he asked quietly, his breath against her ear, "Because I make a mean Ravioli, I think it's the technique I use, opening the can, you see I..." He began to demonstrate an imaginary can opener, stopping abruptly as a broad grin spread over his features. He was able to extract a gentle giggle from the beautiful woman, by means of the folly he displayed so naturally, and her gleaming smile was all the answer he needed.

"It sounds delicious!" she chuckled, her laughter soft and sweet, as if she hadn't a care in the world. Extending an elbow to him, they linked arm in arm, and her respondent escort led her inside. Nicks broad hand slid up the wall just inside the doorway, turning on the soft lights that, Lauren discovered to be, lining the walls of the room. Each frosted covering was delicately shaped like a single white lily, stemming from graceful brass posts that swayed slightly at the centers, green foliage was loosely positioned at the base of each fixture, giving the room a hint of majestic tone. It was a tasteful tinge of grandeur, blended with the authenticity of the rustic cabin. Though the walls were open, and white, each corner of the room displayed a thick, raw, wooden post, richly darkened in a deep pine, auburn hue, the hint of wood aided in the rural design.

As the curious woman examined her surroundings, Nicholas bid her to sit as he prepared a quick meal. He entered a room to the right, past the large rounding staircase that wrapped partially around the spacious den. The beauty of the large cabin was impressive, and unexpected when first presented. Lauren walked into the room, easily stepping onto the thick, fawn colored, carpeting that covered the redwood floor, the majority of the walls were covered in large, tall windows that stood at least six feet in length, they harbored the rear and side walls of the room, and were tastefully draped in heavy, navy colored, swag curtains, that over lapped at each meeting. Behind the drapes, white vertical blinds dangled in uniformity, creating a splash of brightness to the comfortably toned room. Overlaying the fawn carpeting a navy toned shag was thrown, lying at an angle, so as to accent the roundness of the room. Buckskin suede furniture tacked down the throw, conveniently placed to aid in the comfort of the den.

Beneath the broad staircase, and looming largely opposite the windows, a large marble-lined fireplace stood, brass trimmed glass doors held back the chilled breeze from the grand opening, and a marred set of blackened utensils sat idly to the side of the piece. A set of glass and pine tables surrounded both the cushioned sofa, and the pair of large easy chairs, that were quite actually the size of small sofas themselves. The room seemed to be made for company, but an air of loneliness hung sadly throughout it, leaving the woman to reflect on his earlier confessions. She sat curiously on the sofa, and inquisitively tampered with a small remote control that lay on the oblong before her. Pressing a large red button, a sudden burst of light flashed, she dropped the contraption, jumping with a fright. A brightly lit fire blazed before her, dancing and swaying in the immense fireplace. Staring for a moment, she began to feel slightly under keyed in his home, she knew her parents had been well endowed in the pocketbook, but she never recalled such a place in all her years, he just had seemed to be, well in all, too down to earth to possess such wealth.

Looking at her surroundings once more, she noticed several wall hangings, each of which had been created by a well known artist, and each in a depressed state, reflecting mourn, and loss, she grew saddened upon peering on them. How cold it seemed beyond the warmth of the slight colors, no tossed mail or scattered litterings of day to day life, not even a television, or any form of outside reflection, existed to ease the fierce bleakness only isolation and solitude clung heavily to the atmosphere. She shivered at the thought of the deep loneliness, like an empty shell of beauty, it seemed hollowed of any trace of life or love, and it left her in wonder of how he could have existed here without becoming suicidal.

What the room needed was life, and she resolved to acquire something in the morning, to display cheerfully, if need be, in the center of the room. She couldn't bear another moment of imagining the warm, and vibrant, man surrounded by the cold shadow of death any longer. Nicholas suddenly came waltzing into the room, in each hand he carried a glass dish, stone-flecked gray in color, and filled with large Italian ravioli, smothered in tomato sauce, and sprinkled with a dash of freshly grated Parmesan cheese. He approached the suede sofa, that Lauren was perched precariously on,

"Dinner is served," he jested royally as he extended a dish to her,

"I couldn't!" she protested. "Not in here! What if it should spill?" She gestured to the couch and carpeting. Shaking his head Nicholas seated himself beside her,

"Its only furniture," he explained. "It won't hurt anything." He produced two silver forks from his rear pocket and handed the first over to the hungry woman. "Now eat up, I worked hard on this" He waited a moment then smiled slyly, Lauren looked at him a trifle serious for a moment, then her laughter could hide no longer. The hungry pair dually savored the sweet basil and oregano, and their helpings hurriedly disappeared, leaving Lauren feeling comfortably full and content basking in the warm flicker of firelight. The security she felt when Nick was beside her was almost frightening in itself, he was quickly becoming a non-expendable asset to her, as she was beginning to need him more and more with every breath, and her seemingly lost independence was the reason for her fear.

"I think that was undoubtedly the best Ravioli I've ever eaten," Lauren admitted candidly to the satisfied man. Nick innocently studied her graceful features.

"I think, you've got a little sauce…" he motioned to a morsel of the spicy sauce that had dripped inconspicuously upon her chin. Lauren wiped at the remnant, keeping her eyes upon the navigating man.

"No, it's down over." She wiped again, but to no avail.

"Here." He reached his gentle hand to her velvet skin. "Let me help you." Dobbing the drop of sauce from her chin, his long thick fingers brushed her plump lips, tracing their lines easily, her features were so clear to him, that he could have easily traced them time and again with eyes closed. His fingertips gently cherished her flesh, like a fine jewel, ever precious to his simple touch. His hungry eyes met hers, revealing a deep secret that was growing clear, she wasn't the only dependent heart in this game, he was struggling with his own need for the captivating beauty. His fear shone brightly within his cerulean gaze and it grew increasingly difficult to mask with the passing of time bringing them closer day by day.

"You are so incredible…" he breathed. Lauren felt as though he was touching her for the first time, as if his soft lips hadn't yet seared her own. Her nervous stomach lurched as he neared her. "How did I ever exist without you?" His honeyed words hit her heart, penetrating the remnants of the shield that had been built for so long. She suddenly felt as though she were letting go of something, some fragment of her forgotten past that had been restraining her, she had been holding back too long and now she could feel the caution being thrown recklessly to the ever strengthening winds. Their lips met in a fiery frenzy of sweetness, blazing through them wildly. The dancing flames illuminated their entwining silhouettes, casting their flickering shadows carelessly upon the slightly opened vertical blinds. As their lips parted Nicholas rose to his feet, deep within a tremor of warning whispered to his heart, danger, he sensed, stop now, or face the flames and chance the burn, she's not yours yet! Tonight, he begged, just tonight, and this will be my forever … Taking Lauren by her hand, he brought her upright,

"Come with me…" he said softly as he led her toward the rounding staircase, their hearts beat wildly as they mounted the terrace. Both knowing expectantly the haven that awaited them beyond the walls above. Entering the master suite they faced a large king sized bed, it's four post structure a deep honey pine over laying a gray marbled base, the slate blue and white, southwestern patterned, bedding was accented by the similar throws about the room, that lay upon the shining wood floors. For a moment Lauren was taken aback by the majesty of it all, but her thoughts were quickly averted when Nicholas met her squarely upon the frame of the doorway, pressing his heated body to hers and sweltering her with his fevered kisses. How he fantasized of this, taking her over and over again between his satin sheets. The hunger between them left each restraining garment to be flung carelessly from their melting bodies, the hot searing kisses that poured over Lauren's flesh, left her quivering with a wanton desire she could not control. Nick softly tugged at the last morsel of clothing between them as Lauren gasped with a start at his bold movements. Trailing up along her thighs, his nimble fingers found her core sending unbearable waves of pleasure through her quaking limbs, the unsteady woman clasped onto his broad shoulders to still herself under the cruel ecstasy. Staring helplessly into her lover's eyes she could no longer restrain her pleasure, her uncontrollable moans sent Nick spinning with excitement as he pressed her further, yearning for her sweet submission, dangling by a thin strand of composure, to hear her soft and fervent pleading once again. Lauren's mouth found his with an urgency that sent him plummeting over the edge of his teetering resistance, she needed this moment, this blinding passion, to escape the fears she held within, releasing her softness, Nick's trembling hands clasped the woman's shapely hips, pressing the naked flesh of their burning bodies together. His desperate lips hungrily trailed to her neck as he grasped her thigh, conforming her to him and raising her trembling leg to his narrow waist. Closing her eyes, Lauren tried desperately to close out the spinning room, but her world was a whirling twister of incomprehensible pleasures she could not reign in.

"Nick..." she breathed against his burning flesh. His coursing manhood met her with a fervent desire, thrusting within her body. His tensed weight pressed her with cruel pleasure against the doorway, urgent thrusts sent a tremor of exquisite breathtaking sensations through hers. She clung helplessly to his sweating body. As his need increased, his primal sexuality growing intensely, the unmasked urgency behind his exploits touched her with a new excitement, and she yearned for more of his obvious enjoyment. With a sudden movement, he pulled away from her warmth, his pulsing excitement evident. Lifting her supple body from the doorway, he easily swept her to the bed, laying her gently upon the softness of the immense pallet. He sought her eyes for the need he mirrored.

"I've dreamt of this moment..." he whispered, facing the blushing woman. "But my dreams held little justice when compared to your sweet ecstasy..." He kissed her deeply, with a passion that far surpassed lust. Entering her once more, he took in the full richness of their lovemaking, realizing he had never loved another until her, and would never love another the way he did this woman.

The night's air was chilled and thin, under the shimmering glow of the full moon, a distant owl cried out as it sought its squealing victim, the silhouettes that danced upon the large windows of the cabin told of the lover's coupling and the green eyed monster of jealousy peered uninvitingly upon them. It was Lauren who was with the dark haired man, whoever he was, and a deep hatred was brewing in the chest of the sickened onlooker. He watched as the light went out in the master suite and viciously flicked his cigarette upon the ground.

"That bitch..." he spat, to himself. "She'll open her legs to anything!"

He turned, climbing into his Jeep and starting the large vehicle.

"It's not over yet, my dear," he said vehemently. "It's far from over..." With his final words he spun dangerously away spraying a trail of arching gravel over the yard of the secluded abode.

CHAPTER 11

Lauren awoke early the next morning, to hear a loud rapping on the door downstairs, she rose quickly, kissing Nicks' sleeping lips, and donning the robe that she had found in the master bathroom. Hurriedly she ran down the broad stairs, hoping to reach the visitor, before Nick awoke from the boisterous rapping.

Peering out the small peephole, she discovered a young deputy on the front porch; he was preparing to knock again, when the door was opened.

"What is it?" she asked nervously, the officer seemed surprised to find a young woman, clad in a satin men's robe, and his startled brown eyes made a quick sweep of her.

"I'm sorry," he began, "did I wake you?"

Lauren shook her head, "It's all right, have you learned anything new?" Her haste was evident as her heart pounded heavily.

"We're still workin' on it ma'am." He removed his, broadly rimmed, hat. "Actually, ma'am, the chief went ahead an' pulled a few strings, an had me bring the mustang out today." He paused, turning toward the car, Lauren peered at it, drifting into deep thought briefly, something about the car … walking up the broad cedar steps, she turned abruptly, searching for the mustang … The memory was cut off …

"Ma'am," the young policeman questioned, "the keys are right here, he'll have to come down 'n sign for it later."

Lauren shook the picture away.

"I'm sorry?" She blinked in confusion for a moment, as the deputy handed her the set of keys. "Oh!" she said abruptly. "Oh, right! The keys! Thank you, officer." Her thoughts were still on the memory, when she turned and entered the house, she hadn't even noticed the young mans roving glance, at her revealed flesh, as she turned. Climbing the staircase, a thought came to mind. She hurried up the stairs to the suite, and inconspicuously entered the bathroom. She would shower and dress, and then she would head into town for a moment. She had spied a few dollars on the marble desk in the room, and although she felt odd taking it, without his consent, she eased her discomfort with the thought that it was going to be used for his benefit, and truthfully she hadn't the time to search her own cabin for cash.

The morning held evidence of a beautiful autumn day approaching, and the gentle, crisp breeze that wisped through her long hair, brought new refreshment to her well-rested body. The nights events still danced through her mind, as she entered the local florists shop, she greeted the shopkeeper, at the front desk, and then began to search the refrigerated cases for the perfect surprise.

Outside the small store, a large, red and black, jeep loomed, the driver staring into the open windows of the building, and taking repetitive drags from the burning cigarette he held. His blood shot eyes revealed his obvious hangover, as they followed the graceful movements, of the searching girl, his head pounding ever harder as he watched her. He reflected on the last time he had watched her, as she lay quietly sleeping, unknowing, in her bed, she had left the window open on purpose, he conceited, knowing he would watch her … she was sweetly torturing him with every move she made, and he'd done all he could do not to go in after her, but no, he would wait, she would be the one to come to him.

He laughed within himself an evil smile spreading across his charming features, and tainting his handsome face, she would have no choice, he mused. A coy chuckle erupted as he held up the local paper, looking once again at her photo, such a lost look on her face, he admitted, mocking a concerned façade. Tampering with her brake line, had only been meant to leave her in need of a ride, one that he would have readily offered when he showed up to 'apologize'. His plan was foolproof, but he hadn't expected her to disappear after that, he had been certain that she was dead, and the torment of not being able to take her, had kept the bottle to his lips. The unexpected results of his efforts had played beautifully into his cause, however, and now that he knew that she wasn't dead, the need to possess her was exceedingly fueled.

He read the caption beside her picture once again, DO YOU KNOW THE WOMAN IN THIS PHOTO? A loud arrogant bout of laughter, erupted from his broadly smiling lips,

"Of course!" he spoke to himself, still reveling in his ingenious scheme. "My dear Lauren, where have you been?" Another round of the spine-chilling laughter flowed loudly from the gleaming man, he tossed the paper aside, and taking one last glance at the shop, sped away, leaving a dark black stripe of rubber behind him.

Lauren stood over the still sleeping man, peering entertainingly at his relaxed features, she couldn't believe he was still sleeping, but she was glad to have had the time to prepare his gift before he saw it.

"Nick?" she said softly, as she brushed her feminine fingers over his cheek. "Rise and shine…" She kneeled beside him, gently sweeping the locks of black hair from his forehead. Stirring ever slightly, a broad grin spread across his face, as his arms unexpectedly encircled her, rolling her over into the bed. "Oh!" she cried as he straddled her. Holding her arms down over her head, he pinned her to the pillows.

"You little sprite!" he called laughably. "Waking a man from his sleep, with your mischievous teasing!" She squirmed beneath him, laughing amiably.

"If I get out of here, you'll not catch me!" She pulled at her restraints.

"Oh, no?" Nick chuckled. "Then you'll not get out of here!" He leaned closer to her, grinning slyly, his playfulness leaving Laurens blood pumping twofold. Kissing her softly he released her arms, and Lauren encircled his neck, returning the refreshing intimacy, that he offered.

"I've got as surprise for you," she whispered, as he trailed kisses lightly down her neck. He looked up for a moment, surprise clearly in his features.

"Oh," he smiled warmly at her, "and what might that be?"

Lauren grinned mischievously. "It wouldn't be a surprise if I told you, now would it?" She slipped easily away, and headed toward the door. "Hurry down, okay?" she bid him, as she sprightly exited.

A few moments later, the yawning man, came slowly down the stairway. As he rounded the banister, turning into the large den, he stopped, scratching his head with a dazed look. Lauren stepped up behind him, her hands wringing nervously. "Do you like it?" she questioned, biting her lip. Upon the large table, before the sofa, a bright arrangement of festively toned flowers, and ferns sat, glimmering with a livid happiness which emanated, contrastingly, through out the dim room.

"It's … different…" he admitted, curiously studying the assortment.

"You don't like it do you," Lauren sighed, dropping her hands to her sides.

"It's not that," he recanted, "they are beautiful, it's just that some things are meant to be left the way they are…"

Lauren caught a hint of agitation in his tone, "Are you angry?" she murmured. "I didn't mean to be too presumptuous, I'll just get rid of them." She started for the arrangement, as Nick caught her arm.

"No!" he said swiftly. "They're too beautiful to just toss away, I'll just have to get used to them, that's all." He gave her a reassuring grin. "Besides its time for a change in this place, it's too cold in here, now that I …" He stopped himself as he peered into her hopeful eyes. A smile overcame him, as he looked upon the innocence in her face. "It just seems to need a bit more, doesn't it?"

Her satisfied look told of the power his reassurance held, he simply couldn't hold on to the harshness he was projecting, after all, she hadn't known. The flowers could be gotten used to, but letting go of the gray past would be hard, learning to accept his fathers death would be something he would have to do, but somehow the horizon seemed to be brighter with his newfound happiness, for once he held a hope for the future, he had never felt before.

After a light breakfast the pair sat leisurely on the front porch, listening to the sweet melodies of the busy birds, and the gentle rustling of the trees, as the cool currents of wind gusted through their branches. Nicholas studied a dancing leaf, of fiery orange, skipping across the thick green lawn, in amongst the sun-bleached stones, long chutes of wild onions, and wilting native flowers. It bounded along the harsh terrain, until at last it caught the undercurrent of the icy wind and seared easily away, he averted his attention to his quiet companion, she was staring hard at the neighboring cabin, with an expression on her face that was less than pleasant.

"Would you like to go back over there now?" Nicks' question caught her ear, obliterating her concentration.

She glanced at him briefly, flashing an appreciative grin. "I'm not sure I'm ready," she confessed, as she peered at her fidgeting hands. The thought of entering her life again, brought about an unexpected nervousness, that she could not explain, "I'm a little frightened at what I might find."

Nick put his arm around her thin frame, drawing her warmly to him. "There's no hurry, Lauren, you can take as long as you need." He lifted her chin up softly. "Cheer up, at least we're out of the woods!"

Lauren laughed gently, as she faced him. "Nick, I…" She wanted to tell him how cold and lonely it would be without his warm smile, and bright laughter, how long the nights would be without his strong embrace, she didn't want to go back there, not now. She wished they could start all over, together, but she didn't want to push him away with her needs, she didn't want her secret to scare him away.

"It's just that, well, it's so cold and solemn looking over there, it just looks so isolated, I'm just … not ready." The warmth of his smile, told of his understanding, her casual façade was quite transparent as usual, to him.

"Lauren," he started, "I'm not going anywhere." His lips met hers softly, her heart leaping to her throat, he did understand!

The day was crisp and clear, leaving a heavy restlessness in the air that called for a solution, both Lauren and Nick could feel the need to find some means of entertainment on this day. Deciding on a walk around the lake, they set off together, never knowing the circumstances they would find upon their return. As their bodies brushed one another, Nicks' hand found Laurens and he cradled it, softly. He looked away with a boyish grin, revealing the slight laugh lines about his eyes, it had been so long since he had felt the life within him stir, in any other instance the cold, solemn hermit he had begun to evolve into, would have looked at the moment with callous scrutiny. The simple gesture, of holding hands, would have struck him as childish, and frivolous at that. No, this time was different, he'd never felt as vulnerable with anyone, as he did with this woman, and yet his masculine need to protect her, overwhelmed him. He knew what he had feared might happen, had already been surpassed by far, but neither his pride, nor his reluctant mistrust wanted to admit it.

The young trooper waited, patiently, outside the cabin, he glanced at his wrist watch, ten minutes had passed, raising his hand for a fifth rap, a movement to the right caught his eye. Startled, he turned abruptly, only to find the two respondents, he sought, walking toward him. They were at a distance, so to attract their attention he flashed the lights on his patrol car, the quick chirp, and bright flash, brought them hurrying in.

Laurens heart pounded, they must have found something out, her mind was splashed with a mixture of emotion, and anything would be good at this point, right? She questioned if she really wanted to know, and the urge to run was eminent, but Nick's firm hand held her safely, and Lauren focused on the security of that. The officer stepped toward them, a suspicious confusion crossing his features.

"Miss Conklin? I need you to come with me to the station, there's someone … a man, who seems to recognize your picture." He opened the passenger door of his vehicle. Lauren stepped back, her heart pounding heavily, a man? Who could possibly … a memory came to mind, the face she had seen, the name, what had it been? She shook it away with haste, why was she so nervous? Almost frightened, after all, she did want to know, right?

She had agreed to the print up, but yet a chill had set in her chest. Nick's hand squeezed hers in reassurance.

"Well, what are we waiting for?" He said it so dramatically light; that he was sure his false calm was obvious. They climbed into the car, the officer only pausing once to give Nick, a disconcerting look. The ride was quiet, aside from the occasional static from the C.B. and an eerie tension clung to the silence.

They neared the station and Lauren began to wring her hands, nervously, in her lap, her trembling legs barely held her as she climbed from the open door. Nick wrapped a steadying arm around her shoulders, and sensed her tension, his own nervousness had him wondering, but he offered the best reassurance he could muster.

The officer led them into the chiefs office. “Sir,” he stated firmly, “Miss Conklin is here.” The chief motioned them in. a man stood with his back to the door, he was speaking to another officer in the room, his large presence overshadowed many of the other men in the station. Running a large hand through his thick, sandy, hair, he turned abruptly, catching Laurens eyes, his intense hazel gaze locking her attention to him.

A gleaming crooked smile beamed, at her stricken features, the broad cheek-bones, and masculine square jaw struck her, that smile … like flashes of light, the memories hit her, although still vague. She strained, her eyes still searching his, flitting thoughts, emotions, nothing. Nothing except for one fact, she knew him, his name … what was it?

She glanced at chief Ellington, his expression was grim, he looked to her, and then Nick, averting his eyes downward and then back to the stranger.

“Are you sure this is her?” he asked roughly. Without looking his way, the sandy haired man answered with certainty.

“Yes.” His acknowledgement of the others in the room was now barely existent, stepping toward Lauren, he held her gaze. “Lauren,” he began, “do you recognize me? Are you all right?”

She stepped back, and Nick caught her shoulder protectively. He glared at the newcomer, measuring him; he wasn’t sure about this sandy-haired jock.

“Lauren, is he familiar to you? Do you recognize him at all?” Almost reluctantly, she nodded, she did recognize him, but who was he? Why did she feel this strange connection to him that frightened her so?

Chief Ellington spoke up, “Do you know who he is?” the tension in his voice held obvious impatience.

Lauren shook her head, “I recognize his face, I …” she paused trying to explain herself more clearly; “I know him somehow, but WHO he is …” she shrugged nervously.

The chief glanced at Nick, who was still possessively comforting the woman, “Well, do you have the paperwork?”

Nick seemed agitated as the large man handed him a few sheets of legal paraphernalia, he looked over them briefly, and handed them to Lauren. "Apparently this man is your husband." The statement hushed the office, and Lauren could feel her heart jump to her throat, husband!

She fumbled through the paperwork, a marriage license, a legal document from the state of California, containing their blood test results, even a marriage certificate. Lauren clasped her hand to her mouth, in disbelief, this couldn't be it was ludicrous! Surely someone would have known!

The stranger stepped toward her, "Lauren, it's me, Billy, don't you remember me?" She looked up, dropping the papers, Billy Malhoun that was his name! She had remembered, but not a trace of their marriage was evident. She swayed, uneasy, at the newfound matter, only to be caught by Nick, who steadied her weakened limbs.

Billy shot him a look of disgust, "Who is this man with his hands all over my wife!" he demanded. Nick returned the glare, but held his tongue.

"This man," Ellington replied, "is the one who pulled her from the river; I think you owe him some measure of gratitude, Mr. Malhoun." The words came out almost vehemently. Billy glanced to Nick, "my apologies, Mr.?" He held out a hand to the dark haired man, raising a questioning eyebrow.

Nick looked at his hand, and remained still, "Carmen," he stated flatly, "Nick Carmen."

"Well then," Billy sneered, "thank you Mr. Carmen, for … helping … my WIFE, when she was in trouble, I've been so worried, but, well, I thought she needed some time away, to sort things out." He stared at Lauren, who was now very conscious of her situation, Nicks' arm still held her protectively, and his grip had tightened.

Lauren was stiff, the arms that had held her so comfortably these past days, now seemed dangerous, she had committed adultery, although not knowingly, she had still allowed it to happen. Was that the reason for her reluctance, her fear? It must have been, there were no other explanations. Her heart pounded so hard, she was sure everyone in the room could hear it; she suddenly wished she hadn't come.

"Why would she need time away, Mr. Malhoun?" the name came out bitterly, as Nick measured the man's reaction, if Lauren was married to this creep, then obviously there were problems between them.

"Not that it's any of your business," he stated, glancing at the chief as he began to explain, "but married couples do have their little disputes, and I'd never try to keep her if she needed time apart." He grinned almost amiably at the questioning man. "After all, we all make mistakes, that's what marriage is all about, give and TAKE." With an eerie emphasis on the latter, he caught Laurens' eyes once again, but this time there was a strange spark within them that made her shudder.

Her facial hue suddenly darkened, as she felt the heat from Nick's body upon her back. What had she gotten herself into, she had practically thrown herself at him on the mountain, never wondering, never caring, but she wore no gold band, and she had never even mentioned the fact of, well, her husband, to Nick, before the accident. She had even introduced herself as Lauren Conklin, not Malhoun, but why would he have made it up? Besides the documents were real, she'd seen them with her own eyes, and so had Nick, so where did they stand now? What would he do? What could he do?

Billy's ire rose the longer Lauren remained in Nick Carmen's arms, she was his now, his to hold! How she swooned over this pretty-boy, the reluctance in her eyes, that held her there, had him fuming, but it didn't matter, she'd be far from this 'Nick' fellow, soon enough, if he could just keep his cool a little longer ...

"If you're quite finished, HELPING, my wife now, Mr. Carmen, I would appreciate you taking your hands off of her."

Nick glared at him with venomous eyes, "I don't think I need you telling me what to do where Lauren is concerned, if you are her husband, why weren't you looking for her? How could you not wonder about her safety?"

"I was worried!" Billy stepped forward, anger welling up in him.

"She was gone for a week, for gods' sake!" Nick stood his ground, rising to the challenge presented, and stepping ahead of Lauren, so as to keep her out of harms way.

"Who the hell do you think you are?" Billy spat, his fists clenched at his sides.

"Why don't we ask you the same question?" The two came face to face, Billy barely an inch taller, but stockier built than Nick's lean body, the tension grew.

"Both of you need to back off!" Chief Ellington had had enough, but Nick wasn't finished.

"What kind of 'little' dispute would drive a woman away for a week!?" Billy loomed further forward, gritting his teeth; this son-of-a-bitch was getting under his skin. He had to keep it cool, or he'd blow the whole thing.

"That's none of your concern!" His voice rose.

"Documents or no documents, I don't buy it! Laurens not going anywhere with you, until I know she's safe!"

"And I suppose she's safe with you? You wife stealing gigilo!"

Ellington stood up, "That's quite enough!" Lauren was aghast with nerves, she'd had enough, her temper flared, and the fear she had held within had fused into anger.

"I don't know why either of you thinks I need your protection!" she glared at them both, her sudden voice catching them off guard, "I'm nobody's property, and I'm not some naive child! I can't stand this, this disgusting display of male pride, any longer! If either of you wants to help me, than I'll need some time, some answers!"

Billy lowered his fists, quickly taking advantage of the situation, "you're right, I apologize for my behavior," he stepped away from Nick, who was still studying him, and cast his eyes to Lauren. "My temper, where you're concerned, has always gotten me in trouble." He mocked a sheepish grin, and Ellington spoke up,

"More than just trouble Mr. Malhoun, according to your past record." He shot Billy a glaring eye.

"Yes, well, that's the past Bruce; I'm a changed man, that is, thanks to Lauren."

Nick looked up to the chief, for a moment. "Record?" he questioned.

The chief glanced at him. "That's none of your concern, Mr. Carmen, that's not public information."

"Like hell, it's not my concern!"

"Watch it Carmen! Or I'll have you restrained!"

Billy grinned from ear to ear at the situation; things were beginning to take a turn in his favor, "That's right, Mr. Carmen, and she's none of your concern either."

Nick tensed at the words, "That's not your decision to make."

The statement was blatantly spoken, and Lauren could feel all eyes turn to her, they couldn't expect her to make that choice, not yet. It was wrong for her to abandon her past, just walk away, and stay with Nick, but he was part of her life now, her husband the stranger. Even if she had loved him before, what if she never felt that way about him again? What if she stayed with Nick, and someday the feelings she'd had, for her husband, returned? Where would that leave Nick? The situation wasn't fair, and there were still so many unanswered questions, she needed more time, time to think, time to find the answers.

CHAPTER 12

Lauren stared at the ring on her finger, it was a perfect fit at a size five, aside from being slightly loose, which was explained by her weight loss, due to exposure. She sat across from Billy in the chief's office.

"So my parents didn't know?" Lauren confirmed once again.

Billy shook his head, sympathetically searching her eyes. "And neither do mine, they never did get along, we were going to tell them as soon as we closed on the house."

"The house you bought in San Jose'?" Billy shook his head in agreement, as Lauren slowly went through the details once more.

"So we've been married a little less than a month now, but we haven't had very much time to be together, because of the secretism."

"That's right." His answers were cautiously calm and well rehearsed, "Two weeks after our marriage, the accident with your parents happened."

"The plane crash?" she questioned.

"Yes," he began. "When you left for the funeral, I had to go away on business, I'm so sorry I couldn't be there for you, but you did say you would rather be alone at that time."

"So, you assumed I had left again to sort things out?"

"Yes, but I must admit, we did have an argument, I was selfish, I needed you, but you needed me to be there for you, more than I had been…"

"So I left angry?"

"You were fuming! You had been staying in your parents' old cabin, and I came over. I needed to be with you, but you weren't ready."

Lauren thought about what Nick had told her, the night he found where she had lived, it all seemed to fit. "But you've lived here for two years, why hadn't anyone seen me, or known about me?"

"Well, for one reason," Billy began, "we saw each other on business trips, it was usually late nights, or weekends. We spent spring break together, in Orlando. That was when you were in college."

"College?" Lauren questioned, the subject interested her, "Where did I go?"

"Some big-time school in Nevada, I can't remember the name of it, off the top of my head, but I'm sure we've got your diploma packed away somewhere."

"How long did we date?"

"Off and on, about four years, but there were so many complications, this last year, we decided to keep a low profile, our families just couldn't accept our love." He put his large hand on top of Laurens, his palm was sweaty, "Haven't I answered everything now? Or must I convince you further?"

Lauren knew he was right; only one piece didn't fit into this puzzle, everything else, fit, made sense, and he was standing right outside the door. Nick paced like a caged tiger, what was taking so long? How could that jackass just come waltzing up, and change everything? She'd never even hinted to the fact that she might be married, but what he had feared, since the first time they had kissed, was cruelly becoming evident. He couldn't lose her, not after all they'd been through, it had only been barely a week, but in it they had found a lifetime. No, he couldn't let her go, and if she felt the same, they'd get through this too.

The office doors opened and Nick's muscles tensed,

"Mr. Carmen?" Chief Ellington motioned him in. "Sit down, will ya?" Nick fastened his attention to Lauren, who was beside the sandy-haired man now; she avoided his eyes with discretion. "Mrs. Malhoun wanted to speak with you." He seated himself at his desk, and began filling out paperwork. Mrs. Malhoun? The name burned like salt on an open wound; surely she didn't mean to just write him off, just like that?

Lauren glanced at him unsteadily, "Nick, I…" she caught the glare in his eyes, and flitted her eyes away, uncomfortably, an awkward situation if there ever was, she grimaced, "Thank you, for all your help, your time." She faced him squarely now, oh how those words had sounded so cold, so flat, so wrong! She wanted to pour her heart out to him, confess her true feelings, and run back to his warmth, his safety. Inside she knew it wasn't going to happen, though, she knew it wasn't what was right. If she and Billy had once so loved each other, perhaps she would find that love once again, she couldn't just walk away, she had to give it a try, but she didn't want to just leave Nick hanging, and the last thing she wanted was to hurt him.

An icy cold grip, seized at Nicks chest, *'thank you for all your time ... '* the words echoed through his mind, was that what it had been, just a time filler? Is that what he was to her? He remained still, searching this woman's eyes for any trace of the warmth they had shared only hours before in his bed. She'd shut him out, and that burned, but if it was just sex between them, then so be it, no woman was worth going through what he had already, besides, he had been warned, he knew she might leave, that she wasn't his yet, that he might get burned … glancing at Billy, his anger began to rise once again, but he pushed it aside,

"Are you sure, Lauren?"

The softness in his voice seized at her heart, no, no she wasn't sure, about anything, about this man that called himself her husband, about herself, about him.

"Yes." The word stung as she said it, but she had to give Billy the chance he deserved, four years of his life, of their life, was a lot to just give up.

"I'm sorry about dragging you into this mess," she began, "you've done so much, gone so far out of your way…" Nick remained motionless, no expression on his hardened features, surely she wasn't denying there had been something there, something between them. He had no desire to hurt her though, if she wanted to keep those memories private, shield her husband from the truth, he wouldn't betray her, he would do her that one last justice, then he would leave, he'd let her go, back to where she belonged.

"I'm glad I could help." The stale tone in his voice, masked the instability within, he stood, his body tense, "if you ever need anything, Lauren," he shot a look of mistrust in Billy's direction, locking eyes with him, "if you're ever in trouble…"

Lauren opened her mouth as if to speak, but refrained. He searched her eyes one last time, looking beyond her confident façade, looking for Lauren Conklin, the fiery, independent woman he had known, a sign, a trace. She dropped her eyes, and with that, Nick severed his ties, and walked away.

A week passed too slowly, Lauren sat up, gasping, her eyes trying, desperately, to focus in the dark room. She concentrated on her surroundings, calming as reality settled in her tortured mind. Another nightmare, it was an every night affair since she had discovered her identity, days dragged on slowly, and Billy seemed more on edge with the passing of time. She had hoped more memories would surface by now, more feelings toward her husband, she couldn't stand the thought of staying with Nick only to have those old feelings, for Billy, resurface, and hurt Nick more than she already had. Her heart yearned for him, but she kept her distance, in the hope that, soon, she would fall back into her old life somehow,

Swinging her legs over the edge of the king-sized bed, she took a moment to get her balance, as the swaying water mattress stilled. She reached for her robe, which hung on the rocking chair, beside the bed. She wasn't sure how she felt about her new life, Billy's house was too large for her taste, or perhaps it was just the style in which he kept it, she reflected back to Nicks cabin, it had been large as well, but the biased feelings she'd had, weren't based on size. Her dislike of his house had been the reason for selling, Billy explained.

Tip-toeing out of the still room, she headed for the kitchen, she needed something to quench her parched throat, the toddies, that were readily handed to her each night, to help her sleep, always left her mouth dry by morning, and the lingering taste of the liquor on her tongue had her feeling queasy, and nauseous. She grabbed out a bottle of Evian and swished the potent saliva out of her mouth, spitting the taste into the sink; she'd refrain from the concoctions in the future.

As she closed the refrigerator door, a sudden figure loomed before her, Billy. He stepped toward her.

"Billy?" she choked, backing up a step in surprise, he said nothing. Lauren suddenly realized her stature, quickly she gathered her robe around herself, "I needed a drink of water," she explained, "sorry if I woke you, I didn't think you would hear me, from down the hall." Billy stepped toward her, leaning intimately close, as she met the counter abruptly.

"I wasn't sleeping…" he pressed his hands upon the counter top, on either side of her, in the dim light of dawn, the thin night shirt she wore, revealed her shapely silhouette, and more than he needed to see, to keep his quivering need at bay, damn that old robe she kept! Gliding his large fingertips slowly up her forearm, he felt her tense up. His trailing fingers grasped the terrycloth folds of the robe, and roughly pulled them apart, revealing the light covering, which restrained her supple breasts. The nights cool air betrayed her, drawing her soft, pink, nipples taught and firm. A groping hand caught one of her breasts possessively, as Billy's moistened lips sought hers.

"Wait," Lauren pleaded, "please, I, I can't…"

Reluctantly Billy paused, his thumb circling her taught nipple, "Lauren," he began, "it's been a week now…" he tried again to claim her soft mouth.

"Please, Billy." She put her hand between them, against his tightened chest, "give me just a little more time, let me come to you." Softly, she pressed his cupping hand away, and closed her robe, slipping out around him, and hurrying back upstairs.

She had been avoiding any sexual confrontations with him, since he had brought her 'home', but she knew he wouldn't last much more, after all, they were married, and he hadn't lost those memories … only she had. Billy heard her head upstairs, and cursed under his breath. Why wouldn't she succumb to him? He'd been patient, understanding, maybe too much so, his manhood heightened, and pulsed at the mere scent of her, and the painful tightness in his groin was excruciating. Not much longer, he conceited, not much longer …

He couldn't afford to botch things up, with that ill-fated temper of his, at least for now he possessed her, and soon he would consummate this farce, and she would belong fully to him then, mind and BODY. Stifling a painful groan, he stiffly headed toward the guestroom, where he had slept for the past seven days, it wouldn't be long now, and they would be closing on the house, then she'd either succumb to him, or he would take her, she'd have no choice. Once they sold the property, they'd be staying in a hotel room for a night or two, until the deal was set on the beach house, in San José, California, their destination in just a few days. He was grateful that the good doctor there, had still owed him a favor, and when people owed Billy Malhoun, they didn't dare challenge his collecting.

Lauren pulled the covers over her still shaking body, glancing at the digital alarm beside the large bed, six a.m., it hadn't seemed that late already, but at least Billy would be leaving within the hour, to go finish up the paperwork on the house.

"California?" she had said, "but it seems so far away…" but far away from what, had been his next question, and Lauren couldn't honestly answer that, even to herself. It seemed she had no family, no friends close enough to mention, no connections to anyone, aside from Billy, she inwardly grimaced the thought.

Since the day Billy had arrived in her life, she still hadn't an emotional connection to him, just a face in her mind that was all he'd been, and all he still was, she longed for a conversational companion. Billy couldn't look at her, without trying to touch her, let alone talk to her, their conversations were short, and direct, and any other contact was hastily avoided by Lauren, she had spoken to him of his bold sexual advances, but there were unavoidable moments, like that morning.

It wasn't going how Lauren had hoped, she wanted to get to know Billy, maybe even fall in love again, but vaguely, she was beginning to wonder how she could have fallen for him to begin with, after all, he didn't exactly seem her type, she wondered what kind of woman she had been when they met, maybe he was her type back then. That sandy hair, his ever masculine, protruding square jaw, his eyes of hazel, that held a surface longing, but a deeper intenseness, that worried her, he just couldn't capture her the way … *damn!* She scorned herself again, why couldn't she stop thinking that way? Although she'd been denying it, she had been subconsciously comparing him to Nick, and until now, she hadn't let the thought intervene.

She longed to hear his deep voice, to watch the way his lips moved when he spoke, and to remember the way they felt when he didn't. She missed him, and the realization of it hurt. She hadn't seen him since that day at the station, since she'd accepted Billy's invitation back to her past, since he had walked out. Closing her eyes, she pressed her fingers to her temples, she couldn't ponder on whether or not she had made a mistake, it would only be more difficult. Swelling pains burned her eyes, briefly, as hot tears began to well up … No, no she wouldn't allow herself to cry; after all it was still her decision, no matter what the situation was. She needed to see him, just once more, just to say goodbye, just to be sure, she added quickly, before she convinced herself otherwise.

Lauren stepped out of the patrol car, she had received escort without hesitation, "Good luck!" the young officer tipped his wide rimmed hat in her direction, with a broad grin, "I'll be back in an hour and a half, to pick you up, Miss Conkli … I mean Mrs. Malhoun."

Lauren smiled at him in response, "I have trouble with it too." She assured him, "thanks!" slipping his sunglasses back on, the patrolman drove slowly down the gravel road.

Lauren glanced at her old cabin, and then, nervously, she glanced at Nicks place, it seemed quiet, too much so. Swallowing hard, she took a step toward it; unsure of what she would do or say when she faced him. Pausing briefly, she began to have second thoughts, her stature wavering, she quickly turned toward her solemn home, she wasn't ready, he'd want answers for questions she hadn't asked yet, and after all, she'd come out here on the pretense that she'd be packing up her remaining belongings, the ones Billy hadn't boxed up yet.

Inside the cabin, the stale air brought back sudden flashes of memories, memories of her childhood, her parents, only fragments though, nothing fit together, but the rush of emotions, at the realization, that it was all she would have left of her family, seized at her heart. How unfair it all was, she'd lost her parents, and then her memories of them too? She wiped the spilling tears away, and began going through the jumbled boxes and bags. "What a mess!" she whispered to herself, nothing was organized, or folded, just thrown carelessly into containers, and packaged for travel, she was glad she had come over.

After about forty-five minutes of straightening, and repackaging, Lauren sat down at the kitchen table, and took a drink of water. It struck her as odd that nothing hinted at all to the fact that she wasn't single, even the food in the refrigerator was oriented only toward her. Maybe she had been planning on leaving him; maybe their marriage was on the rocks? She had even gone so far as to introduce herself as Conklin, it was odd, but Billy had waved it away, explaining that friends of his parents, who frequented the resort, would have found out their secret relationship.

He had said that they had dated on, and off, what did that mean anyway? She looked at the gold band on her finger, he'd said that she had taken it off during their argument, and left it with him, that was why she hadn't had it on when she had been found. Sliding it softly off, she turned it in her hand, married … it just didn't fit, didn't feel right …

"Cleaning out the skeletons?" a voice loomed dangerously close, behind her, she turned in shock at the sudden interruption of silence, her heart beating triple time. "I didn't think I'd see you again." A deep blue gaze met hers with all the force of a brick wall, and Lauren stammered at the flat and almost bitter statement.

Awe stricken, she struggled to gather her wits, "Nick?" was all she could conjure, as his cerulean eyes held hers.

Briefly, their eyes locked, but Nick broke the connection, as the ring fell from Laurens numb fingers, and panged noisily to the floor, she quickly grabbed it up, and slid it into her tight jeans' pocket.

"What are you … when did you get here?" The hard noises of Nicks' boots, on the hardwood floor, rang in her ears; he looked around at the piled boxes, and then glanced to Lauren. He turned his face from her.

"I saw the door open…" he drew his hands into his pockets, and turned to face her, once more, "What are YOU doing here?" The question stung, she could sense the deeper meaning behind his words, and averted her gaze.

"I HAD, come for my things," Nick was silent, and she could feel his burning eyes, "I'm … we're, leaving, in a few days." Nick shifted his weight.

"I thought your husband already got everything."

Lauren glanced at him, "No. He didn't" Her quiet response clawed at his heart, he wanted to grab her, punish her cruelly, with intimate kisses, for hurting him so, for leaving him feeling like no other woman could ever compare to who she'd been, he strangled the thought. What did it matter anyway, she was nothing to him anymore, she had her own life back now, that was all she'd ever really wanted. Nick turned to leave, he'd done his part, and he was stupid to have let his heart get involved,

"Well then, "he replied coolly," let me get out of your way." He suddenly wished he hadn't come in, she obviously wanted nothing more to do with him, after all, she had tried to keep him at arms length, it was he who had pushed for it to turn into what it had.

"Nick, wait!" Lauren stood abruptly, "I was going to stop in, to say goodbye, to see you one more time…" her voice had dropped low at these last words, and Nick stopped, his body tense at her sudden response.

"Why?" he stated flatly, a deep tremor of emotion underlying his cool reserve.

"I had to see you," she stepped softly toward him, "I had to talk to you once more…" she touched him then, her fingers trembling, her voice almost a whisper, "Just once more…"

Her satin fingertips gently brushed his back, and he felt as though he might buckle under the pressure.

"Lauren, out there, we were free," he paused, not turning to face her, "free from the world, from the past, free from ourselves, but this, this is not 'out there'." He sighed, his head dropping uncomfortably to the side, "I got caught up in the fantasy of it all too, but this is reality, Lauren, this is real life, you're married for Gods sake!" he turned then and faced her directly, her emerald eyes held a quiet sadness that pulled at him, "We can't let what happened between us, stand in our way forever…"

Lauren heard his answer, she heard it clearly, he had felt the same as she, but was he so eager to move on; to forget it all? Did he wake at night with dreams of her, so vivid, that reality seemed to be the dream? Would he be able to go on normally, after this, last encounter, without ever being able to see her again; to touch her again? She knew those were the questions that plagued her so. What did she expect to happen? That when she saw him again it would be over? The longing, the heartache, the sleepless nights? Why couldn't she just move on?

The reality of him, before her, was cruelly more agonizing than any of her dreams, her attraction had not diminished in the least, in fact; he appeared more striking, than ever. Nicks ears were roaring with the rush of blood, which seized him. The words he had spoken, still rang in his head like an endless echo, he needed to feel that freedom once more, it was like an addiction, the longer he stayed away, the harder it was to concentrate, to care. One touch, one taste, left him in need of more, needing to feel the life in him stir. He knew the consequences would be a harder withdrawal, but for just one more rush of freedom from his cold desolate past, for one more hint of light from the endless darkness that lie ahead, would he be willing to risk the pain? Endure the torture of the withdrawal afterwards?

Banishing all thought, Nick grasped Lauren suddenly, claiming her soft mouth with his, her fervent response aroused him effortlessly, as her slender arms, wrapped tightly around him.

"Ah, Lauren..." He breathed against her ear. Laurens searching hands tugged at his clothing, pulling the taught T-shirt, from his blue jeans, urgently she splayed her fingers across his chest, catching his nipples between them, and toying with the dark hairs that encircled them.

Brushing the article out of the way, she softly tugged at them with her gentle lips, and tongue. Could she possibly know what she was doing to him? What he was going through? All the nights he had lain awake, feeling the life drain from him, wanting her, needing her, and she had come back to him. He grasped her, a deep growl of ecstasy rumbling from his throat, pulling her away, he claimed her mouth once more, his large hands caressing her, desperately, everywhere. He pulled at her tank top, bringing it off easily, and reveling in the fact that she wore no brazier.

Firmly, he took her into his mouth, keeping such gentleness about him, that she could not control the urgent pleas that erupted. She wanted to protest, to stop this insanity, before it went too far, but her desire betrayed her, and she clung to her primal need for this man, even if it were just one more time, one more bold act of passion, before ... she shut out the thought.

Lifting her to him, Nick strode to the kitchen table, sprawling her wantonly upon it, Lauren pulled at the restraints of his pants, not caring about the consequences, not caring about anything but the moment and delighting in it. Nick needed her more than anything, more than air at this moment, if she still desired him so, than surely she would not be able to just leave. One more taste was all he'd needed, all he'd thought he'd wanted, but forever was what held him back, he needed to know that she shared his desire, that she'd not closed him out forever ...

"Lauren," he breathed, "tell me that you want me..." His urgent plea was answered quickly, breathlessly,

"Yes, Nick, I want you!" dropping her tight jeans to the floor, Nick grasped her creamy thighs, and brought her sharply to him, his passion unleashed in a swift thrust. Lauren clung to his broad shoulders as he entered her, fully strongly. She felt herself conform to him, drawing herself up eagerly, and responding to his fevered movements.

"Oh Lauren!" he moaned, as her desperate hands caught his hips, needing to feel the powerful, aspiring, passion he possessed.

Her world began to tumult, under the rapturous, bliss he bestowed upon her, she felt him tightening as his movements escalated, the sudden pounding release sending her over the edge, as she closed her eyes tightly, spinning and plummeting out of control, absorbed in the pure ecstasy of the moment. As their bodies collapsed together, the lovers lay breathless, and panting, comforted by their uninterrupted connection, a union that left them feeling whole, complete.

Lauren ran her fingers softly through Nicks, thick, dark hair, what had she done, what had they done? Mixed emotions ran through her as they lay, coupled, upon the table. What now? Nick rose from her, reluctantly, a sudden breeze catching them at the untimely separation. He pulled his jeans on stiffly, casting a warm smile in her direction, "you should get dressed," he began, "after all, we did leave the door open." Lauren blushed at the realization of their haste, sliding her garments on quickly; she slipped into the living room, and shut the door.

She turned to find Nick, leaning casually in the doorway of the kitchen, watching her intently; she felt a strange nervousness she hadn't felt before when he was near. "What are you gonna' tell your husband?" The question hung heavily in the room.

"What do you mean?" averting his gaze, Lauren walked to the fireplace, keeping her face from him.

"I mean," he continued, stepping toward her, "what are you gonna' say to him, about US?" Lauren remained quiet. "He doesn't know, does he?" It was more of a statement, than a question, and Lauren felt her cheeks flush, of course he didn't know, how could she tell him something like that?

"I, I meant to tell him, someday…" she faced him, briefly, seeing something spark in his eyes. *SOMEDAY?* The thought made Nicholas cringe, as he felt the heat rise in veins. "I never meant to hurt you," she drew her arms around herself, protectively, and stepped to the sofa. Nick steadied himself, hurt him? She had no idea what hurt was, he couldn't just let her go now, not after this, he couldn't stand the thought of another man possessing her, loving her the way he had, he couldn't bear it.

"Lauren," he stepped toward her and she jumped, he was taken aback for a moment, surely she didn't think he would hurt her, he would never … "Why did you come here? Why did you let me … why did you do this?"

Lauren shuttered at his anger, if Billy knew … she grimaced the thought, "I … I just needed to be with you … one last time, I never meant for it to go this far, but it did, and now? Well, now we have to go on, we have to get on with our lives, isn't that what you said?" He had said it, but he hadn't meant it, and his pride held him at bay, "What are you gonna tell him?" he pressed her.

"He doesn't know I came today, he doesn't even know I'm here!" Nick looked at her, she never meant to stay.

"I see," he looked away from her.

"I'd better go." Lauren turned to him quickly, she'd had so much more to say, so many issues were unresolved, "I've still got twenty minutes!" she blurted out.

Nick glared at her, his ire rose, "Is that what this was?" She hadn't meant for it to come out that way, she shook her head, desperately. "Am I just a time filler to you? Just a quick fling!" Lauren began to protest, but was cut off once more, "I can't be the 'other' man!" he sneered, "I can't be second place in your life Lauren, ever!" he turned, and strode out the door, tossing his shirt over his shoulder, "GO HOME!" he called back, "GO HOME TO YOUR HUSBAND!"

Tears spilled down her cheeks, as she watched him leave, "But I hadn't meant…" she whispered hoarsely, as a lump formed in her throat, cutting off her words once more. Maybe he was right, maybe she had used him, all she knew was that now he was gone, and she had made a worse mess than before. Sniffing back the tears, and stifling the guilty pangs that ate at her now, she stood straight, and glanced in the mirror, on the wall, straightening her messed hair, and smeared cheeks. It was over, and she'd go on now, knowing how empty her nights would be, and how lonely her days. She pushed the thoughts away, she had been happy once with Billy, or she wouldn't have married him, right? She'd be happy again, she just needed time, and she needed to be as far from her distraction as possible, as far away from Nick as she could be, she just hoped she'd be able to face Billy now, somehow.

CHAPTER 13

The sun shone cruelly over the autumn toned land, and the red-orange glow of trees contrasted sharply with the bright blue sky, giving the atmosphere a crispness, that was heightened by the cool front that had settled in the small town.

Lauren stared out the opened window of her bedroom, so life did go on, she mused solemnly, it seemed a shame to have such a beautiful day before her, and not to notice it, not to care. Quietly she closed the large panes and went down stairs, the house was empty, aside from the few belongings they'd kept back to suit their needs in the days to follow, Billy had been distracted these past two days, and Lauren was grateful for the fact that when it came to business he immersed himself so completely. It was cold downstairs and the large Indigo blue cardigan she wore was most appreciated, Billy had sent someone back for her belongings, knowing that she'd received escort to and from her cabin, to pack her remaining items, he knew that Nick's cabin was right next-door and had shot her a glance of skepticism at the mention of it. Tonight would be her last night in the small town and somewhere deep inside she was almost grateful to get away, too many emotions stirred here, too many distractions kept at her, she needed the escape to try and get her life back, to start again with new memories, new love. A critical sneer of laughter clung to her lips at the thought, love, yeah sure. Soon she would surrender herself to her husband, difficult as it were, she'd stop avoiding him, buckle under his constant perseverance, and then it wouldn't matter, she'd push aside her nausea, the feelings of betrayal and let him think it was of her own accord. She couldn't mend a marriage acting like roommates, besides, he was bound to catch on to her feelings for Nick, he was the only one with her up there for days, he'd surely begin to ponder the thought. She didn't want to face that confrontation, and she surely didn't want him to go looking for Nick, no, it would be easier this way. She'd just get through it, perhaps she'd learn to want him, or at least tolerate him.

Stepping out onto the front porch Lauren noticed a young girl skittering away, casting a quick, nervous glance back at the house, she hurried off, her auburn waves a mass of tangles that tucked beneath the too large flannel shirt she wore. She watched curiously as the girl turned the corner and disappeared, *"that was odd"* she quietly pondered. She shrugged her shoulders and shook it away from her thoughts; it was probably nothing.

Putting on an extra sweatshirt Nicholas Carmen peered uneasily out the large window of his guest room subconsciously searching for movement over at the empty cabin next door, pursing his lips disapprovingly his brow darkened, he hadn't been able to sleep in his own bed now for over a week, the soft scent of woman still clung to his pillow, his sheets, hell the whole damn room still held her there; that soft, musky scent of spring flowers that had graced her skin; the deep aroma of sandalwood caressing the warm essence of her thick raven hair. How could he sleep like that? Yet he found himself unable to remove the linens or simply throw them in the washer. He couldn't let go, not yet, not completely. What he needed was to get out of the house, get away for a while. Reaching into his rear pocket he felt for his wallet, nothing, he searched the second pocket, again nothing, what had he done with it? Combing the whole house, Nick remained puzzled that it was nowhere to be found, thinking back he retraced his steps, he really hadn't seen it since … . Damn; Laurens cabin. He thought for a moment, unsure about making the quick trip over to get it, she wasn't there, he knew, but the lucid mingling of pleasure and pain still hung in the atmosphere of that direction.

It would be there, even if she had found it, it would still be there, forcing him to face the cold hard truth once more, a last reminder of the escape he had found in her, and the imprisonment in which she had left him. A growing anger snuffed out any hidden fears that may have existed, and pushing them away he headed toward the ominous structure, facing his insecurities head on.

Nick stood defiantly inside the dimly lit living room, all the boxes that the room had once harbored were now gone, only a few remnants of paper and dropped items remained. Nick shook his head at the blatancy of her hurry to leave. Stepping into the kitchen he spotted his wallet right away, apparently dropped beneath the table. He quickly gathered it and slid it into his back pocket, trying not to think about how it had gotten there. A few strides to the door and he would be out, just a few more steps, but something stopped him, pivoting on his heels he turned half-way and glanced at the place … empty, lonely, but lacking the bitterness it should have held for him. He appreciatively took in the full effect of the cabin. It was cozy and homey; with a slight Victorian air that easily weaved throughout the woodwork. Curiosity overtook him, and in only a short while he had explored the entirety of the cabin, his heightened apprehension of her lingering presence was averted by a deep concentration on discovery, forcing the threatening pain to become dormant for the time being. Curiosity now overwhelmed him, and Nick commenced more detailed snooping, after all, he thought snidely, what better was there to do. Besides, he didn't trust that Billy Malhoun, not as far as he could throw him, especially with Lauren, maybe she had made her decision, written him out, but this was far from over and Nick was determined to find the answers he sought.

Lauren stared one last time at the fading mountains in the distance, a dim red-orange glow still clung to the luminous masses as dusks icy grip overtook the suns last rays. A small pat on her thigh startled her, as Billy cast a cumbersome glance,

"It won't be long" he started, "and you'll forget all this craziness." Laurens quick release of breath panged at his overzealous pride and he tightened his grip on her leg before returning his hand to the steering wheel, "Maybe then you'll start to relax around me" he growled, "so we can get back to how things used to be…" The thought sent a shudder up Laurens back while at the same time a fire seemed to flash in Billy's eyes. The thought of the waiting hotel room ahead kept his foot on the pedal and an uncomfortable tightness in his jeans. The constant rhythm of the highway soon had an exhausted Lauren sleeping soundly. The day's events had taken their toll and it seemed that every muscle that could ache did. Drawing near the hotel Billy's anxiety was about to explode, he had kept her so busy today, wearing away at her mentally and physically, keeping her from resting for even a moment, drawing all the potential to fight him off, out of her. Tonight there would be no denying him, he'd come too far to leave empty handed, and with the busy schedule he kept, he didn't have the time or the patience for childish games.

Lauren awoke to a pair of strong arms lifting her from the seat of the jeep, "What are you doing?" she queried, somehow it was so hard to open her eyes, "Nick?"

Billy froze for a moment, anger rippling over him briefly, apparently the sleeping pills he'd given her earlier, in her toddy, were working well.

"Don't speak darlin'" he cooed, "Just sleep … ." Lauren's body fell limp as Billy crossed into the room, shutting the door behind him. He quickly laid her on the bed and began pulling off his shirt. Climbing beside her he carefully tested her level of consciousness, shaking her gently, no reply. Pressing further he began to unbutton her blouse, quietly, carefully he opened it, revealing the feminine tee beneath, still no movement. He moved further and unfastened her blue jeans, sliding them gently over her slender hips. His pulse raced at the scent of her, and the sight of her budding nipples caused a throbbing deep in his loins. Fighting the urge to simply take her was nearly impossible by now and it was all he could do to pull the cotton tee from her body without ripping it fiercely in two. Hungrily he grasped her breasts, running his wanton hands over her alluring body. Daringly, his hand sought her panties, tugging them from her roughly. Lauren stirred, but quickly settled in an unknowing trust of her surroundings. Billy's arousal overwhelmed him and he pulled the remaining clothing from himself quickly, lying beside her still form and pressing his heated body against hers. Caressing her thigh, he soon sought her moist core and gently began to stroke. His lips caught her nipple and softly tugged at the hardened peak.

"Lauren," he growled fiercely "You're mine now..." His mouth found hers and obnoxiously he forced it open filling her with his tongue. Gagging suddenly, Lauren gasped for a breath, her heavy lids betraying her straining eyes. The groggy state of her mind left her spinning and numb.

"What are you, doing..." she breathed as her mouth was bombarded again. Desperately, she pushed against him but to no avail, her limbs were like lead, and his body held her down like a stone. Billy overtook her nude form, opening her legs easily.

"Don't fight me!" he growled as she arduously tried to close them.

"No." she pleaded softly, barely able to form the word. Despite her objections, her legs were easily cast apart, and this time they were pinned down by Billy's rock hard thighs, "Don't struggle, Lauren, this doesn't have to be unpleasant for you." The heat of his flat abdomen against hers rippled over her, *"what was happening?"* she tried to think clearly but the clouds overtook her mind. Billy's mouth found hers once more as he kissed her hard giving into his lust. With his craving growing, he sought gratification, entering her fiercely; a gasp erupted from her parted lips as he overpowered her meek protests.

"Take it!" he moaned, "Take it!" his speed increasing. Lauren began to toss and turn, fighting the smothering darkness.

"Stop..." she protested, "please..." her soft cries muffled by her pursuers burning body. As his movements escalated the desperate lust in his loins gave way to primal savagery and his lustrous cries intensified with each thrust. Grasping her hips firmly he forced himself even deeper within her. The sudden infliction of pain roused Laurens slipping consciousness and she became all too aware of her situation, *"Oh, God!"* she thought in terror,

"He's raping me!" Another shaft of pain rocketed through her, bringing a cry of agony from deep within.

"NO!" she cried scrambling wildly from her tormenter. In his heightened state of arousal Billy had released his grip on her, allowing just enough room for her unexpected attempt at escape. Laboriously pulling away, she struggled to gain some control over the chaotic situation before her.

Billy grabbed wildly for her. "Don't fight me!" he roared as Laurens numb and feeble limbs were flung desperately in an impossible attempt to escape his savage brutality. Twisting away, Lauren felt a steely grip upon her as she was hurled effortlessly down once more. A smothering weight was once again cast upon her, and she was again plummeted by the shameful intrusion of her body. Struggling against her captor's restraining grip was futile, the adrenaline she'd conjured from the sudden realization of what was happening, was failing abruptly with each strain of a muscle.

As his movements escalated, Lauren begged for unconsciousness to overtake her, the complete helplessness and shame of the violation she was enduring was far worse than anything she could have imagined. As the crushing pain heightened, a muffled cry erupted from her swollen lips but was dually snuffed out by a large sweaty palm that covered her face. Gasping for air that would not come; Lauren felt herself slipping away as Billy thrust and shuddered atop her, groaning in a disgusting display of self-fulfillment. Lapsing into unconsciousness, Laurens body went limp, livened only by a short gasp when Billy's palm slipped away, signaling his completed desecration of her. Muscles tense and still flexing Billy reflected on his actions, maybe he shouldn't have been quite so forceful, Hell, he hadn't counted on her waking up, but damn the sex was incredible. He pondered his next move, as he pulled away from the warmth of her body, and lit a cigarette, surely she'd remember what had happened, she'd fought him fiercely though weak; what if the charade was over when she did come to? He'd have to keep her subdued until he was sure she was no longer a problem, until then why not enjoy the fruits of his labor? Turning to her still form, Billy's hunger returned with a vengeance, "yes" he thought, "why not take of this forbidden fruit all that I can, while I can..."

Nick rushed into the station and burst through Chief Ellington's door followed hurriedly by the protesting officers that rushed after him.

"He's a fraud," Nick boldly shouted at the startled chief, waving a folded mass of papers in the air, "and I can prove it!" Bruce Ellington stared in confusion at the intruder, his eyebrows raised in amazement.

"Sorry, chief," the young deputy said apologetically, as he struggled to restrain the determined man, "I tried to stop him."

"Wait, what's this all about?" he peered at Nick through scrutinizing eyes,

"It's all right here!" Nick thrust the papers toward the police chief, Nick shook free of the young officers hold, glancing annoyingly at the youth. Chief Ellington slipped his reading glasses over his nose, from the chain they hung on around his neck, he glanced at the two younger men and then peered at the item he had taken from Nick, apparently it was a hand-written log of events. He furrowed his brow in annoyance.

"What is this?"

"I found it at Lauren's cabin," Nick's tone was intense as he explained himself.

"And what were you doing in the old Conklin Place, Mr. Carmen?" The older mans words held a note of disapproval.

"Look, it's along story, but we've got to find Lauren and let her know, she could be in danger!" Nick stepped forward, putting his hands down on the chief's desk, slightly harder than he meant to.

"Now, you look son!" Ellington rose to his feet, the disrespectful gesture striking his ire, "This isn't enough to go rantin' and raven' about, messin up people's lives. It's hand-written, it's not dated and YOU found it! Basically, I need more proof than this to investigate the matter!" he shook the paper in Nick's direction and sat back down.

Nick sneered in disgust, "I should've known. Small town, everybody sticks together..." he turned to leave.

"Now hold on," the chief took the glasses from his face, anger flashing across his features, he pointed an aging finger at his challenger, "Small town my ass!" Nick turned back, his brows raised mockingly. "If I had the proof, just one justifiable shred of admissible evidence, don't you think for one moment that I wouldn't march out there myself and jerk that girl away from him! I don't like that Billy Malhoun any more than you do, son, probably less, we go back."

"I've got my eye on him anyway, he's caused a lot of grief in this town, so don't you walk around so cocked and all fired sure that everybody sticks together!" taking the papers in hand, Bruce Ellington lay them in front of himself and glared at Nicks looming form.

"Look, I'm sorry," Nick managed as he stepped back into the office.

The young officer hurried out, he didn't like to be around the chief when he was in a bad mood, and now was becoming one of those moments.

"I read the whole thing this morning, it's a re-cap of what happened just prior to the accident, Billy Malhoun is *not* her husband! According to this he's an old friend, not to mention his pushy advances towards her…"

"Mr. Carmen, I will look over these and I will see what I can do, you have to understand, we can't just go by some hand-written papers that you've just happened to come across…"

"I know I shouldn't have gone over there, but Lauren and I, well I, I just needed something to remember her by, they'd left a few things of hers, so, I took this book, I knew she'd been reading it because her page was marked with this paper, but when I started looking through it this morning, I discovered her notes!" He needed desperately for him to believe, without the police to back him, how could he convince Lauren of the danger she was in? "Can't you see? He must have forged these documents! He's got her now, and isn't it convenient that their leaving town?"

"Hey, the whole town saw your reaction to the man; do you really think they'll just swallow this story when the girl won't even remember writing this? How do we even know she wrote it?" Ellington sighed, knowing the frustration the other man must be feeling in this situation. "If it helps any, I'll send my best deputy over to check things out," Nick started to speak but was silenced by a wave of his hand, "if, they are still out there, but I don't want any problems out of this you got me? Let me check into it a little, and we'll go from there." Ellington knew Billy's shady reputation, but the papers he'd produced, he'd gone over them himself, and they looked perfectly legitimate. He would have loved to take this story and run all over Billy Malhoun's plans with it, but he knew Malhoun's father would find a way to red-tape the whole thing and Billy would slip away again. He needed something concrete, something that could nail that bastard to the wall, for good! He couldn't afford a slip-up, no more holes for Billy Malhoun to slither through. Nick turned toward the door where the younger cop had stood,

"I'm going with him." He announced. The chief started to object, but just shook his head instead.

"NO problems" he stated flatly, glaring at the determined man.

The patrol car stopped outside of the large Victorian style home, it seemed to be empty and the red and white real-estate sign outside the gate read "sold." Nick was supposed to wait in the car, but upon seeing the hollow state of the house he defiantly exited and headed up the walk.

"Hey," deputy John Harper quickly pulled the keys from the ignition and fought with his indignant restraint, trying to catch up with the brisk man, "Hey, get back in the car!" the young officer hurried toward Nick, "we had a deal!" he caught up to him, slowing his pace as he closed the distance. Nick guessed him to be about 21 or so, a kid, probably just out of college, he motioned to the house glancing at the deputy briefly.

"It's empty," he stated walking toward the front door; the officer ascertained the situation more clearly, this time peering into the empty windows.

"Well, look, just don't tell the chief I let you get out!" Nick shook his head and opened the door, the house was indeed empty, and not a shred of paper was left behind. If only he had found out where they were going, now he may never find her, he only hoped by some miracle that she might regain her memory and escape the danger that threatened her. Until then, he would search for her and the truth.

CHAPTER 14

The burning sun loomed brightly into Laurens sensitive eyes as she slowly flicked them open, her head was pounding with a thickening ache and her slightest movements shot bolts of pain through her swollen sockets. Swallowing dryly, she licked her parched lips only to find them sore and chapped; closing her eyes tightly for a moment she brought herself upright and steadied her dizziness against the firm surface behind her. As she slowly squinted through the thundering ache, her surroundings began to come into focus. Billy turned to the confused woman coming to. *"Shit!"* he thought, kicking himself mentally. *"I forgot the pills in the damn bag!"* reaching over to rouse her swaying form, he roughly patted her thigh, if she was going to remember anything, he'd have to play this off as carefully as possible, already he was formulating a plan in his twisted mind …

"Lauren," he softly mocked, "are you all right?" The voice stirred in her head for a moment, finally translating itself laboriously, a twinge of shock, followed by a bewildered fear, seized her, but her leaden limbs served as anchors for only a moment. She calmed herself inwardly, trying to make sense of her jumbled thoughts, he had hurt her, she surmised, raped her! She remembered that clearly, the sudden pain the humiliation, the helplessness she'd felt! How could he have done that to her! Slowly her tingling muscles began to regain some measure of control. Billy glanced at her features once more, she didn't seem too tense at his voice, but then again, the sleeping pills he'd given her for days now did contain some muscle relaxants.

"Lauren, baby? We're almost there, are you okay?" Lauren cringed inwardly at his familiarity with her, as if nothing had happened, everything was fine in his eyes. *Didn't he realize that she would remember? Didn't he realize what he had done?* Lauren focused more clearly now, they were heading down a highway, scattered palm trees passed by in groves and she could smell the salty sea air all around them, her hair blew back against her face in the warm breeze as she leaned heavily back against the firm leather seats of Billy's jeep.

Reaching over to touch her bare arm, Billy began once more, "We'll be there in no time." He grinned, all the while studying her reactions.

"What is going on?" Laurens voice was hoarse and dry, she cleared her throat, attempting again."What's happened?" She glared at their surroundings once again, exaggerating the gesture.

"What do you mean?" Billy tread cautiously with his words now.

"I mean ... how did we get here?" She shook the last of her confusion away, focusing now on her words "I don't remember the trip..." Billy steadied her once more only to have an accusing glare sent his direction at the gesture. "Why does my head hurt so bad? I feel like I'm hungover..." Nausea swept over her, and she quickly leaned over the door vomiting uncontrollably as her body ejected the forced drugs out of her system.

"You've had a migraine," Billy explained. "I gave you some prescription pain killers' to help ease the pain, but I had to take the pills away from you. I think you may have overdosed."

Lauren glared at him once more, disbelief heavy in her expression. "Or maybe so I wouldn't complain!"

Billy's temper flared, she was a smart mouth little trollop wasn't she? "What do you mean?" He attempted ignorance.

"Why did you take advantage of me!" she spat. The blurred memory coming through in vague pieces. "Why couldn't you wait a little longer, I would have come to you!" her voice broke as the pain lingered vividly. So she didn't know still yet, Billy pondered, he knew he would have to cover that night's event cunningly or she would never trust him.

"Lauren, I'm sorry, It's just been so long, you were a little tipsy from your toddy and when you came onto me, I couldn't stop, It was like old times again, I thought you were into it, too, honey." He watched her wipe the tears from her cheeks as he spoke. "You know I'd never hurt you..." He brushed her hair back from her dampened face only to be met with the sudden retreat of Laurens head as she pulled away.

"Don't..." she warned. Billy pressed on ...

"I'm sorry if I was a little rough with you," he stated flatly, her intolerance of him lighting a fuse, "but I couldn't bear another cold night, when my *wife* was right beside me, teasing and taunting me, drunk or not! If you could have just relaxed a little sooner, I wouldn't have been so pent up!"

Lauren sneered at his overzealous pride, how could he turn this around, she'd had no memory of being drunk or coming on to him, but then again only a few shreds of the event were even comprehendible, even so, there was no excuse for his behavior, she had said "no" and he had ventured onward, hurting her in the process, she didn't want to hear his excuses, but she resided to drop the matter for now, before his thinly veiled temper was released. Their next hour of travel was silent, leaving Lauren to wonder if she had made the right decision on giving him a chance, she tried not to think about what had happened to her, the memory was painful and left her nauseated. She wondered what would become of Nick, if she could ever get over him and leave the past behind her, her "new beginning," wasn't starting out very well, to say the least.

Billy fumed at his companions silence, she had called him "Nick" when he touched her that night, and she only pretended to show interest in him when he was near her, how could he wait any longer to have her! She was his wife, or so she thought, he would have to watch her carefully now, he'd gotten her this far, he wasn't going to let her leave that easily, and if he couldn't have her willingly he would be damned if that tender footed, pretty boy would, no one would!

Nicholas stared hard at the empty cabin next door, it had been over a week since he had seen Lauren last, and the ache in his chest deepened with each passing day. He questioned everyone that Lauren had mentioned in her log, they had remembered the described events, but no one had heard anything about her new ordeal, it was as if Billy had kept her locked up until they'd left, no one had seen her since the paper had run her story. Searching for any shred of prospect was becoming painstakingly difficult, as time passed, he only hoped he could find her before it was too late. He had found out quite a bit about Billy Malhoun since his quest had begun, mostly their were the rumors that ran through the towns gossip chains, Chief Ellington wasn't lying when he said they went back, apparently Malhoun had been tangled up with Mrs. Ellington when he was a youth, there was question about the girl, Sabrina, that she'd had, but the story was tainted with two sides, some said she was Billy's and others were positive she was Bruce Ellington's flesh and blood. Billy Malhoun had quite a list of criminal charges brought on him in his time, those included: grand theft auto, which he somehow got out of, Assault 3rd and 2nd degree, vandalism of public property … the list went on and on, from misdemeanors to suspicion of conspiracy to commit murder, most were never pressed, somehow he'd slithered his way through the cracks, and one statement in particular left Nick wondering with a gut feeling, the name Malhoun seemed to be more than a coincidence.

Mr. Malhoun, Sr. apparently was a lawyer and a dirty one at that, Malhoun was the one that had gotten the drunken driver off, after Nicks own fathers death! He was the slimy, son-of-a-bitch that had blamed it on the seatbelt being the reason for his father's terminal injuries! Now he knew were Billy had gotten his inclinations from, it ran in the family, the notion of getting his hands of the man whom he'd despised for so long, seemed to feed his determination even more, strange how the man who had taken his fathers justice form him, now somehow managed to once again steal the one thing that had kept him from going insane with heartache, it seemed the Malhouns had a knack for finding his weaknesses, and crushing them, but this time Malhoun would not get away with it. He would keep searching until he found them, even if it took forever, he couldn't give up on Lauren, she deserved the truth; she deserved to know who she really was. Nick had posted an ad in the local newsletter, about the situation, saying that it was of great importance that the information be acquired quickly, and that the woman may be in danger, little did he know how right he was.

Lauren was settling slowly in their new beach house, the location was convenient, when she could go out, and the view was awe inspiring, but her depression dulled the beauty of it all. They were still unpacking a few boxes that were left from the move and the need to keep busy helped to subside the turmoil within her, Billy was away this day, business as he called it, Lauren was grateful for the break. When she'd finished unpacking she donned her wide brimmed straw hat and headed down to the beach. Billy never wanted her to leave the house for very long, afraid she might get hurt and not be able to find help. She knew it was an excuse though as he was excessively possessive, and he kept her within arms length when he was home. The hot sand felt comforting on her bare feet as she walked slowly along the shore, her long white cotton gown flowing against her legs in the warm breeze. She inhaled deeply, wishing she could find her happiness once again, right place she'd decided, wrong guy … . NO! She was doing it again, Nick was gone, she'd just have to accept that, she was married, her husband was a successful man, he'd bought her a new home, and a very tasteful one at that, he'd even let her get a new wardrobe, he'd said it was to make up to her for the way he'd acted that night, he knew he'd betrayed her trust and he said he was sorry for it. Still yet, something nagged at her, he always seemed to be keeping something from her, as if he couldn't relax enough to be himself. He was always tense and speculative around her, she secretly wondered if he had known about Nick, and her feelings for him. Wasn't it enough that she had gone with him? She'd stayed true to her vows, once she had found out about him, well except for that last day … she stared out at the rolling waves; she could still feel Nick's burning kisses, his passion; so pure, not like the heated rush that her husband had bantered. She needed to try harder, she resolved, Billy was an attractive man largely built and clean cut; he was always well groomed. As a matter of fact, he spent more time in the bathroom than she did! It was his personality that left her wanting, his short temper and pushy tendencies were what held her back most of all. He was always tense and so, she could not relax around him either. The day was warm and welcoming and the school children were now filtering onto the beach, Lauren watched them frolicking about, children … the thought enveloped her, would she ever have any of her own? Not with Billy she shuddered, he was not cut out to be a father, his patience was almost non-existent and he was very self-centered, aside from trying to buy her affections. No she didn't want to subject a child to this marriage, she wasn't even sure how long they would last, yet in the back of her mind she pondered, she hadn't had a period yet, not since her accident and it had been almost four weeks since then, she slid her hand over her flat abdomen wondering. She wouldn't tell Billy anything, whether she was or not, he needn't know of her anxieties. She walked on silently; listening to the seagulls above and the rhythmic spray of the ocean crashing upon the rocks just off shore, by the time she got home Billy was standing in the doorway.

"Where have you been?" His question was calm, cool, carefully worded.

"I just needed some air," Lauren sighed, as she brushed past him. Billy turned, catching her wrist. Lauren shot him a look of shock at his violent action.

"I told you to stay close by!" his voice held a hint of masked anger, and Lauren pulled free of his steely grip, measuring his stature. He was slightly ruffled, his tie loosened and his eyes slightly reddened, had he been drinking? She took a step back from him. Slamming the door, Billy came toward her, "so where's dinner Lauren?" backing yet farther away from him a fear began to seep into her chest.

"I'll get it now" she started toward the kitchen only to be met by Billy's looming figure. "Excuse me." She stated firmly as she tried to step around him, again he confronted her, blocking her way once more. She tried to slide softly around him only to be seized tightly to him, his rancid breath hot on her neck.

"Not just yet…" he breathed, "Why were you gone so long?" he tilted her chin toward himself, question mingled with suspicion in his eyes. Lauren boldly ventured, her aggravation growing at the accusation in his voice, the liquor clinging heavily on his breath.

"Why?" she asked bluntly, "Afraid I'll leave?"

Billy roughly grasped her arms pushing her hard against the doorway.

"Don't play with me Lauren!" His voice was harsh and luminous in the large house, acoustically amplified by the openness of the floor plan. Lauren flinched at his deliberate fierceness.

"Have you been drinking?" she managed out. Billy blinked; studying her briefly,

"My deal fell through…" He released his hold on her and turned away. "I needed to clear my head." Lauren leaned against the doorway, she didn't like where this was heading, and violence seemed to come so easily to him. "I'm Sorry." His harsh apology was viewed with skepticism as he turned toward Lauren once again. "This doesn't usually happen." He could see her visible discomfort as he faced her. "It won't happen again…" He reached for her, stroking her soft cheek, she almost cringed at his touch, maybe he was under a lot of stress at work, she could understand that, but she was beginning to worry about his ill fated temper getting out of sorts, she wasn't about to walk on egg shells around him because he'd had a bad day.

Turning from him she pushed his hand away.

"See that it doesn't." Her bitterness enraged him even further, he had apologized, even after she'd disobeyed him, that bitch was asking for it, who did she think she was talking to! Turning away, he bit his lip barely able to contain his rage. Breathing deeply he followed her into the kitchen.

"Look," he started, "let's just go out for supper, okay?" He began to put his hands upon her shoulders but refrained when he caught her tensing. Dropping his hands to his thighs he threw his arms in the air. "I give up!" he shouted. "Why do you cringe from me, Lauren?" Staring hard at him Lauren felt her face redden, she couldn't tell him that his touch nauseated her, and that she tried to imagine Nick whenever he'd have his way with her just so she could get through it! She shook her head, her frustration growing.

"I don't know you Billy! Okay! I can't even remember our wedding! Let alone your touch!"She couldn't go on pretending with herself any longer. "Maybe we should separate!" The words hung in the air between them, Billy's expression hard and bitter; an icy glimmer behind his eyes.

"You didn't know Nick Carmon either, did you Lauren!? How long did it take you to open your legs for him?" Lauren gasped at his words, he knew of their relationship the whole time? She started to speak, but turned away abruptly. Covering her face and sliding her hands through her hair.

"You knew?" she softly questioned.

"Of course, do I look that stupid to you?" he spat out as he approached her. "How long Lauren? A day, maybe two! Is he so much better than me? I can't even touch you, let alone make love to you!"

"Ha!" Lauren cut into his statement, turning toward him. "Is that what you call it? Making Love? You don't even ask! You just take, I call it rape!" Billy could no longer control his temper, reaching out he struck her fully across the face, knocking her into the cabinets beside them. The stinging slap left Lauren aghast with disbelief; she ran form the room, upstairs to the bedroom, locking the door behind her. He'd hit her! She wondered if he'd followed or just left, the sobs began to choke her as she sat upon the bed, tears soaking her shaking hands. A knock on the door startled her.

"Lauren, I'm sorry!" Billy's muffled voice came from the other side, "I'm so sorry, Let me in!" The handle shook fiercely. Lauren remained silent, her heart in her throat.

"Go away!" she prayed silently. "Just go away!" A resounding thump on the door caused her to flinch, shuddering at the confrontation.

"Fine," he roared, "I'm going out!" She listened as he stormed down the stairs and slammed the front door. She heard his Jeep revving up angrily and speeding off. Collapsing on to the dark colored bedspread, Laurens tears ran freely, her sobs quieted by the thick pillow she buried her face into; softly she faded off to sleep, her stinging cheek a distant memory, as a dream came to soothe her.

Billy sped down the highway knowing his destination would be Clarrissa's; the high dollar brothel had been his only means of release these past days. If Lauren didn't give into him again soon he was going to lose it! He'd given her everything, the house, the clothing, a life of leisure, even a new identity, but still she rejected him! Even as his wife she wasn't completely his, not as long as Nicholas Carmon was alive! If he didn't crave so much of her, need her so much, he would have already gotten rid of her, just like he had his first wife, that cheatin' bitch! At least something good had come of their wedding license; it had been so easy, using his old paperwork, to create the false documents. He had convinced Chief Ellington and Lauren both of their legally binding marriage, never had he felt so consumed by anyone before; he had to be with her no matter what, she'd just have to accept it!

Swallowing the last of the burning whiskey, he threw the glass bottle out the window, grinning as the shattered object splintered easily over the road, this situation was far from over, he swore, she would be his, or she would be no ones ...

CHAPTER 15

"Are you Nicholas Carmen?" The voice was almost a whisper behind the dark headed man, he turned abruptly towards it. A young girl, with auburn hair, slunk back from his quick movement, she hid behind her hooded sweater, only briefly catching Nick's eyes and quickly avoiding them.

"Who's asking?" he answered curiously, studying the young girl's body language, she seemed so tense, like a rabbit ready to spring and run at any moment.

"I … I know some information, about Billy … I mean those people, in the paper…" She hesitated, licking her lips nervously, "I can't talk right now. Tonight, eleven o'clock, I'll meet you behind his old house … on Avery!" As suddenly as she'd arrived, she hurried away, without a second glance. Nick's heart was racing, could this be it? The piece of the puzzle he'd been waiting for? The young girl had looked so familiar to him, but where was it he'd seen her? She was very young, he pondered, what could she know that would help, but he would meet her as she'd asked, any information was helpful. She'd hurried off for some reason, but why on Earth couldn't she talk to him here? It was a quiet place, not too busy today; he racked his mind for information, riddled now with wonder, as he finished collecting his groceries. Chief Ellington was at the cash register when Nick approached the clerk.

"Chief," he greeted, nodding in his direction.

"Mr. Carmen." The older man nodded back, taking view of his greeter. "Any luck son?"

Nick couldn't help but to grin at the inquiry. "Not much," he answered tiredly, "but maybe something will give." The chief was accepting his change from the clerk as he nodded at the younger mans words.

"Let's hope so." He managed a friendly half-smile with the brief statement, and headed out the door. "We'll see ya' around!" Nick watched him climb into his car after he'd loaded the few items he'd purchased; he started the vehicle and blew the horn once, not pulling out of the parking space just yet. As he placed his items upon the counter he noticed the mysterious young girl coming across the parking lot, from a group of teens that waved to her as she hurried away, his hopes rose, maybe she changed her mind and was coming back to give him the information now, but to his surprise she quickly climbed into the squad car passenger seat, and off they went. Of course! Nick reflected briefly, he'd seen that girl before indeed, it was Ellington's daughter!

Still wondering about the emerging situation, Nicholas Carmen stood patiently waiting, leaning casually against the frame of Billy Malhoun's prior home. A movement caught his eye, and he straightened himself, glancing at his watch, 11:20 p.m., he was getting ready to leave when she'd approached.

"Sorry I'm late," she whispered, her voice heavy with breath, as if she'd been hurrying.

"What's this information you say you have?" Nick inquired. He could barely make out her silhouette in the shadow of the large house. "I hope you're not wasting my time Sabrina." She froze at the mention of her name.

"What?" She feigned ignorance of her identity, how did he know her name? The notion frightened her and she considered running for a moment, was he like Billy? Would he hurt her while they were alone? She'd told no one of her secret, her friends had wondered why she'd changed, no more bragging to them about her sex life with an older man, no more teasing the boys with her sexual antics, and revealing clothing. She could never do that again. The thought frightened her after what had happened. If only she wouldn't have let things get as far as they had. She felt so ashamed, dirty …

"Look, I know you're Ellington's kid, so what's this all about?" Nick's masculine voice interrupted her thoughts.

"I need to go…" she moaned, turning to bolt away. Nick caught her, easily, by the arm, restraining her briefly.

"Wait!" He wasn't letting this go. She knew something and he would find out what.

"Please!" she begged, her voice quivering, "Don't hurt me!" He hadn't meant to frighten her, he only wanted her information.

"I'm not going to hurt you!" She struggled against his tight hold. "Listen to me!" he shouted, stilling her movement. "Why did you tell me to meet you here? What is it that you know?" Sabrina measured the man's words. Maybe she could trust him, if he kept his distance. Relaxing a bit she spoke softly,

"I know where he took her, your friend, Lauren. And I know they're not married, or at least they weren't when I first saw her, not according to what he'd said." Nick's heart leapt with excitement.

"Will you help me then? We need to tell your father this, it's the only way he'll help me!" Sabrina shook her head frantically.

"No! No we can't! Promise you won't tell him I told you!" Her fear was extremely evident as she pleaded, and Nick wondered at it curiously. What kept her so frightened? Why hadn't this come out sooner, how did she even know about them? "Please, Mr. Carmen. Please don't tell him about me!"

The thought dawned on him, her fear when he'd caught her arm. *"Don't hurt me,"* she'd said. *Was her father abusive to her when she disobeyed him? He didn't seem the type, but who could tell these days.*

"What's wrong?" he asked her softly. "Will you get in trouble?" Her features saddened as she turned away.

"I'm already in trouble..." she breathed. Nick ascertained her predicament, obviously she'd snuck out of the house to meet him. She must have known she would be caught by her father when she returned home, only to be beaten for her crucial assistance to Nick.

"Look, I'll go talk to him. Explain you were just trying to help me, I won't let your father hurt you for this." She studied him curiously as he spoke. "If I don't find her soon, I don't know what will happen to her, Sabrina! Please, help me." She shook her head again, measuring his words.

"My father doesn't beat me, Mr. Carmen." Her tone was flat, but laced with emotion. "I know what he'll do to her, I know, because he did it to me..." Her head hung in shame at the confession. "And now I'm in trouble, and nothing you can say will make it go away..." Nicked stared in disbelief at the small girl, his mind still reeling from the thought. That dirty bastard. How could he have touched a child? And possibly his own child at that! He longed to comfort her, cradle her, but he knew she was beyond his reach, she would never be able to be comforted by the touch of a man, not without some help.

"Sabrina, did he rape you?"

She trembled at his words. "I didn't mean to let him," she stammered. "We'd done it before, but he wouldn't stop!" her voice cracked and tears began to spill down her cheeks. "It's all my fault! I'm such a slut!" She buried her face in her hands sobbing uncontrollably. Embracing her gently, Nick stroked her hair,

"No," he whispered, "it's not your fault, no matter what happened before, what he's done is wrong. It's not your fault."

She quieted after a moment, her shuddering slowly subsiding. "I don't know what to do..." she confessed desperately. "I'm not even fifteen yet, my father doesn't know anything, I can't tell him, he'd never forgive me!"

"We've got to tell him Sabrina, and we've got to find them, before it's too late. If he could do this to you, and right under your father's nose, what could happen to Lauren?" He shuddered at the thought, the anger in him growing into rage. The man had already lied to everyone, produced false documents, and even sold his house just to get to Lauren, he was obsessed with her, obviously so, and often times obsessions could turn ugly. He could be like a loaded gun, ready to go off at the slightest test of a trigger, squaring the girl in front of him, Nick looked steadily into her eyes. "Where did he take her?"

Lauren awoke to the sound of the seagulls on the beach; she raised her head stiffly from the pillow, yawning tiredly. The alarm clock read 9:15 a.m., she had overslept. She usually rose at 7 a.m., but a recap of the previous evening's events allowed for her mishap. The door was still shut and locked and Lauren wondered if Billy had even bothered to return that night. Stepping into the master bedroom's bathroom, she stared in the mirror at her reflection, her sea-green eyes were clouded with puffiness from crying, her lips and nose were swollen and red, was this the fear she had felt when she'd envisioned his face the first time, was this the reason she'd fled from him the night of her accident, was she an abused wife? The thought seemed so impossible, surely she wouldn't have put up with it, even now she grew angry at the ominous bruise left on her cheek. What had she ever seen in him?

Undressing, Lauren stepped into the shower, closing the glass door behind her, even if he were in the house, she had locked the door, and she would hear it if he attempted to barge in, consoled in this fact she reveled in the hot water pouring over her. If today held a hint of yesterday's hostility, she would leave.

When she finally headed downstairs, Lauren was surprised to find Billy sitting quietly at the dining room table. She slowed her pace uncomfortably as she approached him, his head hung between drooping shoulders, he seemed small, humble. Lauren wondered when he'd returned, he wore the same clothes he'd worn the day before, and already the growth had become evident on his chin, slowly he met her gaze, squinting through his red and swollen eyes. *"Had he been crying?"* Lauren wondered, the proud stature of the large man was diminisheed this morning, maybe she had been wrong to assume that he'd been abusive, after all, the business was his life, he had said that his deals didn't usually fall through, and he had been drinking …

She studied him closely, keeping her distance in the silence.

"Lauren?" He buried his face in his large manicured hands. "Can you forgive me?" She stared hard at his pathetic presentation, could she? She hadn't the feelings in her to love him, no attachment to fall back on in situations like this.

"I don't know…" She folded her arms over her chest protectively. "I'm not going to be your scapegoat, I won't stay if this ever happens again, and I don't care the reasons." Her voice was stern with seriousness; she needed him to see her strength, not her deep fear, and his reaction would determine her answer. Billy brought his reddened eyes up to hers,

"I know you don't want excuses, but if I could explain, maybe then you could find a way to let us get past this?" Lauren raised her eyebrows in acceptance of his coming reasons. "I just can't stand the thought of another man with you Lauren. You're mine! I was your first and I never have needed someone the way I do you. I've never been unfaithful, Lauren, and I never will, I only wish Nick Carmen would have left his hands off of you!" Billy struggled to keep his tone down, the pounding in his head loomed over his senses in the brightness of the room, his hangover had at least convinced her that he'd felt remorse over the incident; he'd have to try harder to keep his anger in check. He hoped she'd give in of her own accord, if not; things would have to get ugly … nothing he couldn't handle. As if she'd have any say over it.

A sudden rush of memories struck at her, at Billy's words. *"I was your first…"* the picture struck her full force, followed by the emotions behind it. She remembered her first time; the loss of her virginity to Billy. She had felt giddy at the experience, filled with excitement and anxious fear, they'd never made it to the dinner she'd prepared … She gasped at the reflection, a strange tingle in her stomach.

"Billy," she quarried, "I think I, I've remembered something…" Billy froze. Did she know about them, his false documents? Waiting like a stalking tiger, he studied her, standing slowly at her words

"Lauren?" He watched her for any signs of fear, turning her face to him, she clutched her chest.

"Our first time together," she breathed, "in my parents' cabin … by the fireplace…" she trailed away in thought, that was all, no more came to her. Billy started toward her, perhaps this would assist him, if she'd only remembered that first time, then maybe she would buy his story about them, but he had to be sure.

"Is there anything else? Lauren?" Snapping back to reality Lauren realized how close he had come to her.

"No, no that's all…" She backed up uneasily, although her fear of him was somewhat less now. He hadn't been cruel to her as a girl; he'd been quite sensual, although rushed. Maybe her feelings for him would return in time, maybe this had been a one-time mistake. Billy closed their distance easily, putting his arms around her firmly.

"Lauren, are you okay?"

The sudden movement startled her, her breath catching in her throat, the room spun suddenly and Lauren felt herself falling, darkness closing in on her.

"Lauren! Lauren…" Her name from Billy's lip's was the last thing she heard, as she collapsed into him, unconscious.

When Lauren finally opened her eyes again, she found herself in the bedroom, lying on the bed, she sat up, suddenly; unsure of what had happened. Voices came in from the hall and she strained to hear them clearly. It sounded like two men having a discussion. The door swung open and Billy stepped in, a strange look on his face. "Lauren! You're awake…" following him into the room, a small wiry man, wearing a cream colored suit, stepped around the larger man and approached her, a stethoscope hung around his neck and he introduced himself as Doctor Bernard.

"And how are we feeling, Mrs. Malhoun?" He grasped her wrist and felt of her pulse, timing on his watch as he asked the question.

"All right, I guess." She was a little disoriented. "What happened?" The middle aged doctor looked up sharply, his heavy Italian accent evident.

"You took a nasty fall when you fainted, your husband called me immediately, I live just down the road…" He motioned in the direction of his home. "…keep an eye on that contusion there, if there's any swelling, call me. I'd like to run some tests on you in my office, if you don't mind." He caught Billy's glare in his direction, "Tomorrow maybe, if you've got the time." He paused studying her dazed look."Is there a possibility … that is … are you sure you're not pregnant?"

Lauren's face reddened, she noticed the glimmer in Billy's eyes as he awaited her answer, "I'm not sure." She cleared her throat uncomfortably. She looked down at her hands, wringing them nervously as she spoke, "Um, I can't say for sure…" Dr. Bernard nodded understandingly.

"Yes, your husband explained your situation." He stood patting her on the arm. "It may not be. The startle at the returning memory may have been the cause, this can happen." He stepped to the door of the room, with a reassuring nod in her direction. Billy bid the doctor goodbye and turned back to Lauren's worried features;

"We have to talk," he whispered and swiftly showed the doctor the door. "Yes, tomorrow morning is fine, Gordon. I'll see to it she gets there." That said, the door closed loudly and Lauren heard the hurried steps of her husband coming upstairs. He entered the room cautiously.

"Have you been keeping something from me?" he asked suspiciously, eyeing her reddened complexion, "Might you be?" The question stung her ears, she hadn't wanted to let him know of her suspicions, unless she had decided for sure that she would stay, and her newfound emotions toward him confused her further. "Well?" he probed. Annoyance struck her at his pushiness.

"I don't know!" Her voice rose with aggravated tones."I was going to give it a couple more weeks, then I would have gotten tested." Billy glared at her, bitterness gleaming from his eyes. If what the doctor had suspected were true, then Lauren would have to stay with him. If they shared a child, she would be bound to him, no matter what, beside, she didn't know she had any family alive, and he had seen to it that only he managed the finances. She needn't be privy to his money. She might take off if she had a means to support herself, but a seed of doubt grew a plaguing truth, would the child be his? By her reaction he could tell that she'd wondered herself. He wouldn't raise a son born to that bastard, and what if Nick was to find out. If he came for her, he was sure she would leave. He hadn't said a word about their destination to anyone … But wait! Sabrina knew! He'd told her where he was going when she'd come by to tell him she was knocked up, the little tramp. He resolved to take care of the problem, one way or another, but Nicholas Carmen would have to go.

CHAPTER 16

Days past by in a blur for Lauren, the notion that she might be a mother, consumed her thoughts. She hadn't gone to Dr. Bernard's office yet, as he'd asked, she was avoiding the answer to her fears, and the nausea she'd been denying, was growing more obvious now, she hurried to the bathroom, heaving dryly into the commode, if nothing was in her stomach, she grimaced, then there would be nothing to come out. She had avoided eating since the visit from the doctor, her appetite stifled by nerves, maybe her anxieties had been prenatal hormones all this time, she pondered, after all, Billy had kept his word, thus far, he'd been friendly and calm, although distant. Something seemed to be preoccupying him these days; not that Lauren wasn't grateful for his lack of interest in her; but she wondered what had brought about this change in him, surely the thought of possibly becoming a parent wouldn't have affected him for the better, wouldn't it represent less time for him to be with her? But then again, he was still a mystery to her. Her feelings toward him were different now, than before, due to her renewed memories of their past, but she knew nothing of him as an adult; no inquiries about parenting. Today, she decided, would be the day, she would go in to Dr. Bernard's office and have the test done, her stomach churned again at the thought; she only hoped that Billy would react well to whatever the outcome might be. In her heart she could feel a presence, a tiny spark of life within her, but she had been keeping the thought at bay thus far.

Dr. Bernard's office was a cozy little room attached to the basement of his prestigious home, he lived four houses up from them, and Lauren wondered how Billy had known him. She waited nervously in the dark brown polyester chair, adjacent his large pine desk, the results would be in, any moment now, and the tick of the ominous wall clock echoed fiercely in her head. Lauren jumped with a start as the large oak door opened suddenly,

"Well, Mrs. Malhoun, the results are in." He entered the room quickly and closed the door behind him, brushing against one of the large tropical plants that harbored the wall, he seated himself at the desk before her, straightening his white coat and tie. "It seems as though you are going to be a mother." His words barely entered her mind, as her breath caught in her throat.

"Are you sure?" she managed, after a moment.

"Oh, yes, quite sure." His reply was scarcely heard as Lauren brought her hands over her abdomen, a baby, she marveled at the thought, mixed emotions stirring within her. A baby; Lauren was numb. The pelvic exam had determined her to be almost a month along, give or take a week. She wondered on the date of conception. It had to be Nick's, the thought brought butterflies to her stomach and an ache in her heart. She longed to tell him, he should know, he deserved to know, but she knew the truth would only cause more turmoil, would he even have anything to do with her now? The last time she'd seen him, they hadn't exactly parted under the best of terms, he'd made it clear he hadn't wanted to be mixed up with her, now that the truth was out, she was married, and he wouldn't come second in her life, why would he want to step in and play daddy to her illegitimate child. There was, however, a chance that it was Billy's. Slim as it may be, she would have to abandon the notion to contact Nick, and convince herself, and Billy, that the baby was his, she had a sneaking suspicion that if she confessed her uncertainty about the unborn child's biological father, that her husband's resentment of the other man, would convey itself onto the baby. No, she would say nothing, at least her child would be financially taken care of, and she knew she would love it unconditionally, no matter what should happen, she would have to give up on the thought of leaving, for now, she only hoped that things would get better, for her child's sake. At least this way she could have a part of him, even if he never knew, their time together, however brief it may have been would forever be within her child; a beautiful reminder of the true passion they had shared.

It was late when Lauren, heard the front door slam, she had already eaten, and was dressed for bed, in her long silken gown, that had been acquired during her shopping spree for a new wardrobe. She sat before the mirrored vanity, in the bedroom, combing her long dark hair. Billy stood in the doorway, his hungry eyes taking in her sultry image, as she peered into the large, delicately framed, looking glass. His presence was felt suddenly, as she glanced at his reflection just past her own, the look of worry in her eyes did not escape him as she stood, pulling on her long robe.

"Did you go to Dr. Bernard's today?" He had asked the same question since the topic of her possible pregnancy had been brought up, although his usual pushiness had never showed up in the questioning. He seemed to be dreading the answer as much as she had. Her lingering silence answered his question. "Well?" he ventured, annoyance in his tone. "What did he say?" Lauren's hands slid subconsciously to her abdomen as she averted her eyes from his,

"He said that I'm about 3 weeks along," she lied, the blood rushing to her head, inflamed her cheeks to crimson, she was horrible at lying, she ascertained. Billy strode slowly across the room, putting his large hands upon her forearms; he searched her eyes for the truth, a hint of mistrust within him.

"Is it mine?" The question was stern and direct, Lauren felt transparent under his scrutinizing stare, and she sought the strength to convince him of her lie. Defiantly she faced him, her green eyes ablaze with conviction.

"Of course it is," she assured him, the tremble in her pushing to reveal itself. "It could only be yours." She was relieved at the steadiness she was able to convey, she held his gaze coldly, burying her doubts deep within, he would never know, they were hers to hide.

Softly, Billy's hands began to stroke her bared flesh.

"Good," he murmured, bringing her to him fully. "Good…" his lips sought hers with a carefully restrained fierceness, he needed her, now, and her sweet mouth was the drug to embellish his addiction. Lauren resisted, softly, only allowing a brief moment of union before pulling away.

"Billy, I…" She sought refuge in her delicate state. "We shouldn't."

Billy drew her to him once more, claiming her mouth determinedly.

"I'll be gentle…" he rasped, already bruising her restrained arms.

"Please…" she attempted, "…please stop, Billy!" her growing anxiety was beginning to seep through her hardened facade as he easily brushed her robe to the floor, trailing his fevered wet kisses along her neck and shoulder.

"I want you…" he moaned, as his hands tore at her long gown, seeking more of her bare flesh. Lauren gasped as her thin shoulder strap was easily snapped, dropping the bodice of her gown. She quickly pressed her trembling hands to her chest, desperately trying to hold the material in place.

"Billy! My gown!" Her heightened discomfort was obvious in her reaction, devastation was set forth at the realization of his intentions. "Please, don't!" Billy ignored her pleas, intoxicated by the visual stimulant; he roughly pulled the garment from her clinging hands, tugging it off of her slender form.

"We'll buy a new one!" He devoured her flesh, his heated touch growing more fevered with each kiss, her full breasts hung heavily, rising his urgent needs. Lauren pulled desperately away from him, no longer able to dismiss her growing terror, *not again*, she pleaded inwardly, *please not again …*

"It's not the gown…" she boldly attempted, seeing his annoyance begin to escalate into more.

"You are my wife!" he spat viciously. "Now stop these games!" He grasped her firmly once again and swiftly pressed her onto the bed, her meek protests left him undaunted, he would have her, all of her, no more of this charade, he bitterly wrought. He forcefully began to kiss her, his hands roughly seeking her last dividing garment, she struggled beneath him, her fear giving way to a growing terror that grasped her with a choking suffocation, her heart pounding heavily within her chest, *"Why was he doing this?"* she struggled to calm herself under his deliberate assault. Billy pulled himself back for a brief moment, he would have to slow down before he hurt her, the trust, that had begun to return, would be destroyed if he released his frustrations upon her like this, he needed to take her gently, her resistance was futile anyway, no matter how he took her, she would be his tonight. Taking a ragged breath Billy steadied himself upon her.

"I don't want to hurt you..." His words were foreign, to her, in her panicked state; she struggled, still, against the weight of his body. "Lauren!" he roared, stilling her movements. "Stop fighting me! Relax..." He brushed the hair from her cheek, staring into her eyes, he would dominate her, he deterred, and she would give herself to him. Softly he slid his hand up her thigh, reassuring his authority over her at her frightened reaction to his touch. Slowly he began to stroke her velvet flesh, watching for her stricken features to soften, waiting patiently, for her to give in to him and submit. Lauren struggled to calm herself, if she could just get through this, he would be done soon, and then it would be over. She closed her eyes, breathing deeply, if she resisted him further, there was a chance that his roughness would escalate, he might hurt her unborn child. Nick's unborn child. Nick ... she filled her mind with the thought of him. *"Help me through this..."* she pleaded within, visualizing their passionate union. *Yes, Nick ...* she felt herself calming, even as Billy entered her, his rhythmic strokes almost tolerable. Billy studied her still reaction to him, feeling her moistness growing with each stroke, her eyes were closed tightly, her lips softly parted, he could feel himself growing more excited by her obvious pleasure, his movements began to escalate, perhaps there was a chance that she would grow to accept him, if she would just learn to obey him, give him what was rightfully his, without disarray ... Lauren enveloped herself in Nick's memory, he might be out of reach to her, but he would always be in her heart, even now she could feel him, rushing into her, her fingers entwined in his thick black hair, his hard, lean body, hot against hers. Here, in the safety of her mind they would continue to be, passionately making love to one another, she could taste his lips, feel his gentle touch, her own needs being fulfilled … rushing again and again, she could feel herself spinning, falling, crashing into the man she desired.

"Oh, Nick!" she cried, her tumult over the edge so close … Billy froze.

"No!" he snarled, grasping her face between his large hands, Lauren gasped, snapping her eyes open, her fantasy disintegrating at the realization of what had happened. *No!* She cried inwardly. *No!* She closed her eyes tight, once more, trying desperately to escape his reality.

Billy shook her fiercely. "No!" he growled. "Tonight, you make love to **ME!** Not **HIM!"** Determined now, he cared nothing of her pleasure, his suspicions had been forthright; she was still with that damn Nicholas Carmen! No more, she would know her lover now; he held her face firmly, forcing her to look at him.

"Say **my** name, Lauren!" The bitterness he felt was shamelessly obvious as he crushed her ember of pleasure. "Say it!" Tears streamed down her crimson cheeks as Billy thrust himself into her again and again. "I never want to hear his name again!" his voice rose as he pummeled her fiercely, his moans full of anger and betrayal, as he glared deep into her eyes. "Now say it!" He shook her roughly once more.

"Bill-y!" she sobbed out, choking, on her spilling tears, her dignity shattered, her pride no more, she begged for it to be over soon, as Billy's hardened body shuddered upon her, slowing his escalated movements. Breathing heavily, he sneered at her dampened face, releasing her to cover her shamed features with her trembling hands. He rose suddenly, pulling on his clothes, he knew what was going to have to happen, he'd been planning it for days, Nicholas Carmen would no longer be a threat to him, he affirmed himself; No longer.

Nick thrust the last rolled up piece of clothing into his duffle bag, hurriedly zipping his make shift travel pack closed. If what Sabrina had confessed was true, he would have to hurry to make the airport in time for his flight to San Jose, he still had a forty-minute drive ahead of him. The sickened thought of Billy's actions kept at his reeling mind; gnawing at his barely pent fury, when he found them … he couldn't be held responsible for his actions. The recap of Bruce Ellington's reaction, to his daughter's terrible secret, still haunted his memories. *"Daddy," she had pleaded, "I'm so sorry! Please don't hate me." The grief stricken man had fallen to his knees, tears of pain and frustrated anger ran from his eyes as he threw his arms around the sobbing girl, "No matter what" he had promised her, "You're still my little girl! We'll get through this together!"* The scene had touched him deeper than he would have liked to admit, the bond of parent to child was stronger than life, they would get past this, he knew, but the scars of life's sometimes strange plan would always be. Bruce had pulled him to the side after his daughter had fallen asleep, consoled in the fact of his stability.

"That bastard's gonna pay!" he swore, the emotion reeling through his features as he spoke. "You go on after them," he'd said, "and if you don't get him, I will." Something in his eyes sent a chill through Nick, a coldness had settled in his soul, a clear vendetta to murder, burrowed behind his steady gaze, no badge would restrain his fury now. Malhoun had dropped the last straw. Tossing the bag into the blue Mustang, Nick easily started the engine, a clicking sound caught his attention as he reached to close the driver's door, and a sudden flash blinded him preluding an enveloping darkness that swallowed his burning consciousness. A hot searing flash of pain overtook him as he fell back into the black chasm all around him. The deed was done, the Mustang sat engulfed in flames at the sudden explosion that had consumed it, red taillights flared in the cool night air, as the perpetrators red CJ-5 Jeep tore down the dirt road, spraying gravel on the scene of the crime.

Lauren sat motionless, staring off into nothing as she often did these days. She was barely able to fight the depression that had settled on her, everything seemed pointless, just breathing was becoming unbearable. Her only consolation was in the fact that Billy had been away on business since the night he had learned of her secret fantasizing. Rising slowly, she walked to the kitchen for some source of nourishment; she had lost more weight, even though she had been determined not to let her depression affect her health. For the sake of her growing embryo, she painstakingly forced herself to eat something; it was her only reason for living at this point. Biting into the tomato sandwich she had made, Lauren peered out of the wide expanse of large windows that faced the ocean; the view was what made the house she concurred, swallowing the barely tasted food. She watched the seagulls flying overhead, dipping, occasionally, to the rolling tide to snare an unsuspecting morsel, the calming rush of the lapping waves helped to keep her anxieties at bay. Billy hadn't said how long he'd be gone this time, only that it was business out of town, and that it would take a few days possibly, then he had gone to the guest room, where he, consequently, had spent the night, leaving her to cry herself to sleep as before. The notion was becoming quite normal for her, no peace could be found with him around. Finishing her lunch, Lauren Stepped out the back doors, she headed numbly toward the warm and welcoming sand, sandals in hand. As she ventured along the shoreline, she noticed a man near one of the other properties; he wore dark glasses and continually avoided her view. It almost seemed as if he were watching her every move, and desperately trying to go about it unnoticed, she shook the notion from her mind that was preposterous. Who would be watching her? She glanced in his direction once more, needing to assure herself of her folly, but wait! She searched the scene for him, he was gone! He had just been there, she queried, and maybe it was nothing.

Twenty minutes passed by as Lauren walked the sandy beach, the salty freshness of the air all around her enlivened her senses, maybe she could indulge herself in shopping for the baby, of course she wouldn't buy anything just yet, it was bad luck to shop too soon, but the thought did brighten her outlook, as she started for home. Would it be a boy or a girl? What would she name it? Nearing the house, her thoughts were interrupted briefly as she caught sight of the same man in dark glasses; he was walking along the shoreline this time, just to the right of her, at about fifty feet away. Slowing, she paused and glanced at him, he turned from her, thrusting his hands into the pockets of his white, loosely fitting pants, feigning interest in the sparsely scattered seashells that lay before him. Lauren turned, resuming the trip home, only to be startled by his sudden turn of interests. Out of the corner of her eye, she watched him continue to follow her, keeping a distance between them as he did so. Panic seized her as she quickened her pace. *Who could he possibly be?* She reached the house, none-too-soon for her taste, locking the sliding glass door as she leaned upon the wall, breathless with fear. She glanced out of the open glass panes only to have her fears confirmed; he was just out of range of the house's sandy yard, peering carefully toward it now. *How creepy*, she thought. *What could he possibly be doing?* Lauren considered walking over to Dr. Bernard's office, at least then she wouldn't be alone, in the large, empty house. Opening the front door, her breath caught in her throat, another man, wearing dark glasses, stood on the corner, obviously watching the house. She closed the door quickly, grabbing the cordless phone.

"9-1-1," she reminded herself, as she waited to hear the dial tone, no sound emanated from the phone. Desperately, she punched the buttons again, waiting for some sign of response, nothing. A low continuous purr emanated from the receiver, followed by a slight clicking sound, peering cautiously out of the window, she nearly dropped the phone to the floor. A man, dressed in a utility belt and hardhat, sat perched upon the looming wooden pole just outside, apparently working on the telephone lines. Quickly she shut off the phone, her only link to the outside world, stunned at her apparent circumstance. *What was this all about?* Maybe she was being paranoid. She wondered, maybe it was all in her head, just a coincident. She carefully peered out of the window once more, the man in front was gone now, and only the telephone repairman was left, still perched upon the solitary pole, his van parked just below with a largely printed business name on the side of it. Paranoid, she mused, it was nothing, what she needed was some rest; some quality sleep time would help her rationalize better. Lauren glanced out back one last time, just to be sure; no one! She had been paranoid, and how stupid would she have been if she had called the police! Tiredly she headed upstairs, a nap would do her wonders, she derived, but she would lock the door just to be safe.

CHAPTER 17

An ominous thump awoke Lauren with a start; she sat upright staring at the still closed door. The room was dark now, night had crept up on her while she slept and her heartbeat thudded heavily in her chest as she strained to hear what the noise had been. Another thud struck her senses, followed by a series of small bumps and a sudden crash. Stifling a scream; Lauren clasped her hand to her mouth, a growing terror rippled over her. *"Burglars!"* she concluded, trying to rationalize her thoughts, her bedroom had no phone, and the heavy storm window, that harbored the large frame, opposite the door, was too much to move. She sat, very still, for a moment, listening for the intruder to come to her door, dreading the possibilities. A sudden clamor of footsteps erupted up the stairs as a gunshot rang through the air, Lauren's horror overtook her, as her bedroom door burst open, the tall looming figure of a large man came rushing into the room. Lauren sprang from the bed, dashing toward the now open door, only to be swiftly caught up by the intruder's massive arm.

"No!" she screamed, fighting him with all her strength, she wouldn't be taken without a fight. His large hand clasped over her mouth, silencing her cries temporarily.

"Shhh," he pressed his lips to her temple whispering softly, "Lauren! Shut up, it's me." Billy's familiar rasp was suddenly a welcome relief; he released her shivering form, peering out into the hallway once more.

"What's going on?" she questioned, fear trembling in her voice.

"I can't explain right now," he growled, "just pack some things and hurry!"

Lauren was confused but did as told, hurrying in the darkness to escape the unknown danger. Rounding the staircase Lauren gasped, in the full moonlight she could see two men lying on the floor of their living room, the furniture in shambles, lamps and tables strewn about.

"What happened?" she queried.

"Not now!" he spat, pushing her onward, one of the men was beginning to stir, the other lay deathly still, a dark pool staining the white carpet beneath him, she turned away quickly, the scene, horrific in nature, still playing over in her mind as they slipped out of the house.

"We should call the police!" Lauren whispered desperately, tugging at Billy's tense arm. He shook her away angrily, grasping her wrist.

"No cops!" he hissed. "We can't call them!" He drug her forcefully to the Jeep, shoving her quickly into the passenger seat.

"Billy, please!" she begged of him. "What's happening?" Ignoring her plea, he quickly climbed into the driver's seat and started the vehicle, smashing the gas pedal to the floor and speeding away, Lauren hurriedly buckled her seatbelt as the Jeep tore recklessly down the black top. In the distance Lauren could hear sirens screaming through the neighborhood, as red and blue flashing lights emanated from the same direction, everything was happening so fast, it all seemed so unreal.

"Billy?" she questioned desperately. He remained unresponsive. "Billy!" Her sharp tone irritated him.

"All right!" He glanced angrily at her, why did she think she deserved an explanation? If she would just keep her nose out of his business!

"Let's just say I had a run-in with some Columbian farmers," he ventured. "A deal went sour, and they found us..." Lauren realized their situation a little clearer now, drug dealers? What had she gotten herself into? No, her child would not live like this! She would have no part of any of it!

"Let me out!" she shouted at him, his surprise was followed by anger.

"What? Do you have any idea what those people will do to you if they find you?"

"I'm not involved Billy, and I don't want to be!"

"It's too late for that, sweetheart! They've already got a hit out on both of us, you're in deep baby, whether you want involved or not!" Lauren digested his words sickeningly, how could he have put her at risk like this, put their unborn child at risk? How would she ever escape this? It was an impossible feat, and now she was forced to trust the one man she could barely tolerate, with her life! Deep inside she felt herself break; a dark helplessness began to come over her, as if she were drowning in sorrow, drowning, even that seemed a kinder fate than what she'd been dealt. Where would they go? How would they live? Would they live? She sat in silence for the remainder of their journey. Approaching a house, surrounded by chain link fence, Billy parked the Jeep and grabbed the thrown-together carry-ons they had packed. Lauren glanced around at their destination; it appeared to be some sort of docking area, or private boatyard of some kind. Quickly Billy grasped her by the arm, leading her toward the warehouse.

"Let's go! he rasped. "We don't have a lot of time!" Lauren stumbled along beside him, glancing at their surroundings nervously, taking in as much as she could. They approached a small yacht that was docked on the farthest tether of the long pier, two men, of Latin descent, awaited them, Billy spoke brusquely to them in their native tongue, causing a quick reaction among them. They seemed to be clean-cut men at first appearance, their attire a little gruff, but clean. They eyed Lauren briefly, speaking quietly to one another as Billy threw the bags on board. Lauren managed a quick friendly grin in their direction, only to be met with lingering stares. Upon seeing the gesture, Billy stepped in front of the naive woman, growling out admonishments at the other men. He turned to her seriously. "These men may work for me, but stay away from them." His bluntness sent a shiver through her and she avoided any further eye contact with either man. Who knew what else he might be mixed into, she warned herself, she would have to be more careful about trusting anyone associated with him, from now on. Billy stepped quickly away, a flick of his wrist, activating his cell phone.

"Yeah it's me, no … No, I…" he paused aggravation in his features. "I know Dad! Look I know I already owe you, but it's, yes! For Gods sake, would you just listen?!?" He glanced at Lauren, who had been unintentionally privy, to his conversation, glaring at her; he turned and strode down the dock, out of earshot. Lauren thought little of his discussion, she'd never met his father, but he must have been involved somehow too, the apple probably hadn't fallen too far from the tree, she decided. Their journey began that night, as they ventured out into an unknown realm, foreign to the nervous woman. Lauren had no inclination as to where, or how long, they would travel, only that Billy painstakingly tried to keep her at bay and out of sight from the other men. He spoke to them only in their native tongue, barking out orders roughly, and keeping them busy. From the bits of conversation she had been privy to, Lauren had ascertained that their names were Juan and Roberto. Juan was the older of the two, although probably not more than thirty, he wore his jet black hair short and uniform, a small tattoo harbored his forearm, and his manner of dressing was less revealing and indiscreet than that of Roberto, who never seemed to feel the need to don a shirt. His sculptured and browned physique was an impressive one, along with thick waving hair, as black as coal, which reached the middle of his back, and was kept tied back for the most part. His roaming eyes were undaunted by Billy's daggered warnings when Lauren was allowed up top, he seemed to harbor a defiance that ran through Billy like a hot blade, a subtle intervention from Juan kept the two at bay from the inevitable confrontation she was sure would transpire at the current rate of events. The situation was intimidating at best, Roberto's eyes held a deep and dangerous hunger that shone in obvious intention, his youthful pride held no veil to his longing and this intimidated her around him. He was attractive to look at, but Lauren wondered about the various tattoos that harbored his body, mainly the teardrop near his eye, obvious on his high cheekbone, to her knowledge that was a sign of prison time, but he seemed to barely be in his twenties. The notion disturbed her, and she avoided him, all the more, because of it. Her fears were subsided momentarily when Billy finally announced that they would be docking soon. She looked forward to stepping foot onto dry land once again; the never-ending lapping of the waves beneath them was becoming a monotonous thing. They had been at sea for several weeks now and Lauren's pregnancy was just beginning to show, a barely audible bulge protruded from her slender form, 3 months, she pondered, almost out of the first trimester. For nearly six weeks now she had existed mostly beneath the deck, cleaning and cooking for the four of them. The boat was equipped with everything necessary to get by, including an apartment sized washer and dryer, and a small kitchen. Its three bunkrooms were impressive in size and it also contained a dining area and lounge room, where they ate their meals together. She needed a break from it all she confessed inwardly, cabin fever was sure to be creeping in on her by now. Lauren stood beside Billy on the main deck, overlooking the approaching island.

"We'll get supplies," he stated flatly, aggravation apparent in his tone. "Stay below while I'm gone," he ordered, casting Lauren a look of intolerance.

"Roberto will be on the dock to watch for any trouble…" The younger man returned Billy's icy glare fearlessly, the unspoken threat mutually understood between them.

"You just stay below while I'm gone." His intentions clearly defined, he eyed her with finality. Lauren's heart sank, she began to protest, but refrained after catching the warning in his eyes, she grimaced at the thought of being confined any longer.

The boat swayed softly with the rolling waters as Lauren paced the carpeted floor of her bedroom, they had been gone now for about twenty minutes and her annoyance at the situation had only grown. She folded her arms over her chest and peered out of the small window facing the island. There appeared to be a festival of some kind going on, people danced and laughed amongst one another, vendors lined the boardwalk and festive decorations were displayed eagerly along the wide expanse of streets just beyond the beach. How she longed to be a part of it all, just to have some human contact. Even from her contemptuous confines, the Reggae music still emanated, steel drums filled the air with a bubbling sense of carelessness that tugged at her heavy heart. The feeling of being entombed was beginning to overwhelm her. Defiantly she exited her quarters, still leery to go up on deck. She satisfied her need for escape by making her way to the lounge; the windows there were large and open, allowing her to see the celebration more vividly. At least here she could let in a cool breeze and smell the fresh island air that she longed to be in. She watched the festivities for a short time, wondering how long the men would be, she hoped they would be back soon so this torture would end before her longing for freedom drove her mad. Frustrated tears rimmed her eyes as the realization set in, they may be out to sea again, soon, maybe longer this time. How long would it be before she'd even see another person's face? Closing her eyes to the inevitable tears, she hurried to her cabin once more, the thought of being with Billy any longer tore at her, inside, *"Why was this so impossible!"* she queried. *"Didn't he care that she was going to go crazy like this?"* She flung herself onto the bed, neglecting to close the door behind her, not caring who heard her sobbing. A noise in the room caught her attention; she glanced up surprised to see the slender form of Roberto, leaning casually in the doorway, her eyes unintentionally sweeping over his impressive stature. His white cotton shirt hung open loosely, and the gold chain he wore, pressed upon his brown flesh; accenting the chiseled state of his muscular chest. Lauren cast her eyes away embarrassingly for a brief moment, then shot a look back at him in confusion, why was he in her cabin? He stepped toward her, a deep longing flashing in his dark eyes, Lauren scrambled back against the wall of the small room. What did he mean to do without the intervention of her husband? Fear stabbed at her, would he take of her too, the way Billy had? Roberto stopped, studying her trembling features.

"Seniorita..." his voice was deep and soft, it held no hint of callousness. He strode beside her, Lauren closed her eyes withdrawing herself from his direction, waiting for the fierceness of his touch and the cold emptiness that would fill her as he ... The thought curdled her stomach. "Please, I will not hurt you." His gentle words touched her, opening her eyes, she searched his face for the first hint of hidden danger, elation lighting her features.

"You speak English?" Her surprise was laced with a secret excitement, she had been under the impression that they had only been able to speak their foreign language, Spanish, she had guessed. He studied her reaction, a deep passion stirring just beneath his surface.

"Senior Malhoun does not want us to speak to you." He glared skeptically at her. "He says you are his wife?" Lauren paused, comprehending his question.

"Yes … I am." Her hesitation sparked his interest further.

"He keeps you hidden, locked away. Yes?" His eyes washed over her body sensually. Lauren blushed under his personal gesture. "You long to have freedom, no? It may be sometime before we dock again." Lauren looked away, avoiding his captivating stare, the unabashed longing in his eyes left a stirring within her, an uncomfortable reminiscence of the past, that rekindled her dearest memories, feeding the ache within her.

"Yes, I know." She wiped the tears from her wet cheeks, glancing out the small cabin window at the bustling crowd of people. Roberto touched her cheek softly, her cringing bothered him, she deserved to be treated better: he chastised.

"If you were my woman…" His touch lingered, frightening the untrusting woman. "I would not keep you locked up, like an animal." He drew his hand away from her., "Come, my brother has bought some time." He caught her wrist, bringing her to her feet and pressing her to him in the process, Lauren gasped at the strength behind his grip, what did he mean? Bought some time for what? Her fear grew in the closeness of his body to hers, his mannerisms were confusing to her, as if he undressed her with his eyes, but his words and touch remained gentle and restrained.

"What do you mean?" she breathed, his face only inches away, he lingered for a brief moment, as if he wanted to touch her with his lips; then he stepped toward the door of the room.

"I will take you on to the island." He turned back toward her. "If you would like." Lauren's brows raised in surprise, followed by an obvious mistrust.

"Why?" she ventured. "What if we get caught?" Roberto cast a playful look.

"Where is the fun without the danger?" The unexpected reaction caught Lauren off guard, a genuine smile playing on her lips. He reached out for her hand once more; this time receiving her touch and her carefully guarded trust.

CHAPTER 18

The warm heat of the island sun beat down on Lauren's bare shoulders, her soft cotton dress swayed against her slender legs in the gentle breeze. Roberto led her through the crowd to an open square in the center of the small shantytown; the streets were wonderfully crowded with colorful people. Some were buying, some selling; others just enjoying the freedom of the tropical music that filled the air. They had been exploring the many vendor booths on the edge of the celebration for about thirty minutes, the time flying by like seconds. Now, Roberto led her into the town square where several couples had already found their way, dancing alluringly to the island drums. Lauren hesitated, unsure about the gesture, if Billy should catch them ... Roberto's smiling face convinced her to try the daring dance, pressing his lean body to hers they swayed, stepping together seductively in the rhythm of the music. The dark man was expertly instructing his pupil in the ways of the dance.

Spinning her away from him, and just as quickly drawing her back, the pair soon had the attention of the growing crowd, their bodies moved easily together as the music played on. Lauren found herself letting go of the cold darkness that had consumed her for so long, exhilarated by the alluring danger that hovered so close at hand. She flung herself into the enveloping pleasure she was now experiencing, it had been so long since she had felt the rush of excitement that dancing could bring. The fun was captivating. They danced dangerously close to one another, until Lauren could scarcely breathe, she laughed hysterically as they made their way out of the now crowded square. Roberto led her to a quiet place under the boardwalk, slowing their pace.

"We must return now," he explained, the excitement filtering from them now, as they caught their breath. Lauren's disappointment shown through her reddened face.

"I know," she confessed quietly. How she wished she could just stay here in this moment, a spark of happiness barely clinging to her now reawakened heartbeat. The freedom of this day would keep her longing now. Roberto stopped, catching Lauren's hand in his own and turning her to him. Surprised at the sudden movement, Lauren's legs swayed under her, pressing her unexpectedly against the Latin stranger's naked chest, her steadying hand absorbing the heat of his bare flesh, she faced him, unsure, as his full lips caught hers passionately. Still deep in the moment, Lauren dropped her guard, kissing him back, wantonly, his sun browned body flexed against her as he deepened the kiss, pressing his hips to hers and hungrily clasping her to him. Chills swept over her as she fell into the euphoria of it all, the deep trembling within her giving way to a quaking tremor, as Roberto explored her gentle curves.

"Nicholas…" she barely breathed as his lips trailed along her neck, the name had rolled carelessly off her tongue, but had apparently gone unnoticed by her pursuer. The incident struck Lauren like a splash of icy water; her sudden tensing bringing the younger man quickly to a halt.

"I'm sorry…" he began, "I meant no harm." He stepped back, cautiously observing her now. "We should go now."

"Please," she pleaded, "not yet." The look of desperation in her eyes did not go unnoticed.

"We do not have to return, Lauren, we can leave … together…" his hopeful gaze met hers, longing in his dark eyes. "The island is a haven for those who seek refuge."Her hesitation at the notion suggested a fear to him.

"I do not fear Senior Malhoun, Miss Lauren, I know people here. We can escape." His offer was tempting, but she knew it could not be, Billy would never let her leave, and he would never stop searching his overzealous pride wouldn't let him. In her heart she knew it would never be fair to Roberto, to lead him on, in search of only her freedom, her heart belonged to another, the one man she could not escape, did not wish to escape, but yet the sweet ecstasy of his memory harbored her deepest pain, she could never have him, only in her mind could they exist and Roberto had awakened those feelings once again, stirring a new sadness into her guarded heart.

"Please understand," she began, "my heart belongs to another. I carry his child…" her eyes told of her longing but also of her faithfulness to this love. Roberto understood, but a flash of confused anger washed over his features

"Why do you stay? He treats you like an animal! How can you love him?" A sad gentle laugh escaped her lips;

"Billy? I have no love for him, no, I'm not sure I ever did…" she trailed away in thought. Why was she suddenly telling this man her secrets? What was it that made her trust him? Perhaps the fact that they now shared a mutual secret, had loosened her tongue, or maybe the need for human contact had simply overrun her better judgment, whatever the case he now knew the truth that she had been trying desperately to bury. Roberto's features softened, as he touched her abdomen, a gentle smile played across his lips.

"I did not know…" he considered her for a moment, if only they had met under different circumstances, he pondered, maybe before his time "inside" and her impossible decision to marry that cruel man, "You do this for your child." It was more of a statement than a question, but was clearly understood. Tears rimmed Lauren's eyes, she knew that it was the truth, but hearing the words from someone else struck her deep within, was she really doing the best for her child like this? She hadn't had an examination since Dr. Bernard's office call, and her depression had her appetite non-existent, without some sort of vitamin supplements her energy level continued to squander, leaving the tiny being to draw nourishment from very limited reserves. Again she silently cursed the man whose ring she wore, he hadn't a care about the well being of her unborn, only a selfish lust for her body. It was a cruel possession that poisoned his jealous mind; keeping her tethered to him, no matter what the cost. How she missed Nick, longed for his comforting arms to encircle her on those long uncertain nights, it seemed a lifetime had passed since she'd felt his warmth, tasted his kiss … Roberto glanced upward, hearing the footsteps overhead before Lauren. Returning to the present situation, she hurriedly followed the leery man as he made his way to a clear view of Billy's yacht, without being noticed.

Billy approached the dock hurriedly, his temper still lit by Juan's painstakingly long visit to the supply vendors, his trading skills apparently rusty at the scene of his exasperating negotiations with the locals. His searching eyes did not see Roberto. Anger flared at the notion of where he might be and what he might be doing, a murderous glimmer settled into Billy's eyes, even now he could almost hear the soft moaning she would no doubt be doing. He entered the dining area of the boat, not seeing Lauren, angrily he flung their bedroom door open; Lauren gasped, turning abruptly toward the disturbance.

"Billy!" Her presence there stunned him. "What is it? What's wrong?" Her theatrical naivety was playing him well.

"Nothing," he stated flatly. His questioning eyes sweeping over first her, then the room. "We'll be shoving off in a moment." He glanced around the cabin one last time, peering at her skeptically once again before leaving. Lauren exhaled slowly, what she and Roberto had feared to be Billy, was a pair of playful children on the boat dock, but apparently their quick return to the boat was none too soon. Billy had been right behind them. They had cut it close, too close for her taste; the danger of this game was all too real. Billy headed toward the top deck in search of Roberto; if he couldn't stay at his post he needn't be on board, the untrusting man devised. He caught sight of him exiting the upper deck restroom, calling out to him, he questioned the other man's whereabouts in the fast native tongue that seemed to come easily to him, only to be met with a cynical retort that quickly erupted into an argument. Juan came between them, admonishing his younger brother, quietly, for the defiance of their employer. Roberto cast an agitated look at his sibling before turning to leave, he would honor his wishes this time, but his brother would not stop the next confrontation.

Bruce Ellington stood in the cabin where Nicholas Carmen had been living, a bag of personal belongings in hand, looking around he marveled at the younger man's property. He had acquired quite a collection for such a short life. It was a shame what had happened, and he had been the one to discover the incident. The picture still haunted him ... he had come across the Mustang, still engulfed in flames; radioing for the fire department he ran to the scene, hoping to pull the man from the inferno, the flames burned so hot they had singed his leather bomber, on the underside of his forearms, where he had shielded his face from the heat. Try as he may, he could not get close enough to tell if someone was even in the car, let alone pull someone out. He was sure of one thing; it was no accident. From the look of the remains, the following morning, it had been quite a powerful blast. He shook his head at the unfortunate incident once more. It was a shame what had transpired. They'd found Billy and Lauren, had been watching them for days, when word came to move in, Billy had disappeared, this was around the same time the car bombing had occurred. A witness put Billy's red Jeep near the cabin the night of the incident, the evidence was good enough to warrant an arrest, but the operation had soured, leaving one officer dead and another wounded. Collecting the remaining items he'd been sent for, he headed back out to the patrol car. Sabrina stared at the intimidating structure.

"It gives me the creeps..." she was saying, as her father closed the car door and put it in gear. "Oh!" she exclaimed clasping her hands to her protruding abdomen, "That was a hard one!" Her unborn child had been squirming and kicking a lot lately, she had decided to keep the child, after she and her father had considered her options. Abortion was something she'd found herself not able to condone, now that she herself was about to become a mother, four weeks and counting, she reminded herself, soon her child would be a squirming bundle of reality. Bruce smiled warmly at his daughter, she seemed to have grown so much in these past eight months, she and her mother had painted the spare room yellow and trimmed it with everything imaginable for a baby, he watched the wonder in her eyes at the tiny movements that came from within her womb, she was only yesterday an infant herself ... the memories brought tears to his eyes. Blinking them back, to avoid her observant glance, he turned onto the main highway and headed toward his destination, how quickly time passed by, he mused.

Lauren lay awake in her bed, twice now, in the five months since they'd left the island and had been at sea, they had docked for supplies. She had pleaded with Billy to be seen by a physician, for the sake of their unborn child, and finally he had agreed. The pregnancy was proceeding normally; no problems were detected, much to the relief of the soon to be mother. She had been spotting for sometime now and she feared that Billy's relentless persistence with sex might have harmed her child. She now slept alone at night, with Billy next door to her, only coming and going nightly for the brief rendezvous, he craved with her. Their coupling was increasingly difficult for her as she grew larger with pregnancy, and the subtle, but prominent, kicking of her infant seemed to drive her husband away from her all the more. She hoped his intolerance for her pregnant state wouldn't affect his treatment of the baby. Roberto would speak to her privately at times; elated by the tiny probing he could feel when he touched her abdomen. Lauren felt a warm connection with the younger man, the longing for the love she had tasted, long before, still ached in her heart, and she knew that Roberto held certain aspects that reminded her of Nick. It would have been so easy to fall all over this man, but doing so would have only complicated things worse, for both of them. Their relationship remained platonic and neither of them hinted at anything other than this, a quiet understanding between them.

Although conversation was scarce, Lauren had learned enough about Billy and these men to make her wish she hadn't asked. Juan and Roberto were brothers from Los Angeles, California. They had both done time in prison for car theft, and assault on an officer. Roberto had explained how the police officer had beaten his brother when he'd discovered their car to be stolen, he knew they shouldn't have taken the car, but in his neighborhood, the local gang would not accept "no" for an answer when it came to initiation. They hadn't expected the cop to be so brutal and Juan wouldn't fight back because of the authority the other man represented. They worked for Billy in the import/export business, distributing and smuggling illegal substances and weapons. The business was a dangerous one, but the pay was good, and the respect amongst the underground was statuesque. The future wasn't exactly bright for two high school drop outs with eighth grade level skills, and a history of violent crime, this was their ticket out of the land of welfare.

Lauren wondered about Nicholas, if he ever thought of her, she dreamt about him sometimes, but never would she mutter a word of it. This was what kept her going these days, and the fear of having her last link to him severed, kept her enuring and obedient. Soon her child would be here, and her days and nights would be filled with the time consuming tasks of motherhood, she yearned to hold her tiny infant, the love she would give to her small piece of Heaven would help to keep her from drowning in the pool of sorrow she'd filled with her tears of loss and anguish. She prayed to be the best mother she possibly could be, secretly knowing hers would most likely be the only love her child would receive. Her sadness was constant; always lingering behind the smile she'd display at times, pulling her down into the chasm of depression and fatigue that clung to her. She had awoke this morning with an ever nagging ache in her lower back, the pain relievers she'd taken an hour earlier hadn't helped, and by now the growing throb was becoming more obvious. Almost eight months, she wondered, could this possibly be a miscarriage? The doctor she'd seen just ten days back had said everything was all right, aside from her lack of vitamins and low weight gain, he'd even done an ultrasound and the tiny heart of her precious little one could be seen beating strongly, worry overtook her now, as the tightening pain increased in intensity. She rose stiffly from the bed, noticing an obvious stain from beneath her. The deep red spot sent her heart to racing.

"No!" she cried helplessly. "Please, no!" Another tightening wave hit her, bringing her to her knees, scarcely able to catch her breath. After a moment, it subsided enough for her to rise again, she swayed unsteadily against the doorway, was she off balance, or was the boat rocking unnaturally hard? Stumbling toward the upper deck she could hear a deep creaking moan, surrounded by an ever-constant rumbling. What was happening? Upon opening the door a blast of salty spray hit her full force, nearly knocking her back down the steps, she could hear the men shouting over the roaring wind; in the quick Latin tongue they were allowed. Billy appeared, suddenly, before her.

"Get the hell back down there!" he growled, steadying himself against the doorway. "It's Hurricane Emma! She's hit us full force!" Lauren gasped with terror, how would they ever get to land? Would their small yacht survive the tearing storm? Another gripping pain clutched at her now, soaring around her lower back and abdomen in a wave of constricting pressure, she cried out, grasping the metal railing for support.

"Billy..." she moaned, "I need a doctor!" His intolerance of her ridiculous request erupted a mocking laugh.

"We'll be lucky if we make Kawaanii!" he sneered., "Now get back down stairs!" He closed the door on her frail form, leaving her in her pain, alone and frightened. Tears streamed down her cheeks as she slumped to the floor of the narrow hallway.

"Please!" she begged. "Please don't let me lose this baby!" The pain came stronger as the ship was tossed uncontrollably upon the crashing waves. Lauren scarcely noticed the roaring storm outside as she tried desperately to breathe through the waves of pain that struck her full force now, their intensity growing with every rush. A sudden cracking sound filled the air as the boat began to lean exaggeratedly to one side, a groaning erupted from the lower part of the vessel as Lauren forced herself to rise; adrenaline pushing her to flee. Water suddenly burst into the hallway, gushing toward her as she scrambled painstakingly toward the exit above. Grasping the handle, she pushed against the door, no give was detected, she pushed again, and again, it would not budge.

"No!" she screamed as the icy water hit her bare feet. Billy had locked her in! "Help me!" she cried frantically as she threw herself against the barricade. Terror devoured the last shred of clarity within her racing mind accenting the gripping rush of stabbing pains that bombarded her, another wave of constriction clutched at her. "Oh, God," she prayed, "please help me!" Desperate with fear, she clung to the handle of the door as the rushing water filled the small air pocket that was left, rising rapidly. Lauren closed her eyes to shut out the salty sting of the consuming water, a flash of memories struck her at the familiar fear ... *She scrambled to the back of her Firebird, emerging into the pocket of air in the back window ... a man was coming at the glass with something to break it ... Nick. Nick was pulling her out ... pulling her to safety* ... Suddenly the door flung open and strong arms grasped her shivering form. Tearing her up from the water filled room, "Nick?" she muttered weakly as the man drug her over the railing of the yacht.

"Hold on, Lauren!" Roberto's familiar accent penetrated her dazed memories, choking up seawater. Lauren felt herself land softly onto a rubber raft that waved uncontrollably in the water. "I've got you!" His heavy form rocked the lifeboat as he sprang into it from the sinking ship. "Just hold on!"

Pain racked her once again as she clung to the rope that encircled the raft, she struggled to make sense of the rushing memories that filled her mind, but the staggering pain that kept at her, was coming faster now, as the tiny life raft was thrown into the storm without mercy. Billy ... she clamored for the memory to clear, he was showing her the Jeep ... $27.50! Reality slapped her full force.

"No!" she cried in a desperate rage. "That sonofabitch!" Tears poured from her eyes as she clung to the life-giving rope, how could he? All this time she'd been deceived, been kept from the one man that had brought her happiness, brought her love! A lifetime of memories bombarded her through the lifting fog that had consumed her mind for so long. He'd taken everything from her, even her identity, her life, now determination filled her. She had to survive, for her child, for herself, for Nick. Roberto grasped her arm as she cried out in pain once again; the stinging rain pelted them unmercifully, as Lauren tried to breathe through the wave of constriction that enveloped her.

"I see land just ahead!" he cried over the roaring winds. "I'll get you there!"

Lauren could see the lights of the island too, but skeptically she viewed their situation. The storm raged uncontrollably all around their tiny rubber raft as Roberto paddled desperately toward the lights. What if a reef existed just beyond the islands beaches? She worriedly wondered, what would become of them if they struck the jagged rocks? Lauren held on determinedly, praying for a miracle as they rode out the storm. Roberto struggled against the force of the waves as they neared the island, just a few hundred yards left he noted, the muscles of his back straining with exhaustion, Lauren lay back in the small raft her knees drawn up against her stomach in an attempt to thwart the incredible pain that now overtook her. A growing pressure enhanced her excruciating discomfort, as she gritted her teeth, panting raggedly through the experience. They were nearly to the beach now and as Roberto hurriedly scrambled through the thigh deep water, pulling the boat ashore, Lauren felt a burst of hot liquid stream down her thighs, crying out with fear at the sudden eruption she lunged forward grasping the startled mans arm.

"Roberto, I..." she cried, "...the baby ... is ... is ... coming!" The excruciating desperation in her words gave way to a shrill squeal of pain. Gathering her to him, Roberto lifted her into his arms and hurried toward the lights of a nearby shelter, he only hoped they would get her to a hospital in time ...

Lauren lay awake once again, this time in the safety of a hospital bed at Kawaanii St. Reeves Hospital. Hurricane Emma had only clipped the region of islands that Kawaanii harbored, the house that Roberto had found, belonged to a minister and his wife, whom had hurriedly taken her to the emergency room, upon seeing the condition of the woman. A nurse came into the small room.

"Miss Conklin?" The name was a relief from the hellish nightmare that had ensued, she was finally free of her psychotic ensnarer. "Would you like me to bring you anything for the pain?"

Lauren smiled sleepily at the cheerful caregiver, "No, thank you, I'm fine." Her body still ached sorely from the events that had transpired, but the pain reminded her that she was alive, and of the life she had brought into this world. Her seven pound two ounce baby boy had survived his premature birth; although the doctor had insisted that little Nicholas Robert was closer to term than she had thought him to be. His thick dark hair was a puff of frivolous down upon his small round head, she held him tightly to her breast as he suckled contentedly; never had she felt as complete in herself as did she now. She would be released soon and had made plans to bring her son to her parent's house, she had wept with them on the phone, a resounding happiness in the fact that they weren't gone as Billy had so cunningly insisted to her. The coast guard had been alerted to the fact of Billy's possible presence in the area. Roberto had told Lauren the events that had happened prior to her rescue. Billy had been flung from the deck when their yacht crashed upon the rocky reefs encircling the island, but not before attacking Roberto himself for the attempt to check on Lauren, when her cries were heard by the two brothers.

The scuffle had cost him his only sibling, who stepped between the men when a knife was brandished; he had taken the brunt of the blow for Roberto, and had also fallen prey to the chopping waves that devoured the vessel in the end. He wasn't sure if Billy had survived or not, but he wouldn't stay when the authorities became involved. He asked for Lauren's forgiveness in the matter, apologizing for abandoning her here; she understood his reasons, his shady past would never let him be completely free of the burdens he carried, and now he carried them alone. She hoped he would be all right on his own, he was a good man under all the hooded paraphernalia, but it didn't matter what she thought, not in the law's eyes. A gift had been sent to her room the following morning with an unsigned card, but she knew it was Roberto, the package included two new dresses for her, and a collection of infant clothing and diapers for her child. The small note read: *I know what poverty is, thank you for being a friend and looking past my past. Please find your love, he deserves to know his father, don't let him become like me.*

Lauren read the note over and over, the thought of facing Nick again strangely frightened her, she was unsure about the notion, she didn't want him to feel trapped when she presented his son to him. What if he'd already found someone else? Why would he wait for a woman who had left the state with her husband, leaving him to bask in the memories of someone who was unreachable now? Would he accept her, now that another man had used her so viciously, would she be worth the chance? Now with a child to support, maybe she should approach him slowly on the subject. She resolved not to rush back to him too soon, she needed time to heal, physically and mentally, she needed to get to know herself again, to be sure she could survive without him if he turned her away. Deep within she prayed he would still feel the same way she did, still need her the way she had never stopped needing him.

Word had reached Chief Ellington that Billy Malhoun was no longer on the lamb, he was pronounced dead after a three-month search for his body had been called off. He had enquired about Lauren's well being and whereabouts, and had sent a letter to her parent's address, inviting her back up to the mountains to meet his new granddaughter, Shyanne Lucretia Ellington, it had been nearly a month since he'd sent the invitation out, and he wondered if she'd received it yet.

Lauren leaned in the doorway of her mother's kitchen, watching her prepare a Ham Quiche for the luncheon she would be hosting that afternoon, the finger-smeared apron she donned would never have hinted at the débutant she was beneath it. Her dark hair was streaked with silver strands, the only hint to her true age, and she worked tirelessly on the delicate appetizer. Little Nicholas was asleep in the nursery they had prepared for him, when she'd arrived nearly four months ago. She seated herself at the kitchen bar; fingering the worn and stained letter she had received, about three months after she arrived. Bruce Ellington had sent it in hopes of her return to the mountain resort town, but Nick had not been mentioned. So they had learned of her ordeal, she mused, but only Chief Ellington had tried to contact her, she stared out of the large bay window above the sink in the kitchen, considering the idea, as she had so many times before, a nervousness held her at bay, still keeping her from taking the chance.

"Why don't you just go Lauren?" Her mother's comforting voice caught her attention. She smiled supportively at her daughter as she finished her project and removed her tattered apron. "He should know about his son…" She had gently hinted at meeting the man who held her daughter's heart, for some time now, but the incident that she had been subjected to, still seemed to haunt her. Lauren sighed, dropping the letter to the counter.

"I know mother," she leaned her chin in her palm, glancing at the other woman, "but what if he's gotten over me?"

"Oh! Don't be silly!" She furrowed her brow sarcastically. "No man could get over **MY** daughter!" Lauren smiled, a laugh on the brink of escape, if only she knew. Seeing her daughter's obvious expression, she took the initiative to explain. "Now, I know you've left a trail of broken hearts, searching for this one, Lauren." Lauren started to object, but was interrupted by her mother's explanatory statement, "I've waited for years to see you finally open your heart to someone, you've never let anyone get close enough, always afraid of getting hurt."

"Mom…" Lauren glared at her parent, not wanting the lecture.

"Listen, honey, I know you're scared, but if you really love him, then he's bound to feel the same." Lauren considered her words, her stomach fluttering at the thought, maybe she was right, but why hadn't he tried to contact her? Maybe he had left the area, moved on after all the turmoil. Seeing the consideration in her features, her mother took the initiative once more, gently pushing her daughter toward the idea.

"I didn't want to bring it up, Lauren, but Mildred Evans contacted me about a week ago. She'd heard about your return and would really like for you to come visit her sometime." Mrs. Conklin tactfully kept the idea light. "She is alone out there, you know, it must be pretty lonely…" Lauren considered again, perhaps a visit with Mildred was just what she needed, that way it would keep her on neutral ground, and if by chance she decided to look Nick up, maybe while visiting Chief Ellington and his family, she would have someplace to go if he'd forgotten all about her, someplace that wasn't beside his cabin.

CHAPTER 19

The trip was long and tiresome, even when rest would come, Lauren's mind raced with indecision, Nicholas Robert was sound asleep in the backseat of the rental car she had driven down, when she pulled up to the old farm house. Chickens scattered like milkweed seeds from the dusty gravel driveway. Lauren stood beside the car, breathing in the mountain air, it was fall again, she mused; she always seemed to come here in the fall. Mildred swung open the storm door of her quaint home.

"Land sakes, child, has it really been a year!" A broad smile splayed across her face as she hurried toward her much missed visitor, her gray hair streaming down in frivolous ringlets from under her tattered Stetson "It's been too long!" she purred, hugging her young friend affectionately. "Let's get your things brought in, hon, it's gonna be stormin' before we know it!" She opened the door to the Champaign colored sedan, gasping at the now awakened four-month-old that stared, surprisingly at the elderly woman, with large cerulean eyes. Mildred squealed with excitement, "There he is!" she cried excitedly. "You just come 'ere to Grama' Mildred!" Lauren smiled happily at the scene, a warm comfort finally reaching her as they entered the house.

Mildred handed the younger woman her cup of tea, and seated herself before the crackling fireplace, the story she had relayed to her hostess had rekindled some of the feelings she'd been suppressing for months. The sweet taste of honey and chamomile lingered on her tongue as she stared at the dancing flames. A low rumble of thunder bellowed in the distance, bringing to mind the time she had spent here with her rescuer. She could still feel the rush of the autumn wind through her hair, the heady scent of horse filling her senses as the chase ensued, she longed for the freedom she had felt that day, the wholeness she had taken for granted. How strange that her loss had actually been her escape. She had always been complete while in his arms, something that even the return of her memories could not fulfill.

"You know," Mildred began, "that Bruce Ellington was hopin' you'd come by while yer' down, he's mighty proud of that little granddaughter of his." Lauren smiled again, glancing at Mildred's gentle face.

"Maybe I'll go out there tomorrow." She decided it might be nice to see him, and meet his granddaughter. She wondered what had transpired while she'd been away. After all, his daughter was only turning sixteen, an awfully young mother. Little Nicholas stirred beside his mother on the soft blanket she'd laid him on. His thick black hair lying gently across his brow, reminded her of the man she still dreamt of. It would be nice to see him too, she admitted.

The morning air was chilled and crisp; Lauren easily found her way to the police station in town and gingerly entered the building, carrying the infant car seat that harbored her son. She approached the police chief's office cautiously and knocked twice. "Yeah, what!" The familiar authoritative voice brought a smile to her face.

"I have a complaint!" she stated, opening the door slowly.

"What now?" he growled, he'd been swamped with problems all morning and he wasn't sure he could bare another. Standing at the unexpected intrusion, he stared at the familiar smile that met him.

"My name is still on the missing person's board, but I think I've been found…"

His laughter was echoed in his eyes as she entered the small office.

"Well, I'll be!" he exclaimed. "I never thought we'd see YOU again!" She approached him warmly, extending a welcoming arm and hugging his neck.

"Who's this?" he asked, greeting the small one now.

Lauren smiled lovingly at her child. "This," she began, "is my son, Nicholas Robert." Chief Ellington's eyes met hers in surprise.

"Well! Well!" he exclaimed. "I guess a lot can change in a year!" Lauren smiled in agreement.

"Indeed!" She pointedly glanced at the new picture on his desk.

"Shyanne Lucretia Ellington," he announced proudly, "she's almost five months now."

"She's beautiful," Lauren complimented. "Will I get to meet her?"

Bruce Ellington laughed, "You're just the excuse I needed to go home early today!" He phoned his wife and let his secretary know he was leaving before they left. "I'd like to invite you to dinner, Miss Conklin, will you accept my invitation?"

Lauren grinned at the older man once again. "Of course I will!"

The homemade meal of pot roast and sweet potatoes left every member of the dinner table satisfied in appetite, the women chattered excitedly with one another, as Bruce Ellington leaned back in his chair, at the head of the table. He pulled a cigar from his shirt pocket and lit it up, receiving an accusing glare from his wife and daughter. "Dad!"

"Bruce, please take that thing outside!" Mr. Ellington sat forward once again.

"All right, all right!" he laughed, knowing what their reaction would be. He made his way past the admonishing women, shaking his head. Sabrina watched Lauren as she discreetly began feeding her son, glancing at the look of disguised sadness behind her smile.

"Is he Billy's?" Deborah Ellington looked horrified at her daughter's question.

"Sabrina!"

"What mom? I just wondered! If he is, then we're all family, right?"

Lauren was confused. Mrs. Ellington glared at her daughter.

"That's enough!" Lauren seeing the obvious discomfort of the conversation enquired the reason for the girl's statement.

"What do you mean?"

"It's nothing," Mrs. Ellington broke in, "she's ... she doesn't mean to offend you!" Her embarrassment was obvious as she tried to once again silence her daughter.

"Lauren, I'm sorry, I didn't come forward sooner, Mom doesn't want me to say anything, but I can't live with myself if you don't know"

"Sabrina Ellington!" The distraught woman rose to her feet, her face reddened with bruised pride, tears were welling in her eyes as her daughter began to confess the dark secret she had tried so hard to keep hidden, what would this woman think of her now, of them!

"I was scared, to tell about you, not being really married to him, I mean, after what Billy had done to me, I mean I already had enough problems as it was. But Nick was trying so hard to find you and I had to tell someone, if it wasn't for him, well, Shyanne probably wouldn't be here; he helped me tell my parents about it all. Look..." she was breathless with the need to explain herself to the other woman, "I know what Billy was capable of, I didn't want to have it happen, but now Shyanne's here and so is little Nicholas, if we could let them know each other as they grow up, it would be nice, don't you think? They are brother and sister, aren't they?"

Lauren was awestricken, silence lingered too long and Sabrina read the reaction as anger toward her.

"I'm really sorry, Lauren," she said quietly, looking a bit embarrassed now herself. It all had been presented so suddenly that she hadn't digested the situation fully yet, Billy was Shyanne's father? Of course! She reflected she had seen Sabrina before, at the theater that night. The realization, of Billy's crimes, was growing more unbelievable as she discovered them, just the day before she had learned that the intruders in the beach house weren't so called "Drug dealers" as she'd been told, they were the undercover police officers, sent there to incarcerate Billy and release her from his possession. He had known that, and he had actually killed one of them, with his bare hands, after shooting the man. The thought made her shiver with a realization of the danger she had been in for so long. Sabrina had known they weren't married, but how could she be angry with her for not coming forward while Billy was still in town. She empathized with the girls fear. Her mind filled with the mention of Nick, what had she said? He'd been looking for her? Her heart raced at the notion, could he actually still wonder about her? Why hadn't she heard from him? It was easy enough for the other's to contact her.

"I'm sorry, Sabrina." Lauren smiled understandingly at the girl and her mother. "I don't think my son is Billy's." She cast Deborah a heartfelt look of relation, she didn't want her child to be known as a bastard either, especially not conceived from rape, she hoped that they would not feel embarrassed about her knowledge of the situation now, hers wasn't much better. Sabrina stared in confusion, considering Lauren's response.

"Well then whose..." Her eyes widened at the elucidation of who the father must be. Lauren blushed under their knowing eyes.

"I've been putting it off," she confessed, "I didn't know how he would react..."

"You mean Nick?" Sabrina enquired, glancing worriedly at her mother who began to clear the table nervously. "Didn't anybody tell you?" she queried.

Lauren's heart pounded heavily. "Tell me what?"

Deborah hushed her daughter. "It's not your place, Sabrina! You've said enough!" Sabrina stopped short, noticing her father's entrance into the room.

"What's wrong?" he questioned, seeing the paled face of their guest and the reddened face of his wife.

Sabrina looked down at her lap awkwardly. "I'm going to check on Shyanne..." She hurriedly left the table.

"***What*** about Nicholas Carmen!" Lauren demanded, looking to each of her hosts, a growing desperation in her voice. Bruce Ellington's face grew hard, and unpleasant, a look of indecision filled his features.

"Look," Lauren began, "I only want to know for the sake of my son, Nick's his father..." The words seemed to stir emotion into Bruce's eyes; he left the room, returning with a newspaper. Placing it in front of Lauren and covering the front page purposely with his hand. He spoke carefully,

"Now I didn't show you this, Lauren, don't tell Mildred I did." Lauren furrowed her brow in confusion as he removed his hand from the paper, *"Local terrorist attack leaves man critically injured, in car explosion."* Lauren skimmed over the article hurriedly- not expected to live-California man considered suspect-Doctor's give a 10% chance-life support to be taken off tomorrow-Nicholas Carmen to be eulogized by Bruce Ellington. She could read no more. Was he dead? She wouldn't accept it, she read the date of the article; it had happened just days before Billy had taken her to sea. He was gone, and Billy had done it, he'd taken the last chance at happiness she'd had. The horror of reality suddenly struck her, he hadn't tried to contact her, no one had mentioned him, which she had found odd, she had to know, she couldn't accept this, not after everything she had endured, only to lose in the end. She studied the paper briefly, glancing at her son, he would never know his father now, and tears filled her eyes as she stood, placing her now sleeping child in his carrier and securing him.

"It can't be…" she insisted. "I'm going to his cabin to find him!" She threw her white shawl around her shoulders, ignoring the couple's protests, denial closing her ears to any further information on the subject.

"Lauren, please." Bruce Ellington followed the determined woman. "I'm so sorry, I wasn't supposed to tell you." She hurried to the car, buckling her son in the rear seat, trying to hold back the choking cascade of tears that threatened to betray her. "Lauren don't go, he's not at the cabin…" the voice trailed away in the distance as she hurried toward the mountain retreat.

It wasn't possible, she kept repeating in her head, he couldn't be gone, he'd be there, she told herself, desperately trying to convince her own doubting heart. She found the familiar old road easily and rushed toward the cabin, just past her parent's place. Slowing down as she approached, her heart beat furiously in her throat, an unmistakable darkness basked the looming structure, a cold loneliness that speared through her heart like a steel blade. He was gone. She reflected upon their time together, her beautiful son that had taken on his dark features and cerulean eyes, eyes she would never see again … Tears spilt down her cheeks as her sobbing erupted "no," she begged, "please no!" Her heart ached as she wept; her loss too great to comprehend in less than the shattering pain that racked her broken dignity. How would she ever handle this, she'd only feared his heart to be unreachable, never had she considered that he might be gone from existence. She sat, sobbing for the better of an hour before pulling herself together enough to drive back to Mildred's and collect her things. Mildred hadn't wanted her to know, perhaps she was trying to protect her from the heart ache that now consumed her, leaving her to believe that he simply had gotten over her and moved on, but in a strange way the fact that he hadn't abandoned their love, at least gave her a sense of closure. She would have to let Mildred know that it hurt her, that she would keep the truth from her, when she'd known all along. She had even gone so far as to put Bruce Ellington and his family up to not telling her of Nick's murder, the more she thought about it, the angrier she became. A true friendship was subject to complete honesty, how could she have looked into little Nicholas' eyes and known, without saying a word that he'd never get to meet his father! She knew the child wasn't Billy's; he was the spitting image of Nicholas Carmen.

It was getting late by the time she reached the old Evan's farm, the lights were still on in the small house, signaling the fact that Mildred was still awake. Lauren left her son soundly sleeping in the still warm car; this wouldn't take long, she assured herself, as she entered. Mildred sat by the fireplace, sipping her tea, as usual. She smiled knowingly at Lauren's tear strewn face.

"Bruce called," she said softly, setting the small teacup on its saucer. "I guess you know then." Lauren couldn't believe her casualness about the subject. Maybe it was old news to her, but the shock of it all was still raw within her heart.

"He showed me the article Mildred." Tears ran easily from her eyes as she spoke, the quiver in her voice barely restrained, "Why didn't you tell me?" Mildred nodded in agreement.

"I know, I should have told you sooner, but…" Lauren cut her short.

"I don't want any excuses, Mildred, I'm just going to get my things and go home!" She passed the stunned woman as she hurried into the back bedroom where her belongings were kept. "I can't believe you!" she was calling as she cleared her clothing from the chest of drawers. "You have some nerve involving the Ellington's in your ridiculous idea!" She turned toward the bed tossing her suitcase on the mattress to pack it once again, "I mean really!" A falling object caught her eye as she caught it swiftly in her hand. A small cluster of red flowers had rolled from her pillow, she studied them silently; noticing a vase of the same type of plant in the windowsill beside the bed; the breeze from the partially opened window had apparently blown a loose cluster from the bunch. She looked again at the familiar soft points of the red petals, Royal Red Hydrangea, she reminisced, Nick's flower, but why was it in her room?

How cruel that the rare flower he had presented her with, when they had been lost in the mountains, was ever mocking her now, pointedly reminding her of his death. Painful anger welled within her, as she dropped the floral cluster to the floor, perhaps she did need to know why the truth had been kept from her, she had made a mistake coming back here, being treated like a child looking for the pet that had passed on while in school! Why had Mildred let her believe that there was a chance that Nick would enter her life again when she knew he could not? She stormed out of the bedroom and into the living room.

"Why, Mildred?" she enquired sadly. "Why didn't you just tell me he was dead?" Mildred's look of astonishment was matched only by Lauren's confused glare, she hadn't even apologized! "Because I'm not..." Lauren gasped, turning on her heel to face the familiar voice, the blood draining from her face; she stared in amazement at the dark haired man.

"N-Nick?" she felt herself growing faint as he stepped from the shadows into the dim light of the room. Lauren collapsed only to be caught by Nicholas Carmen's strong arms.

"What did Bruce tell her?" he enquired of the older woman.

"He said she read the article, but left before he could explain any further." She assisted Nick in laying the unconscious woman upon the couch. "Yer' lucky she didn't have a heart attack," Mildred admonished. "Why didn't you let me tell her?"

Nick peered at Lauren's soft features, her long, dark hair lay strewn about, she was just as beautiful as he had remembered her, every perfect detail of her face, reminding him of the months he'd spent in rehabilitation, her memory the only thing that kept him clinging to life, and now she was here.

"I couldn't let her think I was dead, she was so crushed..." he gently stroked her cheek; recoiling his hand when he caught sight of it against her porcelain skin. For a moment he had forgotten; he stood, backing toward the darkness once again as she stirred

"Nick!" She awoke with a start, crying out his name, she glanced around the room quickly, catching sight of him once again. "Is it really you?" She strained to see his face, masked in shadow.

Mildred intercepted, "Lauren, I was tryin' to tell ya'. After the accident, things changed. No one expected Nick to pull through, the extent of his burns … well … it was a miracle he survived at all. If he hadn't been thrown from the car when it exploded … Bruce found him just in time…" Lauren peered helplessly at the looming figure just beyond her sight, if she could just see him, know it was really him. She rose, stepping toward his still form.

"Lauren, please don't…" he breathed, he couldn't bare for her to see him like this, his scars had taken so much from him, he knew she would cringe from him should she see them in the light, she continued toward him. "Please…" he begged, stepping back from her, she stopped, staring at him unbelieving. He was alive, she elated, alive, and here now with her, how could he expect her to not come near him, it had been so long. Was he that appalled with her? Well, he would know about his son, she derived, no matter how he felt about her, but how he had he survived? The paper had declared him a vegetable, only kept alive by the machines.

"How?" she breathed. "How did you survive?" Nick studied her, he longed to pull her into his arms; to crush her soft lips with his own and claim what was rightfully his, what had been taken so cruelly from him by the same man who had tried to kill him.

"It doesn't matter…" he answered, a forced calmness masking his urgent need to touch her. "I only came to see for myself that you were all right, to tell you … tell you goodbye." Lauren's heart sank, how could he come back to her only to leave again? She shook her head, turning to Mildred;

"Haven't you told him?" Mildred relayed a "no" and Lauren stepped outside, carrying her son into the house to meet his father, Nick peered at the small boy, soundly sleeping in his carrier.

"Your … son?" His astonishment brought him into the light, as he studied the tiny child, Lauren carefully peered at the man before her, his right hand was clearly visible as he touched the soft cheek of her sleeping child, deeply grooved burns marked his muscled arm, snaking their way up his neck and from what she could see, upon the right side of his face, he glanced up at her, a deep sadness in his eyes, she could only see the man she had loved for so long now, the man that she had dreamt of, longed for. His scars meant nothing to her, held no bearing on her feeling for him. Reaching out she placed her hand upon his; gently brushing his scarred flesh with her soft fingertips, Nick stared at her movement, waiting for her to recoil from him in disgust. Her son was the most beautiful thing he had ever seen, a tiny piece of the woman he loved. He was glad for the shared moment, even if, like all the other memories, it would be all he'd have of her.

He looked away, unable to face her in the light, but unable to draw his hand away from her touch.

"His name is Nicholas Robert Conklin." Her soft voice reached him, gently urging a response, she paused, explaining further, "He is named after his father…"

Nick's eyes shot to hers with a sudden look of shock and confusion as he studied her for a long moment.

"Lauren," he began, "he's beautiful…" Lauren smiled at the admiring man, "But he can't be mine…" his words struck her unexpectedly.

"Of course he's yours," she explained. "He's the spitting image of you." Nick's gentle but insistent disagreeing was beginning to frighten her. "He has to be!" she exclaimed. "The dates don't match up with Billy's…" She stopped at the thought.

"Lauren … I can't … I'm not able to have children…" He stared longingly at the dark-haired boy, a son, he mused, how he wished he could have a son. Lauren clasped her hand to her mouth; he was Billy's son, conceived by rape, a bastard! Tears fell from her eyes once more, a deep protecting love consuming her as she peered at her innocent child. She felt like such a fool, she had assumed him to be Nick's his dark hair and cerulean eyes were identical to his, nothing of Billy could be seen at all in him. Lauren covered her face, taking deep breaths to thwart her sobbing now. Nick longed to comfort her, he had been told long ago that he would never be able to have any children of his own; he had had no idea that she had a child with Billy. The idea of her raising him alone haunted Nick's mind, he couldn't let her face this alone; he wouldn't let her leave again into an uncertain future of loneliness. One last act of cruel intent by the man who had so viciously taken her life away; perhaps, if she'd let him, he could at least be her friend, help to provide for her son, even if she could never love him the way she had before. It would be difficult to keep his longing at bay, but she would never be able to desire his scarred body. Unable to let go of the ugly burden that he now carried upon him, his scars held his heart captive from the woman he yearned for. He would have to accept his celibate lifestyle and help her to rebuild her tattered life. "If you'll let me, I'd be proud to be a part of his life." Lauren wept with mixed emotions now, accepting his proposal.

"I'm so sorry…" she was sobbing, but to her son or to him he did not know, his reassuring hand tightened on her shoulder, opening her to embrace him, she buried her face in the warmth of his neck, calming herself gently in his arms. Nick breathed in the fragrance of her hair, the essence of her heady scent causing a stirring of emotions within him; maybe someday she could love him again, in the darkness of night, where his scars would not matter. "Will you stay with me?" she pleaded, turning to face him. The devastation of learning her one tie to him was not so, was too much to bare, she wasn't ready to let him leave her completely, not yet. The unexpected succession of events that had transpired had left her vulnerable and desperate for support, she had felt herself crumble helplessly before him unable to withdraw her request. Her sea green eyes sought the strength and stability that he represented to her.

"Yes," he responded softly, he hadn't the strength to resist her invitation. He would keep her as long as she would allow, but always in the darkness, he couldn't bare to let her see him fully. Her closeness was growing uncomfortable as the remembrance of his appearance nagged at him. Recoiling from her, he stood abruptly, turning his scarred face from her view. The moment had stirred warmth within him temporarily, he closed the sensation out enveloping himself in the dark coldness that he had grown so accustomed to.

"Get your things, then," he coolly replied. "It's a long ride to my cabin." He crept past them, heading to the safety of his SUV just outside. Lauren rode silently beside her dark companion; she had apologized to Mildred, for her anger over the misunderstanding, and asked her to please return the rental car. She had decided to stay with Nick while she was in town and Mildred anxiously urged the idea.

"It's his pride that's really scarred," she had explained. "He changed after the accident, oh, he never gave up his search fer' ya', but he's become so reclusive, it was all I could do to coax him down here!" Lauren knew it would be difficult to convince him she saw past his scars, but somehow she would open his eyes. She only hoped he could forgive her for leaving him the way she had. He must have been so alone out there, needing the reassurance of her love and compassion, but finding only the cold isolation of solitude.

"Tell me what happened, Nick." Her soft voice penetrated the silence of the ride. "Do you remember it?" She was grasping for conversation, longing to hear a response from the man she still viewed as a ghost.

Nick's features tightened, he could feel her eyes on him. "Why are you staring at me?" His words were cold and carefully guarded, his eyes never leaving the road. Lauren looked away, she hadn't meant to offend him, she just couldn't believe he was really there; the words to explain herself did not come so easily.

"I'm sorry," she whispered, nervousness in her tone. "I didn't mean to…"

"I don't want to talk about it." His retort was cold and calloused, he caught himself. "We can talk later, I'm just tired…" Lauren remained silent the rest of the trip.

They reached the large cabin late that night, Nick was grateful for the covering darkness, he had caught her staring at him throughout the journey and he had felt as though she were scrutinizing his new appearance, he couldn't bare the thought of how she must view him now. No longer was he the confident man she had desired, his scars ran deeper than she knew and the hermit he had become would allow no ease of conscience around her intimidating beauty. He had merely volunteered his financial support to a woman in need, he convinced himself. The cold, platonic proposal, kept his wavering confidence in his abilities, hard as stone. As long as she kept her distance he would be fine, he had gone this long without the need for companionship, he would keep her distant; making sure she never saw him fully, for too long. It was unnecessary to put himself on the line, she would be safe there, with him to watch over her, he had no need for love now, he would only set himself up for more pain, her disappointment was already evident in her staring eyes. He only wished to keep her safe now, as he had always done, he would frighten her no more with his longing of her. A deep fear that she would pity him, played on his heart, she must know he did not need her pity, her charity. He couldn't bare to swallow her false affection. Nick carried her things to the master bedroom, a look of uncertainty flashed through Lauren's eyes at the gesture.

"I'll sleep in the guest room," he announced with a cold acknowledgment of her concern, she sat little Nicholas' seat next to the bed, turning to speak to her new host, only to find herself alone in the large room.

The memories of their encounter here brought a flash of heat over her, followed by a sad longing that crept into her bruised heart. She had hoped to speak to him when they'd arrived, but his obvious disinterest in her left her to reminisce of the things Billy had said about her willingness to sleep with a total stranger, maybe he considered her an easy, naive woman. She had fallen all over him so easily, and then had left with Billy, becoming quickly pregnant by him. Her heart ached at the thought, how would she ever be able to prove him wrong? She felt a desperate longing to be with him when he was near her, but he kept himself so heavily guarded now, she would just have to keep her desire at bay around him, if he only knew how her child had been conceived, but the experience was too painful to confess, only Sabrina could have known her humiliation, her fear. She picked her son up from the carrier and laid him on the bed, undressing tiredly, everything had happened so fast, she needed a good nights sleep, she would at least be consoled in the fact that she was now where her heart had always been, even if the situation was impossible, she would stay with him until he bid her to leave, never again would she leave him abandoned, even if he didn't want her love any longer, she would stay beside him, keeping her longing a secret, and loving him all the while.

CHAPTER 20

Lauren sat, quietly, sipping a cup of coffee at the large oak breakfast table in the kitchen of Nicholas Carmen's cabin. She studied the hand written note that had been placed beside her bed, sometime while she slept. It was pointedly brief and directly to the point. "*Please make yourself at home; don't disturb the guest wing of the cabin, I work at night.*" She pondered on the words, he was so distant, and not the warm, confident man she remembered. He had changed, and it seemed she wouldn't be seeing him anytime too soon. The day wore on, long and quiet, Lauren had resolved to cleaning, to pass the time, soon night fell and as the fading sun disappeared below the mountains towering peaks, the cool darkness of night's starry sky filled the view. Nick leaned ominously in the doorway to the guest wing, on the left side of the huge centered fireplace that stared out from under the spiraling staircase. Lauren startled at the sudden introduction of his presence, he watched her intricately, basked in shadow, stepping forward only to dim the brightly lit lights that surrounded the large room. He approached her hesitantly.

"I'll prepare dinner for us," he paused, as he interjected the statement. Lauren watched him leave the room, her loneliness yearned for his presence, now that she knew he was awake, but instead she headed up to her room to check on little Nicholas, who was now sleeping soundly, content with the feeding he had received prior to the nap. She remained there beside her sleeping babe for the better of forty-five minutes, studying his small features and silently pondering the sad fact of Billy actually being his father, it seemed odd that he bore no resemblance. A creek near the doorway caught Lauren's ear. She turned abruptly, peering into the darkened hallway.

"Nick?" she breathed, her heart beginning to race, as her question remained unanswered, the door opened fully, much to Lauren's bewilderment, she stepped toward her sleeping son straining to see past the darkness of the hall, waiting for a response.

"Dinner will be ready in about five minutes..." Only his deep voice allowed her an answer to his presence, she heard the soft tap of his footsteps as he headed back downstairs. Wondering how long he had been there, she checked her son once more before leaving the room, it was nearly 8 p.m. now and he would most likely sleep through the night. Nick entered the dining room with two plates in hand; he placed Lauren's meal at one end of the long, black mahogany table, and then took his place at the other. He wore a dark turtleneck and blue jeans, from what she could tell in the dim candlelight, always keeping his left side to her, avoiding the revelation of his scars. She seated herself carefully before the plate, waiting for him to begin. Watching her intently as she began eating, he noted her obvious discomfort in his presence, no doubt due to his appearance, he grimaced coldly, damn Billy Malhoun! The meal was carefully prepared and wonderfully flavorful, Lauren conceded. If only the conversation weren't non-existent. She felt awkward trying to find a topic that wouldn't offend his delicate sensitivity.

"I never knew you could cook like this," she admitted lightly. "It's delicious." Nick watched her avoiding his insightful glare, as she delicately nibbled her entree. Glancing at his face, a warm memory, of their last shared meal, came to mind, bringing a smile to her lips.

"The last meal you cooked for me came from a can…" The humor in her eyes softened his hardened heart, creating a spark of emotion, behind his impossible walls. He smiled gently, at her searching eyes, a longing for the times they had shared, however brief, pulled at his heart.

"Yes, I still make some mean Ravioli…" he laughed. The shared memory lingered between them as their eyes met, igniting the flame that still smoldered within them. Nick tore the stare away, the cold remembrance of his unsurpassable scars dividing them once more.

"That was then," he declared. "Finish your meal, I have work to do." He rose from the table and left the room, too quickly. Lauren sighed, a deep ache filling her, she wasn't sure if she would ever be able to reach him. She had escaped from the isolation of Billy's possessive grasp, only to find her loneliness still haunting her even with the man that had stirred her deepest burning passions, she fought the urge to cry at the notion that her heart would never again feel the contentment it had felt in his arms, only the empty hunger that seemed to be the extent of her fate. Her thoughts were interrupted by a small cry emanating from her room, she felt her breasts throb at the recognition of the sound, she would have to clean the mess up later, she decided, heading off to feed her awakened son.

The days wore on relentlessly turning into weeks, and a growing restlessness stirred within her. She barely saw Nick at all, but for a few brief moments in the evening, before he returned to his work. She hadn't yet mustered enough courage to enquire about his work, and what it might consist of; her curiosity was getting the better of her. At times she was sure she could feel his eyes upon her, watching her, caressing her, but she kept a silent notation of the knowledge. She didn't fear him in that way, she knew he would never hurt her, she only feared the pain he might inflict upon her heart; should she attempt to confess her true feelings. It had been so long, and his scars seemed to hold him at bay. If only he could see they meant nothing to her, or could he ever really let himself love her again, they had both changed in one way or another. After all that had been done to her, all she had been put through, was she even worth his time? Or were they both just clinging to the past, a past that was dead and gone, she needed answers, she conceited, not mysteries. She paced the floor restlessly this night, her son had long past fallen soundly to sleep in the crib Nick had insisted she buy him, he was always leaving gifts and thoughtful items for little Nicholas and herself. She was sure that anything she desired he would have gotten for her, no questions asked, and her purse was never left to want for money, but this night her weary head could find no peace. He was never real, she chided to herself, as if she actually were living with a ghost; it seemed he had become one unwillingly, with his intolerance to the day and his mysterious lifestyle. The hours he kept were driving her mad, and her need for companionship was becoming intolerable. He was there, but he wasn't, she was with him, but still alone, she couldn't bare it any longer. Exiting her room quietly, she headed for the guest wing, peering at the digital clock in the hall, 2:15 a.m., it read, she was sure he would still be working. She'd had enough of these shadow games, dancing around his arrogant ride, if he was going to let her past hold him away, then she would leave, being alone completely was better than being near someone who was so unattainable. She crept down the staircase and slipped through the large oak door that fronted the guest wing. The long hall was dark, lit only by scattered candle bulbs that trailed down the length of the wall. The rooms along the way, save one, at the very end, were dark and empty, she assumed this to be his place of work; it was the only lighted chamber in the corridor. Here, at the far end of the hall, she could see a dim glow emanating; she crept toward the light peering in to the room curiously. Nick sat at a large black desk, a brightly lit computer, blaring in the darkness of the room, before him. The desk was neatly organized, with small abstract sculptures gracing its many open shelves, she looked silently around the room, its walls harbored many works of art, mostly abstract in design, ranging from renaissance to modern photography; she was impressed. Bumping the door accidentally, its ominous creak reared a quick response from the dark haired man. He turned abruptly toward the sound, a look of betrayal on his face.

"What are you doing here?" he demanded, rising to face her. Lauren stepped into the room, standing defiantly before him, a disguise of determination masking her nervousness.

"I need to speak with you…" she began, a little unsure now, as he stood before her. Nick's eyebrow rose in enquiry.

"Well? I'm very busy, Lauren." He watched her masked confidence begin to falter, her eyes avoiding his, in discomfort; the obviousness of it disgruntled him as she began looking around the room once again. She walked toward a large sculpture that loomed eerily, beautifully, in the darkness, tracing her finger over its hard design, she tread cautiously.

"So this is your hideaway? It's impressive." He folded his arms securely over his chest casting a speculative eye upon her.

"It serves my purpose…" he stated, his voice a low growl in the large room.

"And what purposes do you get served? May I ask?" Lauren could feel the thinning of the ice she trod on.

"If you must know, I'm an arts dealer. I find the buyers … for the sellers." He held his intimidating stare. "I guess you could say I'm the middle man."

"Middle man?" she ventured. "And this from the one who wouldn't be the other man, the middle man…" The painful memory had slipped in on them, linking the past to the present momentarily. Nick stepped away, avoiding the comment. She glanced at him, summoning her nerve once again.

"Lauren, I doubt you came here to discuss my office, would you please get to the point."

"You're right," she confessed, taking a deep breath. "I've been here for three weeks now." She peered into his watchful eyes briefly, noticing his annoyance at her intrusion. "But I've barely even seen you at all. I don't expect our lives to just fall back in place, to just … well … pick up where we left off, but it would be nice if you would just carry a conversation once in a while." She looked for a response from the agitated man, his glaring eyes swept over her and she felt her confidence failing under his scrutinizing gaze.

"Look, Lauren, I'm a very busy man, I've gotten on with my life, and I like the solitude, I've grown accustomed to being alone, so if you're finished, I need to return to my work…" He turned away from her, heading back towards his computer. He could bare her closeness no longer, already his body was reacting to hers. Lauren stared at his audacity, she was intent on making herself perfectly clear, and after all, he had invited her.

"No," she began, "no, I'm not finished. Frankly, I find you're lack of sociability to be quite cowardly, in fact, this entire masquerade of hiding in the darkness and playing games with my emotions is an act of cowardice all together!"

Her unexpected retort left him in awe, he had taken her in, as she'd wanted, how dare she call him a coward, she had no idea what it was like to have to hide her appearance from the world just to feel accepted, her conceited audacity irked him.

"First of all," he retorted, turning on his heel at the words she had said. "I don't recall offering anything other than support. I tried to tell you goodbye, but you begged me..."

"Begged you!" she squawked. "I hardly think..."

"Yes, begged me, to stay!" Lauren's feathers were sorely ruffled at his words.

"Well, at least I haven't given up on life because of what someone else has done to me!" Nick shot her a threatening look. "My life was just fine without you!" he growled glaring at her flustered expression.

"You call this a life?" She motioned around the darkened room in exaggerated sarcasm. "You keep yourself hidden away, afraid of a few scars! Well let me tell you something, you may not be able to see my scars, but inside, they're uglier than anything you could even imagine yourself to be. I can see past your burns Nick, why can't you?" She turned abruptly, and headed to the door grasping the handle. "I don't know what's worse, Nicholas Carmen." She looked back at him one last time. "Thinking that you're dead, and missing you, or feeling that you are, and knowing you're not..." She turned away before the frustrated tears began to spill. Nicholas' hand caught her wrist unexpectedly,

"Lauren, wait." His voice was filled with intensity. "Please, don't go..." She turned to him anxious wonder filling her eyes, she searched his face for emotions, feeling her pulse quicken at his closeness. "You're right" he whispered, peering intensely into her eyes. "I'm sorry I underestimated you, you are a remarkable woman ... help me find myself, Lauren. I'm not complete without you..." Tears ran down her cheeks at his unabashed confession. Slowly, softly his lips met hers, gently pressing into a passionate kiss, his shaking hands slid over her shoulders, pulling her to him. He ran his fingers through her long, dark hair, kissing her face sensually as she pressed her hands against his tightly muscled chest.

"Oh, Nick..." she breathed. She had dreamt of this moment time and again, as she succumbed to unbearable acts, never again would she be taken from the complete wholeness she felt when he touched her, nothing would keep her from him this time, sweeping her up into his strong arms, Nick carried her silently into the guest room he had stayed in since she had left, his heart raced at the mixing of emotions that the moment brought. He had desperately tried to hide himself for so long that the notion of her perfect flesh against his, intricately scarred body, brought an anxious fear to him, would he please her? Would his less than perfect features disappoint her now? She moaned softly against his ear as he laid her upon the bed. "Oh, Nick," she breathed again, "tell me this is real…" She sought his fiery kiss as he removed her satin robe.

"Lauren…" he moaned, tasting her sweet flesh as he trailed his heated lips upon her neck. She pulled at his shirt, hesitating when he paused at the idea.

"Nick, please, I want you…"Her sweet words filled his mind as he hurriedly removed his clothing, and then hers, their bodies met with a burning fierceness, both needing a part of the other to complete themselves. Yearning for the passion, that had consumed them so readily before, Nick's urgent thrusts subsided gently as Lauren kissed his sweating brow. "My love…" she whispered, "…my life." Nick claimed her lips again, unwilling to release her body and be unwhole once again.

"Let me please you," he breathed, drawing himself from her briefly and stirring her burning need with fevered kisses of ecstasy, she clung to him, helplessly spinning, under his gentle teasing, her body quaked against him as the tremors gently faded into a lingering bliss. She trembled at the splendor of the moment, as if she had never been touched before. All her pent up frustration and anxiety released now, in his embrace. They lay, spent, in each other's arms, a feeling of satisfaction and helpless need filling them both. Lauren rose reluctantly.

"Where are you going?" Nick leaned casually upon his elbow, his magnificent nakedness displayed before her.

"I have to check on Nicholas Robert," she replied gently, wrapping her robe around herself.

"Will you return?" His question caught her off guard.

"I thought you had to work?" she enquired teasingly, Nick's eyes revealed his still urgent hunger.

"Will you spend the night with me?" Lauren considered him briefly, a flash of playfulness overtaking her.

"You know where to find me…" Her seductive smile urged his throbbing member onward; there would be no rest this night he queried. Pulling on his shorts he peered at the darkened room one last time, his hidden loneliness was released now, leaving him with a liberating sense of freedom. Hurriedly following after her, he felt the warmth of loves lingering touch fill the deep chasm within him, no longer would he remain a prisoner to his self-conscious pride. She had accepted him as a man, in whole and breathed light into his darkness. His freedom was just ahead, and life was waiting for him.

CHAPTER 21

Time passed by unnoticed in the bliss of everyday life, Lauren watched her son growing before her eyes, and a deep satisfying warmth filled her as Nick blossomed into the strong and affectionate man he had always been, fascinated by her sweet dark haired boy. They played frivolously in the newly grown spring grass. It seemed only yesterday he was suckling at her breast, dependent on her for every ounce of the nutrient his small body needed, now he carelessly ran to and fro, stealing her freshly baked cookies and giggling at the silly faces Nick would make when she admonished him for taking without asking, his third birthday was only two months away and Lauren marveled at her bright young boy. Nick entered the kitchen with little Nicholas right behind him,

"C'mon, Daddy!" he squealed, tugging at Nick's shirt tail, the exhausted man looked helplessly at Lauren's smiling face, trying to catch his breath.

"Let Daddy rest, sweetie…" She urged her giggling son into the family room for some rest time, watching cartoons.

"I'm completely exhausted!" Nick puffed, glancing at her now as she returned to the room.

"Too much for an old man like you?" she challenged playfully. Nick mocked a look of appalled surprise.

"Old man?" he queried. "Let's just see what this old man can keep up with…" He caught her to him, lifting her easily into the air, her bright laughter drawing the attention of little Nicholas in the other room, he watched them quietly, entertained by their show of affection, violence was never a subject of his young life, only fun loving carefree days filled his little world and he giggled as he watched them kissing now. Stopping at the realization that they were no longer alone, Nick took his stepson's hand in his, leading him back into the den.

"Only PG for you buddy…" he laughingly said, smiling back to Lauren's reddened face guiltily. That evening they lay comfortably in bed together, watching the gentle flicker of the gas fireplace adjacent their bed.

"He's growing up so fast," Lauren softly marveled. "Pretty soon he'll be all grown up and then what will we do?" Nick laughed.

"Don't worry; I'm sure you'll have plenty of grandkids to keep you busy!"

"Don't you mean we will?" She smiled gently at her husband. It had been six months now since their wedding night, but every moment in his arms was just like the first.

"Yes," he agreed, studying her beautiful features as she looked to him lovingly, "we will." Pulling her close, he kissed her forehead gently, slowly trailing down her cheek to find the softness of her mouth. A creaking of the door turned their attention as a small figure stumbled tiredly into the dimly lit room. Rubbing his eyes wearily, he reached for Nick's strong arms to lift him into their bed, as he had many times before; he snuggled securely in between them, smiling at their comforting faces.

"Did you have a bad dream?" his mother questioned, concern lighting her features.

"No, Mommy," he answered looking admiringly at her, "I just missed you soooo much…" A small yawn took his words away quietly; he turned to Nick, studying his face curiously. "Daddy," he enquired, "why does your skin look like that?" A saddened look of uncertainty came over Nick's face at the question, he looked away from the boy's innocent curiosity, not sure what to answer. Lauren's heart dropped, she had hoped little Nicholas would be able to accept that his "daddy" was just a little different, a little special. She interjected quickly,

"Daddy got hurt a long time ago, Nicholas, but his marks are where the angels kissed his boo boos away…" Nick shot a look of unexpectedness at her, smiling appreciatively at his beautiful wife, he wondered secretly if she would ever cease to amaze him. Nicholas' eyes lit up as he stared amazingly at the man he idolized.

"Wow! Really,Daddy?" Nick smiled at his young admirer.

"That's right, Nicholas, but one very special angel kissed my most broken part and made me all better, she fixed my heart so that I can love you!" He glanced at his quick thinking heroin. Satisfied with the answer, the amazed child traced the deep grooves that trailed the length of Nick's right arm, to a large scarred patch of flesh upon the center of his bared chest.

"Right here, Daddy?" Nick stared intensely at Lauren as he answered, a passionate smile revealing the intended message.

"That's it…" he whispered, kissing the boys forehead as he closed his eyes sleepily, yawning once again and giving into sleeps inviting embrace. Nick peered at Lauren gratefully.

"Thank you…" he mouthed in silence.

The birthday party was going over well, the piñata was broken and Nicholas, along with Shyanne and two of Mildred's nieces and nephews, played gleefully with the puppy he had gotten as one of his many presents. Lauren and Nick sat at the glass topped patio table with their company, Bruce Ellington, his wife and daughter, who was subsequently accompanied by Deputy John Harper, the young officer who had aided Lauren and Nick with the use of his patrol car, he had been courting Sabrina for the past three months now, after gaining permission from his superior officer, Sabrina's father. Mildred had come too, with her daughter, Sarah, along with Sarah's eleven-year-old son. The day was gloriously warm, in the high mountain atmosphere, and the frivolous laughter of the children mingled with the buzz of summer insects and chirping birds, creating a haze of unsurpassed comfort. Lauren's mother and father weren't able to make the trip this year; something in their aspiring business had come up, leaving a damper on her perfect day.

A ringing from within the house signaled Lauren to hurry in and answer the phone. Her mother responded from the other end excitedly, they had finished their work earlier than expected and were on their way to the airport to fly down at the last minute. Lauren was ecstatic, she had been hoping for a call like this, she hurriedly snatched the present they had sent up from the kitchen counter, and raced it upstairs to her room, where Nicholas Robert wouldn't find it. They would be able to present it to him now, she elated. She entered the room quickly not noticing the uninvited visitor just inside the door … After sliding the large box into the top of the closet, she turned to leave, a sudden gasp clutched her throat as she stared in horror, her eyes wide with shock.

"Well, well." The cold familiarity of the voice, froze her heart. "Aren't we just the happy little house wife!" Lauren backed up slowly.

"But you're … dead…" Billy leaned off of the wall beside the doorway, a criticizing half grin played on his lips as he considered her words.

"That's right darlin' and so are you…" his fraudulent grin quickly changed into a hard sneer, Lauren glanced past him at the still open door, taking the initiative, she bolted toward it, only to be flung helplessly back by the massively built arm of her attacker. "No!" she screamed, as Billy kicked the door shut and clasped her to him, his broad hand covering her mouth, and muffling her cries. He pressed his lips to her temple.

"What is it with you, Lauren…" His whisper was harsh against her ear. "I could never be good enough for you, could I?" His voice rose slightly in anger at her resistance to him. "Does he make you moan…" he rasped, brandishing a large boot knife, to her horror. He slid the razor sharp tip of the blade down along her blouse, grasping her breast possessively; Lauren cried out beneath his silencing palm, tears running down her cheeks as his hand slid lower, the blade trailing along her abdomen, to the bared flesh of her thighs.

"How is that burned freak better than me?" Lauren cringed at his touch, a feeling of sickening entrapment came over her as he brought the knife back up to her chest; one by one he cut the buttons from her blouse, gazing hungrily at her revealed flesh.

"Well, now it's my turn, baby. I'm gonna make you moan now…" he breathed sharply, his voice growing husky with lust. "You'll be begging me to stop…" He released her suddenly, throwing her onto the bed; desperately she tried to escape him, calling out in vain as he crushed her to the mattress, pressing the knife to her throat. "Shut up!" he spat, as he tore her shorts down viciously. "Don't want to ruin the party now do you?" Lauren cried at the thought of the intentions he harbored, she begged for freedom from his cruel assault on her, her mind reeling with thoughts of escape. In his haste, he faltered with his blade, waving it away from her terror stricken face, Lauren brought her knee up suddenly, catching his groin as he fought to open his blue jeans. The painful blow sent him groaning to the side of her. Springing from the bed, she dashed for the safety of the door …

Nicholas Robert approached his father. "Daddy," he stated, "where's Mommy?"

"She went to get the phone, buddy," he replied, engaged in a conversation with Bruce Ellington.

"I got to go potty, Daddy!"

"Go on in, buddy. Mommy's in there…" He patted the boy on the shoulder, sending him in unknowingly. His calls for his mother went unnoticed as he mounted the staircase toward the noises he heard in Mommy's room, she was up there, he elated innocently.

Lauren grasped the door handle, flinging it open in a rush and bolting out of the room, screaming in desperate terror, Billy charged behind her, his rage unmasked as he wielded the shimmering blade, falling upon his victim. Knocking her to the floor he jabbed the dagger at her again and again, struggling with her flailing body, his blade sunk into a spongy mass, eliciting a tiny cry from the darkness of the hallway. The blood-curdling scream hadn't gone unnoticed as the attack ensued, much to the horror of the startled onlookers. Billy rose upon his knees, straddling Lauren's exasperated form;

he grasped the knife with both hands as he raised it above his head

"You're mine!" he growled, a murderous glare in his psychotic eyes. "Forever!" He plunged the knife toward her as Lauren closed out the horrific scene, throwing up her arms in defense. Billy's sudden release of her body caused Lauren to open her eyes; the ominous crack of splintering bone caught her off guard as she realized what had transpired. Nick was upon the unconscious man, viciously drilling him with unchained fury; his un-resisted kick to Billy's face had knocked him off of her, rendering him unconscious.

"Nicholas!" she screamed as the bigger picture came into view, blood was strewn all over her torn blouse and hands, but she had not been caught by his deadly blade, instead it was the small crumpled form of her young son that tore her heart from her chest. The dark pool of red liquid that ran from him was sickeningly cast about the scene, viciously spread about during the struggle that had transpired. Lauren cried out in terror as she threw herself over his still body. "No!" she screamed. "Nicholas! No!" Nick fell to his knees beside them, tears spilling from his eyes at the horrific scene, a desperate void choking him now. A sudden explosion erupted within the large confines of the cabin as Bruce Ellington stood before them, his smoking gun in hand. A heavy thud sounded behind the grieving parents as Billy Malhoun's lifeless form fell to the floor, his bloodied boot knife still in hand.

The ambulance had arrived in less than five minutes at the alarming call. Dr. Tim Cratchet had worked to stabilize the tiny boy, but his moderate facilities just weren't capable of the pediatric services they would need, the staff of life helicopter was brought in promptly, rushing Nicholas Robert's motionless body to the county trauma center, just down the mountain.

Lauren wept unconsolably as they rushed toward the hospital, forty minutes away; she had begged to ride with her son in the helicopter but was refused due to the lack of room. Now as Nick sped down the winding roads into the town below, she wept as a grieving mother who had already lost her son.

"There was so much blood!" she cried helplessly, staring at the stains on her clothing and hands, her child's blood, she grimaced. Nick touched her trembling hands.

"He's going to make it, Lauren, he has to…"

His heart was racing wildly with the doubt that filled him as they rushed toward the unknown situation ahead; he hadn't raised him thus far only to have him taken away by the man who had robbed him of his dignity, his happiness, his love, no! Billy Malhoun couldn't win, not at the expense of his boy's life, he grieved inwardly as a father losing his son, a deep bond joining him to Lauren's child, he would never be able to give her another child, and his heart ached at the thought of losing the only son he would ever know, even if the boy wasn't his biologically, he would always be his son.

Everyone sat in the emptiness of the waiting room, fear and anxiety loomed heavily in the air as they awaited the surgeon's prognosis, Lauren's parents had arrived at the airport and were met by the good Dr. Cratchet who rushed them to the hospital to be with their daughter and son in law in their time of need.

The door opened and a green clad physician stepped into the room

"Mr. and Mrs. Carmen?" Everyone stood nervously awaiting word on the faltering child. "Yes?" Lauren spoke up, grasping Nick's encircling arms for support.

"He's lost a lot of blood. He's stable right now but if we don't get him the transfusion he needs, I'm afraid he won't make it." Lauren covered her mouth in fear.

"Well, what's the problem?" Nick's mother had arrived just before the announcement. The surgeon began once more.

"Your son has a rare blood type." He directed his gaze at Lauren as he spoke. "Do you have any idea what blood type you are?" Lauren cleared her mind trying to think clearly now. I'm 'O' positive," she stated, a bit confused.

"Well, then we'll have to use his father…" he motioned to Nick to follow him, but was stopped short by Lauren's interruption.

"His father is dead…" The physician turned to them glancing from Nick to Lauren in confusion.

"Oh, I see," he said coherently, understanding the situation better. Her hopelessness over ran her as she began to sob, falling helplessly to the chair she had been sitting in, her son's only chance was gone and there was nothing she could do to save him. Billy's final blow had at last ripped the life from her. Lauren's father stepped forward.

"Don't you have any of this rare blood in stock? Don't you people prepare for situations like this?!" His reddened face shook with indignant anger. The doctor sympathized with the man at the situation.

"I understand your frustration sir," he spoke cautiously and calmly. "It's a very rare type and our reserve was spent just last week, we've given him what was left, but the bleeding was difficult to stop, most of what we gave him was lost during surgery. I'm sorry." Mildred came forward.

"What type is he?" she questioned, hopeful that she might know someone who could loan. "He's AB negative ma'am, he can only accept the same type, that's why we were hoping his mother was a match, but if his father was the AB negative parent and he's no longer living, then we'll have to search our records for donors. If we have enough time..."

A chill swept over Nick at the doctor's words, "I'm AB negative..." he stated, standing abruptly from Lauren's side. Dr. Cratchet watched silently as Nick hurriedly left the room with the surgeon. Lauren's heart was beating wildly. By some twist of fate, Nick had the same blood type as Billy! The rarity of the chance was dumbfounding and Lauren's mind was numb with disbelief, a warm hand on her shoulder interrupted her thoughts. Dr. Cratchet had been privy to the entire conversation.

"Lauren?" he enquired softly. "Might I have a word with you later?" Lauren glanced at him, nodding agreeably. The transfusion was completed and Nick sat with Lauren in the pediatric wing beside Nicholas Robert's bed. He hadn't slept all night as they waited for any reaction from the still unconscious child. Lauren had fallen asleep in her husband's warm embrace as they watched him silently, praying for his return to them. Nicholas began to stir, a soft cry emanated from his dry lips.

"Mommy..." he squeaked, Nick jumped at the small sound, waking Lauren.

"Nicholas?" he breathed. "Nicki?" Lauren rushed to his side.

"It's okay, baby. Mommy's here..." The confused child reached for his mother's embrace, tugging accidentally at the IV in his little arm.

"Ow, Mommy ... !" he cried out, the soreness of his healing wounds hitting him suddenly. She consoled him gently as they bid him to lie back down, comforting his young fears, after a moment he spoke up worriedly. "Mommy, that man hurt me..." his frail little voice, drew tears from her eyes as she patted his hand in response. "Who was he, Mommy? Why did he hurt me?" Lauren turned away from his wide blue eyes, his innocence too pure to have been marred by his biological father, Nick watched Lauren's saddened reaction to the question; he placed a comforting hand on her shoulder.

"He was a bad man, Nicholas, he's gone now; he can't hurt you or Mommy now." His strong words calmed the child and Lauren smiled through her tears at the man she loved, "Thank you..." she mouthed silently.

Awake now, little Nicholas played, as best he could, with the balloons that had been sent to him by concerned friends and family. He studied the bandage on his little stomach that covered the proof of his injury.

"Daddy?" he questioned softly, "Will I get angel kisses, too?" Emotion filled his heart at the innocent inquiry, if he could have taken his place under the assault he would have done so without a second thought.

"Yes, Nicholas," he answered shakily, "now you will have angel kisses..." He kissed the small boy on the forehead watching him play happily now, with the knowledge that he was closer now to being like his hero–his father.

CHAPTER 22

It had been over a week since the incident, and Lauren was overjoyed at the fact, that today, her son was coming home. The hospital staff had given him a farewell party, elated at his quick recovery, Nick had insisted he was his mother's son, a fighter, a survivor, the notion left Lauren glowing with embarrassment, and appreciative of his words.

Dr. Cratchet had left word, with Bruce Ellington, for Lauren and Nick, to come down to his office. He had insisted on the urgency of his call, thus causing an anxious worry in her now. Laurens parents waited at the front doors, to the trauma center, in their white Crown Victoria, anxious to pick up their grandson, for the trip home. He climbed happily into the backseat, brandishing a handful of pictures, he had colored, and a bag containing the gifts he had received, while healing. Lauren looked to Nick, worry and anxiety showing through her eyes, Dr. Cratchet was waiting …

The office of Dr. Cratchet was small and sterile, everything was placed perfectly, and the potted plants glistened, like plastic. Lauren paced the floor, anxiously, as they waited for the good Doctor to finish up, with his previous patient.

"Lauren? Nick?" The voice startled her, as its source, entered the room. "I am sorry to pull you away from Nicholas today, but I have some information that you may find a bit, interesting…"

He motioned them into the small room that harbored his desk, and filing cabinets, opening the cabinet; assuredly, he fingered through the files and pulled a specific chart from them.

"I overheard the rare blood type of your son, AB negative, is that correct?" Lauren signaled a positive answer in his direction. "And you, Lauren, you are, ahhh…" he glanced at another chart, on his desk, sliding his small spectacles down his nose, to clarify his vision, "ah … O positive, correct?" Lauren nodded again, as Nick spoke up,

"What are you getting at, Doc?"

Dr. Cratchet put his hands up, in mock defense. "I'm getting to it, Mr. Carmen … Billy Malhoun, he was apparently the man whom you believe to have been the … father, of your son?" He looked to Lauren once more, in question. Lauren glanced at Nick, who was studying her now.

"Yes," she answered, unsure of where the conversation was going. She explained further, "He is the only one … the only one that could be…" Nick spoke up now, wanting to get to the center of the doctor's questions, "I'm infertile, Doc, impotent, I can't have kids…"

Dr. Cratchet studied Nick briefly, "Are you certain?" he queried. "How is it that you came to this conclusion?"

Lauren clutched her chest, what was he saying? Was there still a chance that Nick could actually be Nicholas' father? Was there any chance at all that he had been wrong about his inabilities? Her mind was reeling with the possibility.

"I'm sure, Dr. Cratchet. The specialist back home ran every test imaginable, my chances were less than a million to one. I'd have a better shot at winning the lottery!"

"Well then," he stated calmly, "I'd like to run a test, or two, myself. Billy Malhoun was not AB negative, he was O positive as well. Nicholas Robert is not his son."

His words clutched at Laurens heart, a chill sweeping over her; she hadn't been with anyone else, other than Nick, but the possibility was so fantastic, she could hardly believe her ears.

"I'd like to run a paternity test on the two of you." He directed the statement toward Nick, as he spoke, "Nicholas and yourself, that is." Nick was skeptical. Ever since he had been told, of his infertility, he had never considered it a possibility that he might have, someday, become a biological parent. He had accepted his inability and resounded to the idea of never being able to pass on his genes; his line would end with him.

Two days later, the results of the test were back, Nick and Lauren were anxiously waiting again, in the sterile office of Dr. Cratchet. Nick paced this time, nervousness overwhelming him, the Doctor had called, and asked for them to return to his clinic, giving no inclination as to the results of the test. Hope and doubt had played on Nicks mind for those two days, which had crept by painstakingly slowly.

The couple had considered all aspects of possibility, Nick was convinced of his unproductive state, he had tried, in his past relationships, for children, without result, and was unwilling to raise his hopes only to be disappointed once again. Although Lauren was in no doubt as to whom she had had sexual contact with, she was in deep disarray over the situation; they had never considered the idea that Nicholas may not have been Laurens! There were many tales of children being switched at birth, and in her case, the circumstances being what they were at the time; it was a possibility they could not rule out. What if neither of them were his biological parent?

They had done the paternity test on Lauren as well, just as a precaution, but the idea terrified her. What would happen if it were true? Would they lose her son? What of her real son? It was too much to handle, and they had decided to stop speculating, and enjoy the time they had before the answers were in. Nick had resolved to not let the answer affect his relationship with Laurens' son, as he came to terms with the possible outcomes, he loved the boy more than life, and nothing would change that.

Nights of camping in the mountains, and baseball games, on warm afternoons, filled his thoughts. Fishing in the lake, and watching football games together, on cool autumn evenings; were assured expectations of his assumed role. He would carry on his fathers legacy, and instill the qualities of their relationship in the boy he considered his son, regardless of genetic ties. Nicholas was his son, no matter the outcome.

Dr. Cratchet entered the room promptly, his stature unrevealing, and professional, Nick was silent.

"Well," the good Doctor began, "the results were interesting, you, sir, are NOT," he paused, carefully wording his statement, "NOT, completely barren, Nicholas Robert Carmen, is your son."

A gasp of released breath sent Lauren reeling into her husbands' arms, While Nick slowly digested his words, emotion welling up within him; HIS son, he elated, HIS son! He crushed Lauren to him, tears of ecstatic joy stinging his eyes,

"He's OUR son, Lauren! MY son!"

"Indeed," the doctor responded, "both tests on the parents came back positive, there were no doubts." Lauren wept with relief and happiness.

"I knew in my heart it was you, Nick! I felt it when he would move within me, and when I looked into those beautiful eyes, the eyes of his true father!"

She kissed him passionately, the euphoria of it all overwhelming her.

Dr. Cratchet cleared his throat, to signal his presence in the room, and Lauren blushed at her uncontrolled actions.

"I am happy for you at this news, but please don't start on your next one here in my office!" His laughter was evident as he spoke, revealing his genuine happiness for the couple.

Lauren took Nicks arm in hers. "Let's go home," she said, a deep calming relief settling on her now. Her family was whole, no more scandalous confrontations to avert, no more worry of badly inherent traits to come, she was where her heart had always been, and she thanked the stars above for the day she had nearly ran an “old” man off of the mountain road. Her journey had been a hard one, full of danger and pain, but she would have gladly taken the same road to have her life fulfilled with the happiness she had found.

Nick lifted little Nicholas, gently, up in his arms, holding him close and thanking the heavens for the chance at being the father he had always dreamed of being. Lauren smiled broadly at the scene, THEIR son, she marveled, and THEIR family.

“So tell me,” she queried, “how does it feel to win the lottery?” Her challenging grin did not go unnoticed.

“I think we should play again…” he ventured, pulling her to him and kissing her softly, “and again, and again, and again…” Her laughter bubbled over.

“I love you, Nicholas Carmen.”

“And I love you,” he returned. “Both of you!”

The End

Printed in the United States
17234LVS00003B/277-315